ASPHALT BLUES

OTHER BOOKS IN THE
DANIEL BYRD ADVENTURE SERIES

MOUNTAIN JUSTICE

A LITTLE BIT KIN

SELF RESCUE

A DANIEL BYRD ADVENTURE

ASPHALT BLUES

PHILLIP W. PRICE

LANIER
PRESS

LANIER
PRESS *a Division of BookLogix*

Alpharetta, Georgia

ISBN: 978-1-6653-0875-5 - Paperback
eISBN: 978-1-6653-0876-2 - eBook

These ISBNs are the prope rty of Lanier Press (a Division of BookLogix) for the express purpose of sales and distribution of this title. The content of this book is the property of the copyright holder only. BookLogix does not hold any ownership of the content of this book and is not liable in any way for the materials contained within. The views and opinions expressed in this book are the property of the Author/Copyright holder, and do not necessarily reflect those of Lanier Press/BookLogix.

Library of Congress Control Number: 2024915183

Printed in the United States of America

♾This paper meets the requirements of ANSI/NISO Z39.48-1992 (Permanence of Paper)

0 7 3 1 2 4

DEDICATION

To George W. Weaver, October 31, 1941 to June 27, 2024.

A Green Beret medic in Vietnam, an Atlanta police officer, the first District Attorney of the Appalachian Judicial Circuit, and a Defense Attorney till the day of his death.

George was the inspiration for the character Jerry Mason. He lost the DA's job over incidents highly fictionalized in Mountain Justice. *Some said George was tilting at windmills. I say George had a clear idea of right and wrong and sought to do something about it.*

He was a mentor and a friend, and he owes me several thousand dollars' worth of hamburgers.

FOREWORD

The first reference to a substance being banned was in the Book of Genesis. God told Adam and Eve there was only one fruit they couldn't eat. I think you know how that worked out.

In 2005, and even today, Metro Atlanta was the epicenter of methamphetamine distribution on the East Coast. In a few short years, methamphetamine, smuggled by Mexican Drug Trafficking Organizations (DTO), was cheaper than the homemade product that had proliferated in the mountains of North Georgia (as described in *A Little Bit Kin*). The method of smuggling methamphetamine across the country in liquid form was just showing up on law enforcement's radar in 2005. The meth oil would be converted to crystal meth for sale on the streets.

On the other hand, the scourge of prescription drug abuse has been with us for a long time. Legislation has been written on both the state and federal level to address the problem; but people are people.

PROLOGUE

Daniel Byrd was cold as he climbed the stairs out of the tube station into the daylight and his knees were stiff from the long plane ride. The London Underground was crowded with lunch goers. Byrd paused to be sure he had gotten off at Embankment Station. The city was overcast and there was a light rain falling. Byrd took a left, and with the help of his smart phone, followed the route to his hotel, which only happened to be a very short walk from the station.

Byrd crossed the street, almost getting hit by a passing car when he looked the wrong way for oncoming traffic. After fifty-three years in the US, old habits were hard to break. Byrd was more cautious as he stepped up to the next curb, and then followed his phone west. Until that day, he had never been outside of North America. As he marveled at the old buildings and the new; he felt lost as a ball in tall grass.

He was startled when found his hotel and there was a top-hatted man at the front door. The man, in a morning suit with tails, pulled the door open for Byrd and welcomed him in. Byrd looked around in awe at the lobby of the hotel. There were well-dressed customers standing all around. The country boy felt badly out of place.

Before him, a man stood and stuck his hand out. "Special Agent in Charge Byrd. How good it is to meet you at last. I know we've spoken several times on the phone but it's always helpful to put a face to a name."

Byrd stood still. "How'd you know me?"

"Your director's office was kind enough to send us a photo."

Byrd looked the man over as he shook his hand. "Detective Chief Inspector Ashwood?"

Jonathan Ashwood, with the London Metropolitan Police Force, was a lean man a couple of inches shorter than Byrd. He was dressed in a conservative black suit and dark tie. "How was your flight?"

"Long. But I slept some on the plane. Do we need to get a taxi to get to your office? I'd prefer to keep moving. If I stop or sit, I might go to sleep."

Ashwood shook his head. "It's close by. We can walk. We'll just drop your bag with the clerk."

Byrd dropped the bag near the desk after alerting the clerk, and turned back to Ashwood. "When you made my reservations, did you get some kind of government rate? I can't imagine the GBI paying for a place like this."

Ashwood chuckled. "We simply told the director of your Bureau that this was the closest place to our offices. His comment was, 'He can't sleep on the street.'"

Byrd wrapped his overcoat around himself as they started out. They walked along the Victoria Embankment on the Thames toward Scotland Yard. "Your agency has a long history. You guys are pretty much the original police force," Byrd declared.

"We have been the police force of this area since 1829. Quite a long record of service. Your department was probably formed about the same time?"

Byrd laughed, "Well, 1936. But I've worked several cases with the Texas Rangers. They're the oldest *state* law enforcement agency in the US. They go back to 1823, I believe."

Ashwood nodded. "Ah, Texas. Cowboy hats and boots. I've seen them portrayed in many Western movies."

Byrd didn't want to know what he must think of Georgia from the movies. He somehow doubted Ashwood would have been a fan of *Smokey and the Bandit*.

Byrd enjoyed the view as they walked. He could see Westminster Bridge ahead and, through the trees, he could make out Big Ben. "What's all the mystery with this meeting? My boss told me the Met Police wanted me to discuss an old case and were willing to pay for my travel. The GBI wouldn't allow that, but they gave me the nod to fly over. What can you tell me?"

Before Ashwood could answer, Byrd saw the famous revolving sign in front of a plain-looking building along the river. It read "New Scotland Yard" and Byrd was excited to be there. He made a mental note to avoid standing with his mouth agape as he took in the historic buildings.

Ashwood was striding toward the building when he noticed Byrd had stopped. "Everything okay, Agent Byrd?"

"I grew up reading Sherlock Holmes, and this is almost like a dream."

Ashwood chuckled. "The Metropolitan Police Force is always happy to make dreams come true."

Byrd was disappointed to discover New Scotland Yard was simply another office building with little character inside. After passing through the security station, they took the lift—not the elevator—up to the fifth floor and Ashwood led the way to a conference room.

The room was walled in judge's panels of dark wood

and there were no windows. In the center of the room was a large conference table with several comfortable-looking chairs spaced around it. When Byrd came into the room, he could smell tea brewing. A man stood by the oak conference table and extended a hand to Byrd. He wore an expensive-looking suit and was neat to a fault. Tall and thin with white hair combed straight back, he looked like the man Byrd would have imagined to be a boss at Scotland Yard. "Detective Chief Superintendent Baker. You must be Agent Byrd."

Byrd shook his hand. "That would be me."

Baker motioned to a seat. As he made his way to the chair, Byrd saw another man, probably in his late sixties, sitting along the wall. He didn't introduce himself, but he was watching everything that transpired in the room. Byrd dropped into the chair he'd been offered, even more acutely aware that his knees were aging at a faster pace than he was.

Ashwood stood by a cabinet against the back wall. "Would you care for a whisky? We have Scotch and Irish. I'm afraid we don't have any American, though."

Byrd waved his hand. "Thanks, but I'm on the clock."

Baker sat at the head of the table. "We are waiting for someone else. But I can tell you the Crown is seeking information on an investigation you were a part of in the past. You happen to be the only officer still working in law enforcement."

"The Crown?" Byrd was puzzled.

"British government," Baker explained. "Does the name Rojo ring any bells?"

Byrd smiled. "He's been dead for about twenty years, I think."

"Nineteen to be exact. We have matters of interest to

the government that you may be able to shed some light on." Baker took a folder from the middle of the table and pushed it toward Byrd.

Byrd opened it without comment. It was similar to most of the other case folders he had examined in his life. There were no names on the tab, only a case number. Byrd opened the manila folder and saw what appeared to be crime scene photographs. The focus was on a man sitting on a park bench. Byrd struggled to find anything in the photos that had any meaning to him. The man was dressed in a business suit and was sitting upright on the bench. The background looked like a park. His position made it hard for Byrd to make out a face.

As he fanned the pictures out on the table, a new man came into the conference room. He was about forty, well dressed, and tanned. Byrd thought that was unusual for England in the winter.

The new man found a seat and put his overcoat over the chair beside him. "Agent Byrd. It's been a long time."

Byrd searched the face. There was something about him that rang a bell. Then it hit him. Byrd couldn't believe his eyes for a moment.

"It *has* been a while," Byrd remarked smoothly.

The new man nodded. "Nineteen years, I think."

CHAPTER 1
OMAR NO MORE

MONDAY, MAY 30, 2005
9:35 A.M.
EL PASO, TEXAS

Omar Warren squinted at the bright West Texas sun. He had been inside the building behind him for just a few weeks, but he'd been held in a cell far from any sunshine. Omar glanced back at the building, then spat on the sidewalk. He'd be twenty in a few weeks and his time in the El Paso Adult Detention Center had worn on his soul.

Adam Benjamin, Omar's traveling companion, shook his head with a frown. "No need to poke the bear. Spitting on the sidewalk is probably an arrestable offense in this corner of hell. Let's get going."

Omar admired Adam, an experienced mercenary who had worked for Omar's father for as long as Omar could remember. During the last year, Adam had become a surrogate father to Omar.

Omar Warren had joined his father in a drug smuggling enterprise with a Mexican drug lord called Rojo. The operation had worked well until a team of Georgia Bureau of Investigation agents caught Omar's airplane on a clandestine runway in northwest Georgia. Adam had been seriously wounded in the gunfight that followed. Omar's dad, General Mitchell Warren, had escaped using his contacts from the time when he was an operative for the CIA, while Omar and Adam had been charged by an Assistant US Attorney in El Paso, and the two had been transported to face those charges.

Omar bounced down the short flight of steps, arms and legs limber. He didn't walk like a man who had been jail-hopping across the country since Valentine's Day of this year. However, Adam was moving noticeably slower.

"Where to?" Omar asked.

"Your dad has a house in Cambodia. He's headed there now. We'll need to take a circuitous route to get there, though. The feds may come looking for us any time."

Omar's eyebrows shot up. "You mean the charges weren't dismissed?"

"Nope, kid. Some lawyer who owes your dad a favor is in town. He's some hotshot from the Department of Justice. He dropped some bogus papers on the county. We need to make tracks."

"Won't the cops be looking for us?"

Adam laughed and then began to cough. He gripped his right side and went pale.

"What's wrong, Adam?" The two had been separated during their incarceration.

"If I had to guess, I'd say I'm bleeding internally. They got the bullet out at the hospital, but the skill level of those surgeons left something to be desired. I've kept it under wraps, though." Adam fought to stand erect. "Not a big deal, but I'm weaker than I should be. Just be patient with this old man."

"Why didn't you say something to the jailors? Those assholes would have to get you checked out."

Adam took a deep breath, teeth gritted. "That would have made it harder to get us out. We needed to be able to walk out the jail door as soon as the paper dropped. We've got to get moving, kid."

Omar didn't understand. "They released us based on *something*, right?"

Adam winked. "I didn't see the paperwork but, if I had to guess, the Sheriff's Office got a teletype from the Justice Department. It said to release us immediately and the paperwork would follow by US mail. Something like that."

Omar wasn't convinced. "Can we at least get you to an urgent care? Somebody to get you fixed up?"

Adam leaned against a bench on the street. He shook his head. "Kid, I'm sixty years old and I've been shot half a dozen times. I know I'm hurt bad this time, but I'm not going to lie down and die. So, let's get this show on the road."

Omar chose not to argue. Like his dad, Adam was hardheaded. "Where to, then?" Omar asked. As an after-thought, Omar asked, "How long do you think we have?"

Adam shrugged his shoulders. "I'm hoping your dad's people came through. We need new names and some money to travel with. As far as the cops looking for us, it could be an hour or it could be a day. Either way, we need to beat feet."

Adam stood and looked around. After a couple of seconds, he grunted. "See that taco truck? Help me get over to it."

Omar took Adam's arm and helped him make his way down the block to the truck. When they got to the window, the young girl working inside asked, "What do you gentlemen want?"

Adam put both hands onto the counter. "Do you have fresh shrimp in your tacos?"

The girl shrugged. "Sir, we ain't got no shrimp tacos. We got all kinds of meats . . ."

A man came from inside the truck and leaned out the window. "Sorry, she didn't know you had called ahead."

He thrust a bag out and Adam took it. Adam crammed the bag in his pocket and walked away. Omar followed, looking over his shoulder at the girl who seemed as confused as he was.

"Do you know that guy?" Omar asked.

Adam sat down hard on a bench. He pulled the bag out of his pocket and offered it to Omar. "You want a taco, kid?"

Omar shrugged and opened the bag. After he examined the contents, he looked all around them. He didn't see anyone watching.

"What did we get?" Adam asked.

Omar spoke softly, "A couple of passports, a handful of driver's licenses, a credit card, and some cash."

"How much cash?"

Omar looked back in the bag. "Two bundles of US currency. The bands say ten thousand."

Adam nodded. "Twenty grand should get us going. Good. Let's get a taxi to the airport."

"Where are we flying to?" Omar asked.

Adam's smile was wry. "Nowhere."

Omar used a bogus Texas driver's license to rent the car. He swiped the credit card from the taco bag. Then he tried to look cool and calm as he waited to see if the man behind the desk would call the police.

After a wait that seemed to go on forever, the rental car

agent handed over the keys to a midsized sedan. With no luggage, they had plenty of room. Omar piled in behind the steering wheel and waited for Adam to slump into the passenger seat.

"Where to?" Omar asked.

Adam closed his eyes. "We're headed to Vancouver. Once we're on the Canadian side, maybe we can get directions to a friendly doctor."

Omar headed the rental car north. By midnight, the pair had made it to Green River, Utah. Omar found a cut-rate hotel willing to take cash for a room. Adam struggled out of the car and, with Omar's help, made it to a bed where he flopped down. In short order, Adam was softly snoring.

The next morning, Adam seemed to feel better. He woke up and dressed before Omar rolled over. Omar watched him as he prepared a cup of coffee with the little pot in the room. Then Adam went outside without saying a word.

Omar showered, dressed, and was ready to go when Adam reappeared. Adam took a map they had gotten at a service station and began working on a path north with a pencil.

"What's up?" Omar asked.

"I made a call to someone who will help us. We're going to meet him at a place called Bonner's Ferry, Idaho. This guy will get us into Canada. Then we'll get a plane out of Vancouver to Japan."

"Sounds like a plan," Omar observed. "Can we stop at a thrift store and get some clothes?"

Adam nodded. "Good idea, kid. Stinking and dirty is not the way we want to cross the border. I want some new clothes and a shower to get the smell of a jail out of my nostrils."

Twenty hours later, Omar parked near a motel in Bonner's Ferry, Idaho. Omar had driven all night, fueled by coffee, fast food, and the need to get out of the US.

The small city was nestled among the mountains along the northwestern border. The morning was crisp in the Idaho border town and Omar was happy to be away from the Texas plains.

He noticed a tour bus near the entrance to the motel and a group of men and women standing around. This was the group they were to join.

Abandoning the rental car here, Omar helped Adam climb out and walk over near the tourists.

They climbed on the half-full bus and, sitting separately, made themselves comfortable. Adam seemed to have rallied and was exchanging pleasantries with a retired couple from Independence, Missouri. Omar pretended to sleep.

When everyone was comfortably seated, the driver pointed the bus out of the parking lot and gunned the old diesel engine, and the smoking bus chugged toward the Canadian border.

When the bus made its mandatory stop at the border checkpoint, Canadian customs officials boarded the bus. The tourist bus crossed the border twice a day, and the Canadian officers simply asked each passenger to hold their passport open beside their face. The officers glanced at the faces of each passenger, comparing the passport photo next to them, and paid no attention to the two fugitives.

"So far, so good," Omar mumbled under his breath.

There would be no record of them, of their real names or the names on the new passports, since they left El Paso.

Omar glanced over at Adam, who looked gray. Omar hoped they could find a place to get Adam some medical help.

The bus ride was shorter than Omar had expected. The bus pulled into a parking area beside a duty-free store. The white and blue metal building had seen better days. As soon as the bus came to a stop, the tourists began to empty. When the others were off the bus, the driver pointed to an old Range Rover at the corner of the parking lot. Adam pushed five hundred dollars into the bus driver's hand as they climbed down and headed for the next leg of their journey.

Adam stumbled on the curb leading into Vancouver International Airport. The Range Rover had dropped them near the departures area and quickly disappeared into traffic. With their flight scheduled for early the next day, Adam recommended they check into the hotel near the international check-in counter. Omar helped Adam onto the elevator and the men rode up one floor. Adam walked with Omar into the hotel lobby and then Omar strolled over to the front desk as Adam slumped in a comfortable chair with a cap pulled low over his face.

"I need a room for one night, please," Omar said to the lone employee.

"What credit card would you like to use, please?" The man eyed Omar suspiciously.

Omar leaned in, conspiratorially. "I'll be holding the room on this card, but I was hoping to pay cash." He pointed to Adam. "My friend over there is a bit of a recluse. He doesn't like to leave a record behind. His wife has attorneys breathing down his neck and we'd like to keep this stop off her radar."

The clerk scowled. "I can run your card, if that's agreeable. When you check out, we can zero your balance."

The clerk pulled a form from under the counter. "I will need you to fill this out and then let me copy your passport."

Omar leaned in. "I have them both right here." He handed the bogus passports to the clerk and waited. When everything was ready, the clerk passed Omar a couple of pass cards in an envelope.

Omar walked over and helped Adam to his feet.

Omar had slept poorly, anxious to get to Asia. He gave up and rolled out of bed around four a.m., pulling on his pants and making coffee in the dark. Once the tiny pot was full, he quietly padded over to the other bed, where Adam lay still.

"Adam, we probably ought to get going pretty soon." When he didn't get a response, Omar tugged at Adam's shoulder. His fingers brushed Adam's neck and Omar was shocked to find his friend and mentor cold to the touch. Omar felt unsteady as the truth sank in. The kindest man in his life, and his true father figure, was dead. *We were so close to the finish line*, Omar thought.

He sat on the bed, feeling lost and alone. He didn't cry, but the emptiness was almost unbearable. He shook his head and tried to decide his next move. This life of his father's, this clandestine world he had been thrust into, was less attractive each day he sat in jail. Adam's death brought into focus the ugly reality of the path he was on.

After several minutes, he stood and went through

Adam's pockets. He was surprised Adam's body was already stiff. Omar took Adam's fake passport and any other identification and crammed it into his own pockets. Then he took a last look at his friend. He hung a "Do Not Disturb" placard on the door handle as he left.

Omar rode the elevator to the front desk. He made eye contact with the clerk on the morning shift and the man bustled over. "What may I help you with?"

"We need to have the room for one more night," Omar said.

The man frowned. "That may be a problem. I'll see if we can extend your stay?"

The clerk checked his computer, clicked away for several seconds and then returned to Omar with a smile. "It is arranged."

Omar grinned. "Thanks so much. Our flight departs at midnight tonight. We'll be out of the room later this evening."

Omar went downstairs and passed through airport security. He found a seat near the gate and slumped over with his eyes closed. His hands were cold and yet he was sweating profusely. His ears were ringing and he realized he hadn't eaten anything all day, yet he wasn't hungry. At that moment, Omar realized he had never felt so alone. He hadn't felt this alone in the little twin-engine airplane flying hundreds of pounds of meth across the country. He wanted to just sit and cry, but this was no time to draw attention to himself.

There was nothing to do now but wait. Barring any surprises, he would be in Tokyo by midnight.

CHAPTER 2
BULLET RESISTANT

Georgia Bureau of Investigation Special Agent Daniel Byrd had put the wild events of last May out of his mind. A major drug investigation spanning half the country had collapsed when General Warren, his son Omar, and Adam Benjamin had disappeared. The last four months had seen him return to the routine cases of a regional agent.

Now, Byrd was in the dark, literally. He sat in the passenger seat of a government surplus armored vehicle the GBI had gotten from the Air Force.

Byrd had been called earlier in the day to act as a negotiator for the GBI Special Response Team, a tactical unit made up of agents from across the state. Byrd had been certified to act as a negotiator after attending a training class in Florida in April. He had rushed to the city near the South Carolina border, only to end up sitting.

He was seated next to Gary Thomasson, the designated operator for the armored truck. Thomasson had been recently assigned to Region 8, the same office in Gainesville as Byrd. Thomasson had been a well-respected officer with the Georgia Department of Natural Resources before being hired by the GBI. Both men were well out of their office territory, in Franklin County in the Northeast Corner of Georgia.

Byrd spoke to the place in the dark where he thought Thomasson was sitting. "Didn't you have a hand in the GBI getting this vehicle?"

"Yep. I still have contacts in the Air National Guard. The Air Force used these for base security," Thomasson sounded relaxed.

The men sat quietly for a moment, then Thomasson asked, "Did you get a brief on this guy? All I know is he took a shot at a deputy."

Byrd nodded without thinking Thomasson couldn't see him. "Yeah. The guy who lives here is named Oliver Tarvin. He decided to beat the living hell out of his live-in girlfriend last weekend. She asked for a Temporary Protective Order against Tarvin and happened to mention her boyfriend has a gun he keeps near the door of the trailer. Being a convicted felon, the Sheriff's Office took a warrant for him. When a Franklin County deputy came out here this morning to serve the arrest warrant, Tarvin took a shot at the deputy with a Mini-14 rifle. Deputies and troopers surrounded the place and tried to get him out. Sometime in the afternoon, the Special Agent in Charge of the Athens Office decided to call in SRT. But by the time the GBI got enough people to the location, the sun had set. Now they want us to get the man's attention while the tactical team tries to get close to him."

"I wish we had some night vision goggles. This sitting here in the dark is for the birds," Thomasson observed. "No offense."

Byrd laughed. "No offense. And yes, I wish we could see something."

"We have the target in sight." The voice was team leader Lamont "Monty" Davis calling over the GBI radio. "He's outside the trailer. Can the negotiator call him on the public address system?"

"Will do," Byrd responded into the microphone.

Byrd fumbled around and turned the PA system on. Once the system was active the inside of the truck was slightly illuminated. "Mr. Tarvin. We need you to come on around here and put that gun down."

Oliver Tarvin pointed his flashlight at the sound of the PA. Suddenly, Thomasson and Byrd were blinded. Seconds later, Byrd saw a bright flash and heard what sounded like a hammer hitting the truck above his head. Monty Davis shouted, "Shots fired!" over the radio channel.

Reflexively, Byrd leaned down near the dash. Byrd shouted into the PA, "Mr. Tarvin, you don't need to do that."

The man had disappeared into the dark.

"I thought I saw a gap in the armor over here," Byrd asked Thomasson. "Is that possible?"

Thomasson grunted. "That's why the Air Force got rid of these. The armor doesn't completely overlap. There are small gaps that, I am told, are too small for a bullet to get through."

"Fuck! How is this thing considered bulletproof?" Byrd asked.

Thomasson shook his head. "Not bulletproof. It's bullet resistant."

Byrd sighed. "Great!"

Tarvin fired again. Byrd heard the bullet slam into the vehicle near his head, again. "Monty, can we light this asshole up? We are blind here."

"No, no, no!" came the quick reply over the radio. "If you do that, you'll silhouette the team."

Byrd wasn't happy. "Got it," he growled into the radio mic.

"Team two," Davis reported calmly over the radio. "He is coming your way. Use caution."

Byrd strained to see anything in the dark. Suddenly the man's rifle fired, this time away from the GBI truck. A millisecond later, Byrd heard what sounded like a flutter of wings. Byrd knew the sound. The buzz of a suppressed MP-5 machine gun used by one of the SRT operators.

The radio suddenly became a torrent of jumbled signals. "Shots fired!"

"Target down!"

"Any of our team hit?"

"We need a medic right away!"

"Someone get us some light!"

Thomasson pulled the armored vehicle into gear and turned on the headlights. He could see the tactical team gathered around a man lying on the grass. Byrd grabbed the trauma kit from the back of the truck. As Thomasson brought the hulking vehicle to a sliding halt, Byrd jumped down and dropped the trauma kit.

Byrd fell to his knees beside the man. He didn't look much older than Byrd. Tarvin lay on his back, his eyes staring sightlessly at the sky. Byrd heard Tarvin sigh loudly and then stop breathing.

FRIDAY, OCTOBER 21, 2005
11:53 P.M.
CANTON, GEORGIA

Daniel Byrd trudged up the steps to his apartment near downtown Canton. Because he hadn't been involved in the shooting, Byrd had been dismissed from the shooting scene and had made the two-hour drive home.

He kicked off his shoes as soon as he got in the door. He turned on the lamp near the door and was surprised to see Violet Childs sleeping in his bed. Violet worked as an Assistant District Attorney in Canton. She and Byrd had been dating since her divorce became final in September. Last week, Byrd had given her a key to his apartment.

Byrd pulled his clothes off in his guest bedroom as quietly as he could. He had driven home on autopilot, pushing his government car hard, as soon as he had been released from the scene. He had considered it a bonus the GBI didn't mandate counseling for those who hadn't fired shots in the incident. He had given a statement and was given permission to head home.

Once he had undressed, Byrd tried his best to shower without waking Violet. He leaned on the wall of the shower stall and let the hot water run over his head and back. He stood for a full minute as the water rinsed the day from his body. For several seconds, he let the stress roll out. He was startled when Violet began to rub his shoulders.

"Sorry," she said. "I didn't mean to scare you."

He looked back at her. "It's okay. I'm sorry I woke you up."

Violet looked at his face. "Are you okay, Danny?"

Byrd pushed off the shower wall and turned to Violet. They stood face to face in the spray from the shower. "Did you come over here to check on me?" Byrd asked.

She watched for his reaction. "No, but I didn't come over here to sleep either."

She held his face in her hands as she leaned in and kissed him. Byrd wrapped his arms around her and closed his eyes.

She led him to his bedroom where their love making was gentle, slow-paced, and perfect for the moment. The post-coital snuggling was the salve Byrd needed.

Within a couple of minutes, Violet lay softly snoring. Byrd rolled onto his side, hoping for sleep.

Then his new Bureau cell phone rang.

Byrd sat up on the edge of the bed.

He clicked the phone open (in spite of the name, it wasn't possible to flip it open). "Byrd."

"Teddy?" the voice asked.

"Who's this?"

"It's Clete Petterson."

Byrd smiled. "Good to hear from you." Then Byrd followed up with, "Who told you my nickname?"

Petterson laughed. "It's all over Texas."

Clete Petterson and Byrd had become close friends when they both investigated a smuggling group led by General Mitchell Warren. The group was operated by Warren's son, Omar. Less than seven months ago, the smugglers were intercepted running hundreds of pounds of crystal methamphetamine from the US border near El Paso to a farm in Georgia.

Byrd grunted. "You called me in the middle of the night to tell me that?"

Petterson shifted gears. "Nope. I called you to give you some information. I think it might have something to do with one of your defendants."

"Okay."

"We got a call from the Royal Canadian Mounted Police up in Vancouver. They had a John Doe body found in a hotel at the Vancouver International Airport in June of this year. He didn't have any ID and the names used to check into the room were bogus."

Byrd grabbed a pad and started making notes. "Go ahead."

"Since Vancouver is right there on the border, they ran his prints through the FBI. They got a big zero. One of the Mounties, just as a precaution, sent the prints to the US Military Records Center in St. Louis. About a month ago, they got a hit. Some guy named Clarence Edenfield. Was a Green Beret and served in just about every conflict since he joined the Army."

"When did he get out?"

Petterson checked. "The records I have show he was never discharged."

"So, what has any of this got to do with Georgia?"

"At the same time the Mounties were checking through the military, one of their lab folks decided to go through John Doe's clothes. The lab guy found a man's sock filled with quarters and knotted. He recognized it as a prison weapon. He checked for identifying marks. Seems our fellow had a pair of socks issued by the El Paso County Adult Detention Center."

Byrd thought about the possibilities. "I'm guessing it was Adam Benjamin?" Byrd asked.

Clete's voice had softened. "Right. He died from the gunshots from over in Georgia. According to the medical staff at the jail, he refused follow-up after he got here and told them he was fresh as a daisy."

"What about Omar? I thought they both made it to Thailand or Cambodia or somewhere that didn't extradite to the US."

"It looks like Omar made a flight to Japan using a stolen British passport with his photo added, and then he disappeared."

Byrd sighed. "I guess I need to get word to the Bureau. My bullet killed Benajmin. I assume that'll bring on more talk."

Petterson was ahead of him. "The Director of the Texas Department of Public Safety is reaching out to your director. They'll be sending him a copy of the entire package of information. I just wanted you to know what was going on."

Byrd's voice was barely audible. "So, I've killed another man?"

Petterson replied quickly. "He chose to keep his circumstances hidden from the jail staff. The medical examiner in Canada says there is no reason for him to have died other than lack of medical attention to his internal bleeding."

Byrd nodded absently.

After a too-long silence, Petterson asked, "Are you okay, buddy?"

Byrd nodded again. "Sure. Just a little overwhelmed on a Friday night."

After more small talk, Petterson rung off.

Byrd poured a shot of vodka in a glass and followed it with cranberry juice. He held up the glass and examined the liquid before he took a sip. As he held the glass to the light, he heard Violet come into the kitchen. "Drinking this late?"

"I'm not even TDI."

"What?"

Byrd shrugged. "Two drinks in."

Violet scowled. "Couldn't it just as easily mean three drinks in?"

Violet came over and wrapped her arms around him. She pressed her head into his back. "Danny, what was that call about?"

Byrd shook his head. "I shot a man back in May during a dope deal. He appeared to be fine when he was released from jail out in El Paso. The Mounties found him dead in Canada a couple of days later. He died from complications from *my* bullet." Byrd looked her in the eyes. "And then tonight, the Special Response Team had to put a man down."

"Were you a part of that too?" she asked.

Byrd shrugged. "I was just there as a negotiator. My job was to try to get him to give up. When that didn't work, I kept him occupied until the team could get close to him."

Violet stepped back. "So, you didn't cause his death either. Both men died from their own bad decisions."

Byrd hung his head. "That's not what the guy tonight said to me." The next words were a whisper. "Well, he said it with his eyes."

Violet frowned. "What?"

"I was looking into his eyes when he died. I actually saw the lights go out."

Violet felt guilty. "I guess I'm prying."

"I guess you're right. It could mean three drinks in." Byrd pulled away and went to the counter.

Byrd took the glass from the counter, refilled it, and drank it down. He looked at the empty glass for a moment. "Sometimes I drink just to get the taste of the day out of my mouth."

Violet watched in silence. Then she grabbed a glass and poured a shot of Irish whisky Byrd kept for visitors. She didn't add anything to the glass. "I've been a prosecutor for four years now and every day seems harder." She took a gulp of the whisky and then, after a quick breath, finished it off. "That may be the smartest thing I've ever heard anyone say. It may not get all the taste out of your mouth but it sure does make it better."

SATURDAY, OCTOBER 22, 2005
7:55 P.M.
CANTON, GEORGIA

Byrd and Violet were boxing up all his worldly goods. Violet looked over, examining his profile in the dim light. "This is a big step for you, isn't it? How long before you close?"

"The surveyors finished yesterday. The lawyer says the first week in November should be a good target."

"Aren't we getting ahead of the game? You'll be living here a couple of more weeks."

Byrd stood up and stretched his back. "Yep, but a big case could pop off. This is a pretty big deal for me. I guess this won't be my last weekend as an apartment dweller, but I want to be ready. Thanks for helping me pack."

Violet grinned. "Happy to help! If my back wasn't out of whack I could do more."

Byrd sighed. "You're doing plenty just by keeping me on task."

Violet stood in front of him. "You seem satisfied the house and property will work for you."

Byrd thought about the little house just outside of Canton. Byrd's uncle had bequeathed the forty-year-old farmhouse to him when he died last August. "Uncle Jimmy's house has some years on it, and there are going to be projects for the foreseeable future, but the property will give me lots of privacy."

Violet pursed her lips. "At thirty-four, it's about time you settle down."

Byrd ignored the jibe. "I only have to pay off the last loan my uncle took on the property. I'll be paying a lot less for the house than I'm paying in rent. And I'll own something."

Violet laughed. "You and the bank."

Byrd laughed, too. "Really, more the bank's house than mine."

Violet shook her head. "I can't believe you fell into a house with ten acres. That will be amazing."

Byrd nodded and grinned. "There's a great place to shoot out back. And a hot tub on the deck, if I can ever get it working."

Violet cut her eyes over. "You boys and your toys. Sounds like this'll be a good place to hide out. I may need a place to hide soon."

Byrd scowled. "What?"

Violet giggled. "My boss, the Chief Assistant District Attorney, thinks I was sleeping around before I got my divorce."

"Is that a problem?"

Violet shook her hair and tugged it back into a ponytail. "Maybe. He thinks it's an act of moral turpitude. Like I'm the only one in the office who has slept around."

Byrd took the box he had just filled and taped the top. "He thinks or he knows?"

Violet laughed bitterly. "One of the guys in the office couldn't keep his mouth shut. He told someone else he was having a relationship with me."

"You had an affair with a coworker? I can see that being a problem. How long ago was it?" Byrd heaved the box on top of the others near the door of his apartment.

"I quit seeing him last year."

Byrd rolled up a bathroom rug and tossed it on top of the boxes. "He can't plan to discipline you over past history like that, can he?"

Violet scowled. "He acts like a prude, but the talk on the street is that he has his own skeletons. He's made a big deal of how often I've missed work over my back issues. It's his way of getting back at me for my alleged indiscretions."

Byrd dropped into one of the kitchen chairs. "But you're under a doctor's care, aren't you?"

Violet stared out the window of Byrd's apartment. She didn't like where the conversation seemed headed. She knew other cops like Byrd, and they all saw drug use as very black and white. She didn't consider herself a druggie but, if she were candid with Byrd about the number of painkillers she was taking each day, he wouldn't see it that way. "Well, I've been to a few doctors. All they want to do is give me painkillers and suggest back surgery."

Byrd glowered. "They aren't doing anything to treat the problem?"

Violet wouldn't make eye contact. "They treat the symptoms. The pain. I've tried chiropractors and massage therapists. Nothing seems to help the pain."

Byrd tried to sound casual. "You have to watch those pain meds. They can get to be a problem."

Violet laughed. Byrd thought the laugh seemed forced. "That's why I keep a big strong man like you around."

Byrd ignored her and pulled a box from his bedroom.

"Are you taking everything out of the bedroom?" Violet asked.

Byrd shook his head. "No, I won't be able to move in till next weekend. Just getting everything I can set to go."

Violet nodded. "Good. No vodka, then. I'd like to have one last wild night in this place."

Byrd squinted. "What is it you're saying?"

"Don't get into the vodka until you've had your way with me," Violet stared back.

"Some things are better than drinking. But technically it sounds like *you're* having your way with *me*."

"Daniel Byrd, boy toy!" Violet's laugh seemed genuine.

Byrd winced. "I've been called worse."

CHAPTER 3
PASSING OUT SOME JUSTICE

MONDAY, OCTOBER 24, 2005
11:02 P.M.
JASPER, GEORGIA

Daniel Byrd quietly pushed through the doors to the courtroom. Byrd made sure he rode the door as it closed. He didn't want to draw attention to himself.

The judge watched Byrd make his way across the courtroom to the table reserved for the prosecutor.

Judge Reginald Lance's prematurely iron-gray hair made him seem older but, at fifty-three years, he was one of the youngest Chief Judges of Superior Court in his home state of Georgia. He had become the Chief Judge of the circuit when Judge Thomas Pelfrey, long time jurist and feudal lord of the mountain counties in north central Georgia, killed himself rather than go to jail. And then Pelfrey's daughter and successor, a meth-shooting nut-job, had been appointed to the Georgia Court of Appeals.

Judge Lance looked over his glasses at the man in front of him, held in place by a Pickens County deputy. The man wore an orange jumpsuit and was visibly shaking as he stood in the front of the courtroom.

Judge Lance had been known as Reggie to his friends

growing up near Athens, but since moving to Ellijay after law school, he had been hung with a different nickname. As a young prosecutor, straight out of school, then the District Attorney for the circuit, and then finally as a no-nonsense judge, he was known as "No-Chance Lance."

Lance addressed the man standing in front of him. "Mr. Johanson, you will be appointed an attorney to represent you as soon as possible. In the meantime, you will be held in the common jail of Pickens County until such time as a hearing can be scheduled to address any possible bond. Is that clear enough for you?"

The man frowned. "Your Highness, I need to get home and take care of my young'uns as soon as I can. Is they any way you can speed up a hearing?"

"Mr. Johanson, your children are in need of care because you stand accused of beating your wife so badly that she is currently still hospitalized. Therefore, your children have been given into the custody of the state. Even if an attorney made an argument convincing me to release you on a surety bond, I don't anticipate you'll be the caregiver for your children."

The man hung his head. "I guess that means I ain't getting out no time soon?"

Judge Lance gave him a stern look. "That's exactly what it means."

The man wanted to protest, but the deputy pulled him out of the courtroom through the side door reserved for detainees.

Judge Lance looked at Byrd. "Agent Byrd, to what do we owe the honor?"

Byrd glanced up. "Just here to do my sworn duty, Your Honor."

Lance chuckled. "I assume that means you're here to testify in some hearing I haven't heard about yet."

Byrd grinned.

District Attorney Jerry Mason slapped a stack of papers on the prosecutor's table, then stood and faced the bench. "Sorry, Your Honor. I was trying to negotiate a plea on the case coming up this afternoon."

The clerk handed the Judge a piece of paper. Lance glanced at the heading and read aloud, "The State of Georgia versus Thomas K. Gordon?"

Mason nodded. "The State has offered Mr. Gordon a plea of life with the possibility of parole for the murder of his father and mother."

Judge Lance laid his glasses on the bench. "And Mr. Gordon thinks he can do better in front of a jury?"

Mason shrugged. "He confessed to Agent Byrd here." Mason pointed at Byrd. "Mr. Gordon believes that he was cleansing his soul. He thinks anything he said to Agent Byrd should have been confidential. He saw it as a religious moment protected the same as priest/penitent statements."

The Judge shook his head. "Well, what do you propose?"

"If Your Honor will agree, we would like to have a Jackson-Denno hearing for the limited purpose of ruling on the admissibility of the confession."

Judge Lance scowled. "Who represents Mr. Gordon?"

The door to the courtroom swung open and local defense attorney Lane Sims walked briskly toward the front of the courtroom. "I do, Your Honor."

Judge Lance shook his head. "Are you planning on filing a motion for this Jackson-Denno hearing?"

Sims held up a piece of paper. "I have the motion right here."

The Judge gave Sims a hard look. "Does your motion explain to the court how your client's mistake of belief, if it's real, becomes a question of voluntariness?"

Lane Sims couldn't suppress a smile. "Your Honor, my client is willing to enter a plea *if* you rule his confession is admissible."

Judge Lance looked from Sims to Mason. Neither man spoke as Lance rolled the idea over in his mind. "You want this on the record?" the Judge asked Sims.

Sims shook his head. "I think this might be left to our own recollections. Later examination might not be favorable to any of the participants."

Lance scowled. "That's what I thought. I doubt this is anyone's finest hour."

Lance looked at the deputy sitting near the door. "Have Mr. Gordon brought into the courtroom."

The deputy spoke into his radio microphone and a moment later, a second deputy brought Tommy Gordon into the courtroom. Gordon was a tall, skinny man with dark hair and a scraggly beard. The ill-fitting jail uniform with matching handcuffs and belly chain didn't compliment his appearance. He nodded to his attorney and to Daniel Byrd as the deputy escorted him to the front of the courtroom. Before the deputy sat Gordon in the defendant's chair, he motioned at the handcuffs.

Jerry Mason shook his head. "You can leave them on, for now."

Judge Lance nodded in agreement. "He's fine for the purpose of this motion."

Mason stood at the podium and started his argument. "Your Honor, the State believes that the statement made by the defendant is properly taken and legally able to be introduced at trial."

Judge Lance turned to face the defendant. "Mr. Gordon, would it be sufficient for your purposes if the court were to question Agent Byrd and then give a ruling?"

Gordon looked questioningly at Lane Sims. Sims nodded and Gordon turned back to the Judge. "Yes, sir."

Byrd stood and walked to the witness stand. He stood by the box as Mason gave him a stern look. "Do you swear to tell the truth, the whole truth, and nothing but the truth in the matter before this court?"

Byrd stood awkwardly and nodded. "I do."

Byrd climbed into the witness box and took a seat.

"Agent Byrd, have you ever been a licensed doctor, a licensed psychotherapist, or a minister by any definition?" Mason didn't waste any time.

Byrd shook his head. "No, sir. I've been a cop for my adult life."

Mason nodded. "And, Agent Byrd, have you ever held yourself out to be a licensed doctor, a licensed psycho-therapist, or a minister by any definition?"

Byrd shook his head. "No, sir."

Mason dropped his papers on the table. "That's all the State has, your honor."

Lance looked over his glasses at Jerry Mason. "Anything the State wants to add?"

When Mason shook his head, Lance looked at Lane Sims. "Mr. Sims?"

Lane Sims stood awkwardly and shook his head. "No, Your Honor. I think you have covered the matter."

Lance leaned back in his chair and steepled his fingers. He looked at a spot in the ceiling for several minutes as everyone sat quietly.

Finally, Judge Lance looked harshly down at Tommy Gordon. "Mr. Gordon, I find no merit in your argument that your statement was coerced. I will work with your attorney, Mr. Sims, to set a date for you to offer any plea you may wish to present."

Tommy Gordon stood by Lane Sims as the Judge announced his decision. Gordon seemed dazed. He stood, head bobbing up and down, as his attorney interpreted what had just happened. When Sims finished, the deputy grabbed Gordon by the arm and took him out of the courtroom.

Once Gordon was on his way back to jail, Judge Lance looked at Daniel Byrd. "Agent Byrd, there is a matter I would like to address to you in chambers. Would you please join me?"

Lance thought Byrd looked confused by the request, but he quickly circled around the courtroom and out into the hall. The first door on the left was the Judge's chambers.

Lance heard Byrd tap softly.

"Come in."

Judge Lance was seated at his desk, and he motioned Byrd to a chair in front of him. The Judge lit a cigarette—in violation of the courthouse rules. "Agent Byrd, you know you are still under oath?"

Byrd nodded uncomfortably. "I do."

"Agent Byrd, is it true you've had sex with every available woman in this courthouse?"

Byrd's face reddened. He started to sputter an answer when Lance spoke up. "Sit down, Danny." Lance motioned at a seat. "I just wanted a cigarette."

Byrd sat down hesitantly. "Shit, you scared the hell out of me."

Lance laughed. "I didn't think you wanted to answer that question."

Byrd seemed to relax. "Judge, I thought a good lawyer didn't ask a question he doesn't know the answer to."

Lance nodded and inhaled the cigarette smoke deeply. "You've got me there."

Byrd crossed his legs as Lance worked on finishing the cigarette.

"What happened to you and that hot redhead in the DA's office?" Lance asked.

Byrd struggled to answer the question. "I guess things just didn't work out with us. She outgrew me."

Lance puffed again. "You know she'll be finishing her degree soon. She wants to go to law school."

"I had heard she planned to. She'll be a good lawyer, for sure."

Lance stood up, took a last, deep draw on his cigarette, and shooed Byrd out the back door. "We need some good lawyers up here. That's for sure. Now, let's go back out and get Mr. Sims to buy your lunch. I know that tightwad Jerry Mason won't buy!"

Byrd chuckled. "Even if he would do it, the GBI has a pretty strict policy about taking gratuities."

Lance nodded. "Sims would just try to bill the county for the meal . . ."

Daniel Byrd led the trio of lawyers out the side door of the marble monument to justice in the heart of Jasper, Georgia. The white building was almost blinding in the bright October sun as the four men in dark suits walked out onto Main Street in search of lunch. The streets were quiet as the men ambled along.

"I can't believe we went through that charade about that statement," Jerry Mason observed.

Lane Sims didn't break stride. "There's more than one way to grease the wheels of justice."

"So, was anything that happened this morning legal?" Byrd asked.

Judge Lance stopped and looked at Byrd. "Danny, the law is as much spirit as letter. We observed the spirit today. I guess you could argue that we failed in the letter of the law, but Mr. Gordon got a better deal the way we did it than he would have if a jury found him guilty."

"Which they surely would have done," Jerry Mason observed.

Byrd had turned to comment when he heard a crack like a whip. The sound of a bullet passing near him caused Byrd to push the group of men toward a doorway. "Everybody, get down!"

Each of the men had heard the crack, but only Byrd had recognized the sound as a bullet breaking the sound barrier.

Judge Lance was startled. "What the hell are you doing, Danny?"

Byrd had his pistol in his right hand and stood scanning the area. "Somebody just took a shot at you, Judge."

Felisha Gomez had been stretched out on the floor of the pickup truck bed. She wore dark jeans and a dark top. She had been able to angle her body across the bed and still lie low enough to be hidden by the boxes of produce by the back tailgate. After Felisha had taken the shot, she pulled down the door of the camper top.

Felisha lay quietly, angry with herself for the missed shot, and disassembled the AR-7 Survival Rifle she had used. She put the main parts of the rifle into the stock in their appropriate compartments, and then slid the thin black silencer into her front pants pocket. She noted the black cylinder was warm to the touch after a single shot.

She quietly crawled through the back window into the driver's seat of the truck. She fired up the four-cylinder engine and backed out of the parking spot. When she shifted into drive, the little engine shuddered before it lugged the truck along Main Street toward Highway 53.

At almost forty years old, Felisha felt strong and agile. She was a distance runner and unabashed gym rat. Her features hinted at her Mayan heritage, with almond-shaped dark eyes and jet-black hair. She dreaded having to let Rojo know she had failed. Rojo had offered to use a contact of Warren's to give her better information about the man, Byrd. Now she'd have to admit to Rojo she needed help.

She hit her thigh with her right fist as she drove, and shouted at the roof of the truck, "*Mierda!*"

The streets of Jasper had been peaceful and quiet just an hour ago. Now Main Street was teeming with police officers from every agency in the area. The Jasper Police Department blocked the streets in the courthouse area. The Georgia State Patrol had converged on the courthouse square, and troopers were standing alongside deputies at each of the courthouse doors. Sheriff Bobby Wilton, the man responsible for courthouse security, and several of his deputies were going from business to business on Main Street looking for witnesses to the shooting.

Tina Blackwell, the Special Agent in Charge of the GBI office in Gainesville, and Jackson "Doc" Farmer, an Agent in the Gainesville GBI office, had shown up on the courthouse square to offer support.

When Byrd saw Tina striding up, and Doc close on her heels, he headed their way. Tina stuck out her hand and shook. "Teddy, what happened?"

Byrd pointed at a mark in the marble foundation of an office on the corner by the courthouse. "That's a bullet mark. We found a lead projectile laying on the sidewalk not far from where it hit. Looks like a .22. The sheriff is personally talking to everyone on Main Street he knows, which is practically everyone, but he can't find anybody who saw a shooter. In fact, he's having a hard time finding anyone who heard the shot."

Tina looked over the area. "There's no doubt someone took a shot?"

Byrd shook his head emphatically. "Tina, I've been shot at before. I heard a crack like a bullet breaking the sound barrier. Honestly, I didn't hear a shot either. I'm wondering if the shooter used a silencer."

Doc Farmer rubbed his hand through his hair. "Are you sure the shot was meant for the Judge? Who all was he with at the time?"

Byrd thought the question over. "The Judge is the most likely target. I guess someone might want to take a shot at the District Attorney. Jerry Mason has pissed people off, for sure."

Tina nodded. "Just you three?"

Byrd chuckled. "Well, there was a Defense Attorney named Lane Sims. I can't imagine anybody trying to kill him—except maybe a cop he embarrassed on the witness stand."

Tina gave Byrd a sharp look. "What about you? Any angry husbands or girlfriends we need to know about?"

Byrd cut his eyes toward Doc.

Doc turned his hands palm up. "Don't look at me, Teddy. We're in a small office and people talk."

Byrd pursed his lips. "There's nobody out to get me. Not that I know about, anyway."

Tina pressed her lips together. "You're probably right. The Judge would be the most likely target. He certainly has a reputation in this area."

Doc grabbed Byrd by the arm. "Teddy, do you want me to carry this case? You seem to have a lot going on lately."

Before Byrd could answer, Tina spoke up. "You're the case agent, Doc. Danny will be carried as a witness."

Byrd pointed at Doc's chest. "Are you sure your ticker can handle a case this big? Did your doctor clear you?"

On May 30th, Doc suffered a massive heart attack. His heart blockage was at the beginning of the left main artery, commonly called the "widow maker" for good reason. Doc was lucky to be alive, but he had made a full recovery.

Doc shrugged. "You think Tina would let me come back to work if I wasn't cleared? And I can prove my heart is working right. Can you, Teddy?"

Byrd laughed. "I guess you've got me there."

Tina motioned for Byrd to follow her down the street as Doc turned to get a better look at the bullet mark on the wall. Byrd strode alongside her. "Is this about the dead guy in Canada?" Byrd asked.

Tina stopped and turned to face him. "They train us to approach these things with sensitivity. Offer emotional support. I don't know if you make things easier or harder."

Byrd looked over her head, avoiding eye contact. "Am I in trouble?" Byrd asked.

Tina shook her head. "No, the investigation of the shooting stands. And the Canadian medical examiner was pretty clear in his report. He died from keeping his symptoms quiet. Not something you could control."

"He shot first," Byrd offered.

Tina nodded. "On a lighter note, I hear you're buying a house. That's pretty grown up, isn't it?"

Byrd grinned. "I close on it in a few weeks, unless the bank figures out how little I earn."

Byrd turned to leave. "Where are you headed?" Tina asked.

"I haven't had lunch!"

"Take care of yourself," Tina offered to Byrd's back as he headed for his car.

He stopped and turned. "Tell Doc I'll come back in a little while and give him a statement."

Tina Blackwell strode toward him. "Why don't you buy my lunch? I want to hear about your house."

CHAPTER 4
SOME OF MY EX'S LIVE IN TEXAS

WEDNESDAY, OCTOBER 26, 2005
2:22 P.M.
CIUDAD JUÁREZ, CHIHUAHUA, MEXICO

Vincente Acosta-Hernandez realized he was one of the most feared men in Mexico. He was known on both sides of the border as Rojo. Rojo waited for the man on the other end of the phone to answer. While he waited, he watched the old man who cleaned his office go about his chores. Rojo had grown tired of the young women his men hired to clean. They either wanted to lure him into sex for money or prestige, or were so timid they never met his eyes. The old man came in and did his job, quietly and efficiently. That was exactly what Rojo wanted in his inner sanctum.

When the voice came, it was slightly garbled by distance and the electronic circuits that encrypted the call. "My friend," the voice said. "It is good to hear from you. I hope the most powerful man in Mexico is doing well?"

Rojo looked out the window of his villa in the heart of Juarez. The view was gorgeous by any standard, but this day was particularly stunning. The sun was brilliant, and at this time of day, the mountain air was still icy cold.

He nodded to himself. "Yes, I am well. How are things in Asia? I understand that is where you are now."

"You are well informed. Yes, I am in Cambodia. My family has established a nice home here outside of Phnom Penh. We are enjoying the experience." The American let the comment hang. He wouldn't admit the constant rain since his arrival and the clogged drainage system, even in the expensive neighborhood where his home stood, was less than a paradise.

"It must be late there?" Rojo asked.

"I am a night owl."

Rojo cleared his throat. The two men had spoken rarely since their smuggling operation had blown up earlier in the year.

General Mitchell Warren offered, "By the way, I have a friend in Washington who was able to supply me with a complete report of the shooting of your son. It is directly from the FBI, who investigate all shootings by federal agents. It contains all the personal information of every person who was interviewed. I paid several thousand dollars to a senior member of the FBI staff for it and I would be happy to provide this copy to you," Warren sounded pleased with himself.

"That would be an interesting document," Rojo declared. "But I also have friends in your FBI. They sold me a copy for much less. This is not my hobby, friend General. I must be informed to survive."

Warren chuckled. "A reminder to never underestimate you."

Rojo observed, "It is."

Warren seemed to have something else on his mind. Rojo waited patiently for the American to continue.

Warren said, "I understand your soldier missed in the United States. Was there a problem, or just bad luck?"

Rojo became very quiet. "The soldier was not effective. I can offer no excuses. She says the next attempt will be successful."

Warren lowered his voice, conspiratorially. "The assassins I employed have no connections back to you in Mexico. They are men and women who will kill for money, with no particular political affiliation. They come to the area and leave without a trace. They are Vietnamese but speak perfect English. They travel on a variety of Asian passports."

Rojo pointed out. "The murder of a high-ranking Texas Ranger is no small undertaking. I understand that finding the right men may be difficult. Even *you* may have repercussions from the assassination of American police officers on American soil?"

Warren responded slowly. "The death of my soldier at the hands of the GBI cannot go unavenged. This man worked for me. He and I have fought in many countries around the world. He had been my most trusted ally in business and in combat. His name, at least the one I used, was Adam Benjamin. He died from the bullet of an agent from the state of Georgia named Byrd. Byrd is the target I passed to your people."

Rojo pursed his lips as he leaned back in his chair. "And I feel the same about the loss of my son. I need vengeance."

Warren sighed. "Vengeance is a strong word. But I think there needs to be a balancing of the books, so to speak."

"Our ships are still on course. And this method leaves almost no traces of the origins of the contract. My people kill your Byrd, while your people eliminate the Texas

Ranger." Rojo willed himself to be patient. He paused and then shifted gears, "There is another matter. A strictly business matter."

Rojo despised asking for help, particularly from the arrogant American who had the support of the CIA.

"I am calling to see if you might be willing to organize a shipment from south Texas to your home state of Georgia?" Rojo asked.

Warren didn't hesitate. "Of course. I would be happy to support your operations. What would you require?"

Rojo hated to ask the man for anything more, but he was in a pinch. "I need one hundred sixty gallons of liquid moved. It will be delivered to a location we have in Woodstock, Georgia. My people have rented a warehouse in a secluded location."

Warren sounded pleased. "Of course, we can help with that. I must assume this liquid you're asking me to move would be of significant value?"

"It would be worth fifty thousand dollars to me," Rojo spat it out.

Warren quickly countered. "I think we should speak more about the value after I make some plans for the operation."

Rojo sighed. "Please provide me with a plan within the next week and we will finalize the price. My cousin is my point man in Texas, and he can help with some logistical matters."

"I will try to do this operation as cheaply as possible, but the price could fluctuate once I work out the details," Warren mused.

"A week, please." Then Rojo broke the connection as he grumbled to himself, *"Cabrón!"*

THURSDAY, OCTOBER 27, 2005
2:44 P.M.
EL PASO, TEXAS

Texas Ranger Lieutenant Clete Pettersen drove his pickup truck northwest on Interstate 10 as he neared the New Mexico border. The day was bright and sunny, and the air was turning cold. The afternoon sun was blinding as it steadily dropped on the horizon. As Petterson guided the car along Interstate 10, his eyes were drawn to the left. From the highway, he could see into Mexico. Petterson tried to pick out the mansion sitting on one of the hills that guarded Ciudad Juárez from the western winds. The big house situated near the Camino Real was one of the homes of the drug lord known as Rojo.

Petterson reflected on the tumultuous series of events directly linked to Rojo that had resulted in his marriage to Montana. Petterson's wife, Texas Trooper Montana Petterson, had begun her law enforcement career in Canton, Georgia, as a city police officer. She had known Daniel Byrd, the local GBI agent at the time. Petterson met Byrd two years later when he saved Petterson and newly appointed Texas Ranger Adeline Riley from cartel assassins.

Since the attack, Rojo had been declared public enemy number one by the Texas Rangers. Rojo had run drugs into the US for many years and was, he felt certain, a billionaire. Rojo's network of spies, murderers, and smugglers stretched across the US and beyond. Until recently, he had been a prime target of the Drug Enforcement Administration.

Petterson had been livid when word had come from Washington that Rojo wasn't worth the DEA's effort. Federal agencies were targeting other drug groups working along the border. This sudden change in priorities caused the Texas Department of Public Safety to take a look at their options.

Petterson had done his best to ignore the political infighting and spent his time following up leads after Rojo and General Mitchell Warren's smuggling operation had been broken.

Petterson had spent the morning working with his wife, cleaning the house they shared before the winter cold got a strangle hold on West Texas. They had vacuumed and mopped, cleaning everything in sight. Petterson had to protest when Montana started clearing out his gun cabinet. Montana relented and passed over Petterson's guns, but she suggested Petterson go to work and leave her to clean.

Their marriage, in front of their new friends from the GBI, had been a whirlwind. Then the fallout from Petterson's being wounded in Mexico had thrown a dark shadow over their first months of marriage. The United States Attorney for the Western District of Texas had threatened to empanel a Grand Jury about Petterson and Addy Riley's ill-fated visit to Mexico to collect evidence. It took the involvement of the Attorney General of Texas, and proof a special counsel from the US Department of Justice had authorized the trip, to get the pressure off the Texas officers.

With their lives back to a state of relative normalcy, the pair had begun to enjoy their relationship. The last couple of months had made them feel more like what they were, newlyweds.

Petterson enjoyed the challenges of his work. Montana, relatively new to the state of Texas, was learning the ropes.

Today, Petterson planned to drive by a residence he suspected of housing a fugitive. He took a circuitous route through the extreme western border of his home state. He planned to jump off the interstate at La Tuna and take a back route to the house. He'd have to be sure to establish the house was inside of Texas once he found it.

With over twenty years in law enforcement, observing everything around him was second nature for a ranger. He had noted a silver automobile pacing him as he drove the speed limit. He noted the car didn't have a front license plate.

Pettersen decided to slow down and see what the sedan did. He let his foot off the accelerator and casually watched the rear-view mirror. The silver vehicle didn't slow. Petterson scowled, and reminded himself every suspicious car wasn't a potential threat. Even in a border town where law enforcement officers could be targeted by drug groups simply for doing a good job.

Pettersen adjusted his focus to other vehicles on the road.

He continued to dawdle in the slow lane as the sedan overtook him and came even with his door. The passenger stared at the ranger as the car passed on the left. When the sedan had passed, Petterson noted it had a New Mexico license plate. He read the tag, a habit, but thought little about it.

Pettersen thought ahead to the route he wanted to take to get a look at his target house. A horn honking caught his attention. He looked over to see a compact car jump in front of him as they dodged the slow vehicle in their lane. The silver sedan from New Mexico slowed down sharply and Petterson almost passed the car.

Petterson glanced over at the silver car just in time to

see the passenger point a pistol out the window. Petterson slammed on the brakes. The last look he got at the silver car was an Asian man pointing a pistol toward him. Petterson swerved his big truck off the freeway and onto an exit ramp.

The sedan suddenly accelerated and Petterson immediately lost sight. Petterson tried his best to get back on the highway and catch the silver car. He slammed the gas pedal to the floor and thought about activating his lights and siren, but he knew the chase was over before it began. The car was nowhere to be seen.

Petterson took a deep breath and continued on his way.

THURSDAY, OCTOBER 27, 2005
2:44 P.M.
EL PASO, TEXAS

Adeline Riley strode into the El Paso offices of the Texas Rangers. The dour-looking five-story building located just off Interstate 10 was shared with several other state agencies.

The tall, lean ranger with long, auburn hair tucked into her western hat had been promoted a few months ago. She was still learning the ropes as a ranger. She had served as both a trooper and a narcotics agent for the state of Texas over the last fourteen years.

She had been called to a meeting with the regional supervisor for the West Texas area, Major Stetson Crosby. Adeline, Addy to her friends, took her hat off and carried it in her left hand as she negotiated the constricted space.

Addy saw Major Crosby standing in the hall near her

cubical. He turned and waved at her. "Ranger Riley. How are things going?"

Addy dropped her hat brim up on her desk. "Good, Major." She dropped her voice. "I hope you're not about to tell me something that might change it." Addy was painfully aware she was still on probation as a ranger.

Crosby shook his head. "No. Well, at least not directly." He motioned her toward his office. "Come on in and have a seat."

Crosby, at six feet, seven inches, ducked as he went through the door. Addy followed him in and waited for him to take a seat.

Crosby had turned and waited for her to sit. Crosby chuckled and pointed to her chair. "Sorry, I may outrank you, but my mother said I should always stand until a lady is seated."

Addy grinned. "You had a good mama."

They sat and Addy leaned forward in her seat. "What's going on, Major?"

Crosby put both hands on his desk. "I got a call a couple of hours ago from the Lieutenant Colonel. This is coming straight from the governor's office. Word has come down from the DEA that Rojo is no longer a priority target. The joint task force here in El Paso is being redirected to other targets."

Addy shook her head. "Why? He's probably responsible for more drugs crossing the border than anybody else."

Crosby shrugged. "If I had to guess, off the record, I'd say friend Dagget from the Department of Justice had a hand in this."

Addy groaned. "I never would have believed something like this could happen. He tried to get a ranger killed, and me too for that matter, and he gets a pass?"

Crosby looked grim. "It would seem that way."

Addy stood up. "Major, this is bullshit."

Crosby motioned for her to sit. "I have to agree. That's why we've been authorized to create a task force of state and local officers to go after Rojo."

Addy nodded. "I'm glad to hear that." She pushed her hand through her hair. "I know rangers don't normally get involved in drug cases, that's what the Narcotics Service is for, but I sure would like to be a part of the task force when it gets going."

Crosby pursed his lips. "You're right. Rangers steer clear of drug cases normally. But this isn't a normal circumstance."

Addy moved to the edge of her chair. "So, any chance I could be on the task force?"

Crosby shook his head. "I'm afraid that won't work." Crosby watched Addy's face fall. "You can't be on the task force and lead it at the same time."

Addy blinked. "What? Can you say that again?"

"The colonel wants you to run the task force."

Addy grabbed the chair as she almost slid off the edge. "Holy smokes, Major. That's great news!"

"It won't be an easy job, but I think you'll be a perfect fit. I've got calls from several of the sheriffs in our company area. I'll be getting you a list of people to choose from to staff the task force." Crosby pulled a file toward him as he finished. "Get your other cases closed out and get ready to hit the ground running."

Addy stood. "Yes, sir! And thank you for your confidence in me."

Crosby glanced up at her. "You earned that silver star on your chest. Now you'll be learning what it takes to keep it."

CHAPTER 5
FROM ONE PEN TO ANOTHER PENH

FRIDAY, OCTOBER 28, 2005
11:44 A.M.
PHNOM PENH, CAMBODIA

General Mitchell Warren sat in the big chair in his office. He had a magnificent view of Phnom Penh but for the incessant rain this time of year. He sipped at his breakfast scotch as he pondered his next move.

His son, Omar, sat quietly watching the rain come down. Omar had felt the weight in the room as soon as he walked in. His dad had some bad news for him, that much he was sure of. Omar assumed it would be another smuggling mission and hoped it wouldn't take him back to the United States.

"Son, our friend Rojo is offering us a substantial amount of money to engineer the transportation of a product from Texas to Georgia. His offer is, as they say, too good to turn our noses up at." Warren turned to stare at his son.

Omar returned the stare, stunned his father would ask him to go anywhere near Texas or Georgia, Rojo's area of operations. Omar had worked on their relationship since he got to Cambodia. Mitch was treating him like a fellow operator rather than his child. Omar understood the potential for cash when working with Rojo. He also had a feeling his dad was willing to go out on a limb to impress the Mexican drug lord; potentially at Omar's expense. "I'm not keen on walking myself back into the hands of the Texas Rangers or the GBI. I have to assume they have at least some kind of poster, or whatever they do nowadays, with my face on it."

General Warren nodded. "I'm not keen to have you in their hands, either. And I detest the idea of having to call that prick Dagget to get you out. He seems to have an inflated view of his place in the world."

Omar turned back to the rain. "I didn't meet him, but I heard he left a trail of people behind who hated his guts."

Warren shook his glass, watching the brown liquid swish around. "He is memorable. But he did get the job done, I'll give him that."

"What does Rojo want us to do? I assume it has to do with drugs."

Warren nodded. "And we have an arrangement to do some wet work for him. In turn he is going to close the file on your friend, Agent Byrd."

Omar stood and ran both hands through his thick hair. "I wish I could be there when it's done. I owe him for Adam."

Warren leaned his elbows on his desk and steepled his fingers. "I owe Adam, as well. He would expect some accounting. But we can't afford the trail to lead back to us. Rojo is going to have him taken care of."

"How much?" Omar asked.

"We kill the Texas Ranger who killed his son."

Omar raised an eyebrow. *"Strangers on a Train?"*

"What?"

Omar shook his head. "An old Hitchcock movie. I

would have thought you would have known it. It's more in your time than mine. I've seen it on late-night TV."

Warren winced. "I'm not familiar with it."

Omar changed the subject. "Are you expecting me to hunt down this ranger?"

Warren shook his head. "No, no. I have enlisted the help of a couple of men who do that sort of thing for a living. They're from Vietnam and travel wherever the work is. No ties back to us if things go wrong."

Omar mulled over what his father said. His dad had a way of keeping his hands clean, even as those around him got dirty. "How soon do I need to go back to Texas? I feel like I need to change my looks. Maybe grow a beard."

Warren turned away. He didn't want to face his son when he answered. "We'll be moving about twelve hundred pounds of methamphetamine across the country for Rojo. We'll make a smooth half-million dollars for a couple of days' work. A week at the most."

Omar was impressed. He did a quick calculation in his head. "Rojo is going to get rich off this. Even at wholesale, the load is worth over eight million."

Warren nodded. "His actual estimate is closer to five million. They are using a new method to complete the meth in Georgia. You'll be hauling some fifty-five-gallon drums. Rojo claims the police will not be looking for this."

Omar smiled slowly. "I hope that load doesn't stink as bad as the finished product. Hauling that shit inside an airplane gave me a major headache. Literally!"

Warren put his arm around Omar's shoulder. "Son, I've seen you in action. I know what you're capable of. Let's show Rojo how to smuggle drugs. Moving twelve hundred pounds is chicken feed. I want you to go out there to Texas and show these Mexican Mafia guys how to get a job done. Does that make sense to you?"

"I'm sure there's a better way to do business than the process Rojo is using. Hell, he must have realized that too. He just can't figure out what it is. Otherwise, he'd do it himself."

Warren nodded. "I hoped you'd see it that way. I need you there sooner than later. There's a flight leaving Phnom Phen for Seoul at midnight, tonight. We need to be on the ground making arrangements. Can you make that?"

Omar headed for the door. He paused long enough to say, "No surprise. I'll pack a bag. What's my cut, by the way?"

"One hundred twenty-five thousand a load. A fourth. A fourth to you, a fourth to me and half directly into business operations. We have to keep the whole family solvent."

Warren tipped back the glass and swallowed the drink. His son had grown into a man in the last year. The experience of running a cross-country smuggling operation, going to jail, and seeing his friend, Adam Benjamin, die as they fled the US had all hardened the boy Warren had known.

Warren leaned over and took one of the phones on his desk off the hook. He dialed a number in Langley, Virginia. The connection sounded hollow as the phone began to ring.

"Stover Hardware, how may I help you?"

Warren knew the call was encrypted, but he didn't

believe for a minute that the NSA wasn't listening in. "Mitchell calling from a job site."

The line became quiet for a moment. "Mitchell, what can I do for you?"

"I'm going to need some things for an operation. They must be able to pass close inspection. A passport, a credit card, and a driver's license for one person. All US."

"You'll send the photo and legend?"

Warren responded. "Yes. I need a rush, if you can."

"What state license?"

"Texas."

There was a pause on the line. "You're going back there? I hear there are some folks over at the Puzzle Palace who'd like to see you fade into the sunset."

Warren sighed. He recognized the veiled reference to the powers that be at CIA Headquarters. "I'm sure your neighbors at the headquarters building would like to see me dead. But until they get the balls to do me in, or I grab my chest one last time, I go where the work is. The papers are for my son."

"I've got what I need for him. I'll have it available for pickup when he lands. What airport will he be going to?"

"El Paso will be his destination."

"You know where to tell him to pick up? And should I also include a bust-out kit?"

"I know where to send him. Yes, I think a bust-out kit might come in handy. Can you do both?"

"Of course. That's what I do."

Warren sighed. "I can always count on you."

Warren heard the grunt on the other end. "You're a fucking thrill seeker, you are!"

FRIDAY, OCTOBER 29, 2005
6:44 P.M.
EL PASO, TEXAS

Omar Warren hailed a taxi outside the El Paso International Airport. He was exhausted.

Omar had taken a flight from Cambodia to South Korea using a British passport his father had kept from their days at the Farm. Mitch Warren had kept a stash of passports for himself and everyone in his family to use in an emergency or, as it had developed, to run from the law.

After an uncomfortable seven-hour layover in Seoul, Omar had hopped on a flight from South Korea to LAX. The last leg, from LAX to El Paso, included an eight-hour layover. The journey to El Paso took just over thirty-three hours.

Once on the ground in El Paso, Omar had the cab wait as he made a quick stop at a public mailbox store. The package waiting for him was in his real name. He knew the business wouldn't be able to cross-check with any police databases, so he took the package back to the taxi with his newest identity.

As he sat in the back of a taxi to his motel, he examined the passport and license and marveled at how authentic they looked. Both had been roughed up to make them appear used. He memorized the name and birthday on them and then stuffed them in his pocket. His dad had insisted his source include a 'bust-out kit,' with a completely clean identity which Omar hoped he wouldn't need. Omar hoped Bill Kleinman of Midland, Texas, would be able to avoid any encounters with the law.

Omar checked into a motel on the east side of town, he burned the old documents and then flushed the ashes. His dad had reminded him the motel staff in most places in Texas were on the payroll of the US government or the Mexican Mafia. Or both.

Once all the administrative tasks were done, Omar crawled into the bed with a too-soft mattress. He was immediately asleep.

SATURDAY, OCTOBER 30, 2005
10:44 A.M.
EL PASO, TEXAS

Reyes Acosta Hernandez was a distant cousin of the man known as Rojo. He was known as Rojo's fixer in the US. Reyes had lived his entire life in the El Paso area, having been born in Texas. He was Rojo's most trusted man on the Texas side of the border. He had been sent to meet the spy named Omar to organize his cousin's next shipment of drugs to the East Coast.

Reyes was an average-sized man with black hair and Castilian features. He wore his hair in a businessman's cut with a trimmed goatee. Reyes preferred nondescript clothes and plain-looking cars. He eschewed the glamour and glitz that could have come with his enormous income and lived a simple life west of the Franklin Mountains in northwest El Paso. At thirty-five, with four children in private school, he served as the CEO of a private consulting firm whose only client happened to be Rojo. He had mostly managed to fly below the law enforcement radar.

These were the things Omar's father had told him before he left Asia. Omar had been reluctant to return to El Paso so soon after his release from jail there, but Rojo had insisted his man preferred not to stray far from his home.

Omar sat low in the rented car and looked out of the window as Reyes drove south on the interstate, away from El Paso. He was jetlagged to hell and back. Omar glanced over at the man as he drove. The silver streaks in his hair were, to a nineteen-year-old going on forty, indications of an ancient birthdate but the broad shoulders and chest spoke of strength.

"How long is the drive?" Omar asked.

Reyes glanced over at the boy. "Less than four hours, now."

Omar was surprised. "Shit, that long?"

Reyes smiled. "Texas is a large state, my young friend."

Omar grunted, "I know."

Reyes focused on the road ahead. "We'll be checking on the status of the shipment. Our men have brought over a couple of the drums to this side. But they must float them across the river at night when the Immigration Police are less active. We will see how many barrels are ready to go. Then, next time you visit, you will know the city."

Omar scowled. "From one visit?"

Reyes chuckled. "Presidio is a small city."

As they drove farther from El Paso, Omar began to relax. He sat up in the seat and watched the mountains come and go in the car windows. "How far from the border are we?"

Reyes shrugged and gazed out the passenger window toward Mexico. "Never far."

FRIDAY, NOVEMBER 4, 2005
2:44 P.M.
EL PASO, TEXAS

Omar was tired as he walked through the El Paso airport, head down as much as possible, and hurried to the rental car lot. The flight from Atlanta to El Paso had been uneventful. His seat had been in the back, and he had managed to sleep for most of the flight.

He was on his way to Presidio after making his first trip following an eighteen-wheeler to Atlanta. Rojo's men had disguised the steel barrels loaded with methamphetamine by surrounding them with several tons of onions in wooden crates. The tractor-trailer truck had crossed half the country from Presidio, Texas, to Woodstock, Georgia, without a hitch.

The travel had been slow and tedious. The trip had been punctuated by road construction in Louisiana and a four-car pile-up near Birmingham, Alabama. The entire excursion had taken over twenty-eight hours, between problems, routine fueling, and rest stops.

The driver had been forced to stop several times to be weighed and inspected. One inspector, in Mississippi, had been particularly suspicious. He had made the driver open the trailer and had examined his load. He told the driver his agency had sent out a bulletin about drugs loaded in trucks carrying onions. The barrels of meth oil had been intentionally tied down in the front of the long trailer. The inspector wasn't willing to unload the trailer of onions.

The off-loading of the drugs was tedious, with the team first having to move the wooden boxes of onions, then pulling the three barrels of oil out and finally reloading the onions. With the barrels safely in the old warehouse in Woodstock, Omar's job was completed. He helped the driver dispose of the crates of onions to get an idea how hard that task would be each trip. They had gone to a local market in Cartersville and offered the onions for free to any takers. The next inspector might be more willing to unload a cargo of onions.

The operation took eight days from start to finish. It seemed like a lot of work for twelve hundred pounds of product. Omar decided there had to be a better way.

MONDAY, NOVEMBER 14, 2005
2:44 A.M.
WOODSTOCK, GEORGIA

Omar stood beside the trailer as a forklift unloaded the pallet of meth. Once more, the load was only three barrels. The remainder of the trailer again was filled with onions. A cold rain was coming down, but Omar hardly noticed. He felt some pride in the pace of the loads. But there were concerns with this operation, Omar thought.

The second tractor-trailer truck had successfully crossed half the country from Presidio to Woodstock much as the previous load. Once more, the ride had been slow and tedious, with Omar tagging along behind the driver. He had done as much to learn the ropes as to provide a level of security.

He had noted the greatest amount of law enforcement attention was devoted to the westbound side of Interstate 20, the side on which the money would travel back to

Mexico. Marked police and sheriff cars were posted adjacent to the highway, watching for a driver who matched the profile of a money hauler. Omar knew the money movement would be his next hurdle, but first, he wanted to get the drug shipments going smoothly.

The road construction in Louisiana was still there and a car fire, near Meridian, Mississippi, took over an hour to clear.

The new driver had been forced to stop several times to be weighed and inspected, just like before. Then, a near catastrophe when the driver failed to move over for a stopped tow truck. The trooper in Tuscaloosa, Alabama, had stopped the truck driver to investigate his inattention. After an attempt at communication, punctuated by many hand gestures and waving on both sides, the trooper confronted the driver about his paperwork. The documents had been printed hastily before they left Texas, and the dates were wrong. The driver's poor English and the troopers poor Spanish almost resulted in the trailer being impounded.

Omar was forced to sit, watching from a distance, as the trooper walked around the truck, checking for violations. The trooper had called for a dog. The K-9 and handler arrived on scene and the dog spent several minutes running around the truck, sniffing every cranny. Once the dog failed to alert, the trooper let the driver go with a warning.

When the truck arrived in Woodstock, the unloading of the meth and the reloading of the cover load took several hours. All the businesses nearby were closed by the time the truck pulled out of the parking lot.

Omar told the driver, using signals and motions, to take

the load of onions and sell them in Arkansas. The driver would pocket anything he made.

Omar was concerned about getting rid of the produce they were using as cover. He thought unloading the truck at night in the quiet industrial park would eventually draw unwanted attention. And the paperwork for the drivers needed to be flawless or the drivers needed to be English speakers.

Omar was convinced there had to be a better way to accomplish what they wanted. He planned to spend the flight back to Texas figuring out what it was.

CHAPTER 6
COWBOY UP

Omar met Reyes at a nondescript Mexican joint on the eastern edge of Marfa. Marfa is a dusty city in northeastern Presidio County. The town sits squarely in the Chihuahuan Desert and, if everyone is home, Marfa has a population barely over fifteen hundred. Recently, Omar had made it fifteen hundred and one.

The restaurant was a popular eating spot in the little desert town, but the evening crowd was still an hour away. The tables and chairs looked old and worn and the room was dark. Omar felt comfortable there. The restaurant was empty except for a waitress behind the scarred wooden bar along the left wall. She wiped the bar with a cloth and watched the men find a table.

Reyes examined the menu. Omar had become a regular and knew what he wanted.

"Have you tried the menudo?" Reyes asked. "That dish is a good measure of the quality of a Mexican restaurant."

Omar watched Reyes's face closely. "Are you screwing with me? I know what menudo is made of."

Reyes shrugged. "Good menudo is good. Like your southern chitlins. Menudo is also known as pancita. That means little gut or little stomach."

Omar shook his head. "It's soup made with cow's stomach and loaded with red chili peppers. I don't eat it. I also don't eat chitlins."

Reyes laughed. "For a young man, you are not afraid of much. I have heard my cousin talk of you flying the aqua from Juarez to Georgia. He says you are a fearless pilot. Is that true?"

Omar snorted. "Hell no! I was scared shitless the whole time. What are you afraid of?"

"My cousin," Reyes answered earnestly. "You call him Rojo but to me he will always be Vince. We have been close since childhood. But I am under no illusions. If we make a mess of this operation, he will kill me as surely as the sun will come up tomorrow. And he will kill you. He will kill my wife and family. I am afraid of him, that much I know."

Omar was somber. "I understand your concern. We made a lot of money off those first two loads. I want to find a different way to haul. I was hauling a couple of hundred pounds at a time. We need to move tons of the stuff to feed the need on the east coast."

Reyes was defensive, "The plan is working. It may be tedious, but it is effective.

Omar toned his enthusiasm down a notch. "This truck thing is good, but the drivers we used looked shady as hell. I want to find a driver who'll pass with ease. And I need someone bilingual, if possible."

Reyes nodded. "I can see that. I can put feelers out in El Paso. I know you don't want to go there if it can be avoided. You can stay here in Marfa until I get someone lined up."

The waitress had come to the table. She stood with a pad in her hand. "Drinks?" she asked.

Reyes nodded. *"Dos cervezas, por favor."*

Omar spoke up, *"Una cerveza y una margarita."*

The waitress wrote on her pad. *"Sí, ¿como siempre?"*

Omar nodded. "With two beef tacos."

She turned to Reyes. He shook his head. "Beer only, *por favor.*"

As soon as she was out of earshot, Reyes leaned in. "My cousin wants very much for this operation to go smoothly. He has enough of the barrels to make millions from his contacts in Atlanta. Whatever method we use, it must be smooth. My cousin has much invested in these barrels of aqua and he can only afford to lose so much."

"Aqua means meth?"

Reyes looked over his shoulder. "It is a term sometimes used."

Omar nodded. "Well, we have a lot riding on this too. My job is to set up a pipeline and keep it flowing. I want it to be as simple as possible. And I want a routine established in the next couple of months. That's how we all make money."

Reyes sat silently as the waitress brought the beer and margarita. "I will be back with the tacos in *uno momento,*" she said.

Omar shook the margarita on the rocks. Once it was cool enough, he took a gulp. He grinned at Reyes. "They just don't taste as good when I try to make them in my room."

Reyes smirked. "You're missing the secret ingredient. For gringos, the bartender pisses in the drink."

Omar took another gulp. Then he shrugged. "In Cambodia, the drinks had piss in them too. But there you had to pay extra."

FRIDAY, NOVEMBER 18, 2005
9:04 A.M.
EL PASO, TEXAS

Sheriff James "Jim" Hallman sat behind his desk at the El Paso County Sheriff's Office in El Paso, Texas. His office was in a sprawling complex on the southside of the Fort Bliss military reservation.

Hallman was the very image of a Texas sheriff. Just over seventy years old, with gray hair and a bushy mustache, Hallman was seldom seen outside without his white cattleman's style hat. At that moment, he had his worn cowboy boots propped on the corner of his desk.

Hallman heard the phone in his hand click and then a voice came on the line. "Commander Estrada."

"Lenny, this is the Sheriff."

"Yes, sir."

"Do we still have someone on the DEA Task Force working on Rojo?"

"Sheriff, I guess you didn't get the word. The feds disbanded the task force."

Hallman dropped his boots to the floor. "What?"

"There was some kind of political bullshit. DEA says they have other priorities."

Hallman shook his head. "What the hell?"

Lenny Estrada hated to be the bearer of this obviously volatile news. He acted quickly to calm the sheriff. "Sheriff, we do have one of our Narcotics Officers we plan to assign to a new group the State has established to work on Rojo. I've heard rumblings the group has been made a priority for the DPS Narcotics Service."

Hallman snorted. "Well, maybe the State can do what the feds don't seem to be able to do. Can you have our agent give me a call? I have someone he needs to talk to. A potential informant who's been approached by one of Rojo's people."

"It's she, boss."

"How did you know the informant was a female?" Hallman barked.

"No, Sheriff. Our agent is a she."

Hallman laughed. "Sorry, you had me backing up for a minute." Hallman squinted out his office window. "That might work out for us, though. The source talking to me is a female. Have that agent call me on my personal cell phone right away."

Looking out the window at the skyline of El Paso, Hallman considered whether the drug units were worth the effort. Men like Rojo, who used the porous border as a refuge and a defense, made a mockery of law enforcement's efforts. Life on the border had been like that as long as Hallman could remember. He knew from the old timers, still around when Hallman began his career, that alcohol had been a commodity in years past and women were enslaved and forced into sex work for the powerful groups in Juarez. Now, it was drugs, and when the drug market faltered, it would be something else.

He grabbed his hat, putting it squarely on his head. As he walked out of his private office, he leaned down to his secretary. "Marge, I'm going to be out for a few hours. Call me on my cell if something comes up."

He walked out to his big four-wheel-drive truck. Hallman climbed in and pointed the truck north. He took Gateway Boulevard then turned left on Woodrow Bean Transmountain Drive. He passed the Border Patrol

Museum on his right and followed the mountain road as it climbed into the Franklin Mountains. He rolled the windows down and turned the heat up. He pulled the truck over at an overlook and got out. He pulled on his leather jacket and walked to the guardrail. He was rewarded with a spectacular view of the city. And of Juarez. He stared in the distance, unconsciously comparing the two sides of the river.

He was about to sit on the guardrail when his phone rang.

"Hello," Hallman's voice was unintentionally gruff.

"Sheriff? This is Deputy Raelynn Michaels. Commander Estrada told me to call you at this number."

Hallman was embarrassed. "Thank you, Deputy Michaels. I was having a bad day at the office, though no fault of yours, and shouldn't have barked into the phone."

"Thank you, sir. But there's no need to apologize to me."

"Yes, there is. I understand you're a hard worker and have made a reputation at the task force. I just wanted to pass on some information that came my way on our old friend from across the river."

"Rojo, sir?"

"None other. I got a call from a woman who did some work for me at the house. She says she might be able to help us get him. And I want you to work with her."

Hallman took off his hat and wiped his forehead. He wanted to do more to make up for growling into the phone. "I also want you to know that your work hasn't gone unnoticed. That deal you worked with the GBI was first rate. I want to keep you at my agency."

"Thanks, Sheriff. That means a lot coming from you."

Hallman shifted gears. "This lady is a little different.

Hardheaded and kind of rough on the edges. I just hope she can deliver."

"Me too!" Raelynn said.

FRIDAY, NOVEMBER 18, 2005
12:44 P.M.
CANTON, GEORGIA

Daniel Byrd sat looking at the paperwork he had just signed. His mouth felt dry, and his breathing was shallow. He still couldn't fully comprehend the weight of the step he had just taken. He had bought a house.

Byrd sat in the comfortable conference room of a local law office. The attorney who handled the closing was exclusively a real estate attorney and wasn't well known to Byrd. But Byrd had seen him in the courthouse in Canton and Jasper on occasion.

"I guess I've signed my life away," Byrd declared with finality. "This must be what it's like to take a guilty plea. You sign a whole bunch of papers and then your life is never the same."

The lawyer neatly stacked Byrd's copies of the paperwork. "Mr. Byrd, or should I say Agent Byrd?"

Byrd shook his head. "Either one. Or just Danny is fine."

"Danny, you have just inherited a house. You'll be paying less for the loan payment than you were paying for your rent since all you have to cover are back taxes on the property. If you decide to move, you can actually sell the house and maybe make a little money."

Byrd still felt numb. "I know I got a good deal on the house."

The lawyer laughed. "You got a hell of a deal. Twenty thousand for a property worth probably a couple of hundred thousand for the land alone. When your uncle bought the place, he planned it as an investment. Too bad he didn't live to realize what the place might be worth."

The lawyer pushed the papers toward Byrd. "Relax. We do this several times a day. Hell, some people are actually excited to buy a house."

FRIDAY, NOVEMBER 18, 2005
2:22 P.M.
EL PASO, TEXAS

Raelynn Michaels felt conflicted, she realized as she drove south on Interstate 10 toward a meeting with a pharmacist. She had been a narc with the El Paso County, Texas, Sheriff's Office for barely two years. She had worked uniform for a couple of years but knew her true calling was to be a drug investigator. The strong-willed woman with curly blond hair wondered if her career was stagnating and she couldn't decide if she cared or not. She felt pressure from her bosses to test for a sergeant position, her next step in a career path.

Her job had been to work on a joint federal/state/local task force investigating drug cases in western Texas. She had worked with a partner she trusted with her life. Then last May, her old partner, Adeline Riley, had been appointed as a Texas Ranger, leaving her position with the Narcotics Service.

Rae had been excited for her old partner's promotion to one of the most prestigious jobs in Texas law enforcement.

But it didn't change the fact Rae had to work with people she barely knew. The task force almost folded in June, and new people from various agencies were assigned to work with her. Rae was the only person left from the old group.

She knew she was liked by most of the agents and the bosses. She had a sharp tongue and a quick wit. She bonded with informants, the life blood of any drug unit, and had a reputation as an excellent witness in court. But she had begun to feel she didn't fit in with the direction of the reorganized operation. And then to cap things off, she had gotten a call this morning from personnel informing her the sheriff planned to move her to a new position. And the lady from personnel didn't know where she was going.

At twenty-nine years old, she wondered if she should go back into uniform and seek advancement or look for a job with the State. She worried that either one would be unsatisfying or worse, boring.

When her phone rang, she assumed it was the pharmacist calling to see if she was lost or her new boss calling to assign her some dead-end tip. Her boss, new to drug enforcement, had no idea what sorts of leads were important.

Then she recognized the number. "Hey, girl! How's life in the Texas Rangers?" Rae was surprised to be so excited to talk to her old friend.

"Just living my best life. How are things with the task force? I hear there's been some turnover," Addy Riley asked.

Rae snorted. "You could say that. I was the only one left and I found out today that I'm being moved. The sheriff was pissed when he found out that Rojo is no longer a target of our unit."

Addy Riley paused for effect. "Word on the street is your sheriff may assign you to a new State-run task force. Any truth to that?"

Rae laughed. "I just talked to the sheriff a few minutes ago but he didn't mention where I would be assigned. He gave me a lead on Rojo he wanted followed up, and then he told me to come by the Commander's office and officially get my new assignment."

"Sheriff Hallman didn't mention that you had been requested by one of the new supervisors on the state task force."

Rae groaned. "What have you heard. Is it someone I'm going to hate?"

Addy chuckled. "I hope not. It's a new ranger named Riley."

Rae whooped, "You? That's awesome! When do we start?"

"My husband is working late tonight. Let's meet for dinner and talk things over."

Rae hadn't felt this good in a while. "I should be able to meet you around six, if that works for you."

Addy suggested a place to meet and then broke the connection. Rae whooped again.

CHAPTER 7
HOME SWEET HOME

SATURDAY, NOVEMBER 19, 2005
2:36 P.M.
CANTON, GEORGIA

Byrd heaved the box out of the back of the truck he had borrowed from Cherokee County Sheriff Willie Nelson. Nelson had offered to help with the move, and then got a call from a frantic county commissioner whose gun had been stolen from his unlocked car.

As Byrd lugged the last box out of the truck, he saw Violet Child leaning over, emptying one of the boxes. "Violet," Byrd said too sharply, "You don't need to be bending over like that. You have enough trouble with your back as it is."

Violet stood, stretching backward. "I just want to help."

Byrd rushed to her side. "I know you do but I don't want you laid up while we celebrate my first house."

She nodded. "I know. I remember when my husband and I bought our first house. I hope this place lasts longer than our marriage did." She sat on a full box and massaged her lower back with her left hand. "Is there wine in that cooler you brought, or just water?"

Byrd grinned. "We can't celebrate with just water."

Violet stood up. "Good! I'm going to pour a glass of wine and take my time getting these boxes taken care of. When is your agent friend meeting you to get the furniture?"

Byrd consulted his watch. "Gary Thomasson is his name. He should be at the apartment any time. If you're okay here, I'm going to head that way."

Violet leaned forward to stretch. When she stood up, her face had reddened. "Okay, I'll be fine. Go get your stuff."

Byrd drove the borrowed truck up the long drive. Thomasson couldn't get over the size of the property. "Man, how long is this driveway? Can you even see the house from the road?"

Thomasson had been in law enforcement for over ten years. His deeply lined face and perpetual squint were a product of years in the field as a Department of Natural Resources game warden.

Byrd grinned like a kid with a new puppy. "I haven't measured, but I'm guessing it's about fifty yards."

Thomasson gave a low whistle. "Wow. How much land came with it?"

"Ten acres and some change."

"I heard that you have a place to shoot out here," Thomasson said as he looked around.

Byrd nodded. "There is a natural wall and plenty of protection down by the creek. I looked it over, and it is perfect. The neighbors might not like it, but I won't be shooting at night."

Thomasson shook his head. "You got a creek too."

"It's the property line."

When they were near the little house, Byrd swung the

truck around and backed up to the front porch of his new home. The little house sitting in the quiet wooded property had a single bedroom, a small living room with an adjoining dining area, and a kitchen on the first floor. This space had been essentially the same since the place was built after World War II. Byrd's uncle had added two small bedrooms and a bathroom in the A-framed ceiling space.

When the pair squeezed the couch through the front door, Byrd saw Violet sleeping on the floor. He sat the couch down gently. "She's had a rough day! Let's be as quiet as we can and let her sleep."

Byrd and Thomasson moved the little bit of furniture that Byrd owned into the house. They were as quiet as they could be until it came time to move the refrigerator.

Try as they might, the big appliance was challenging to get into the house. They hooked up the water line and the power, but pushing the heavy box into place was a struggle. The floor of the old house was uneven in most places, but the kitchen had the added issue of a brick floor. They took several tries, with much grunting and shoving, to get the fridge into place.

Byrd noticed Violet didn't move during the fight with the appliance. He went over to check on her and saw her breathing was rhythmic, but very slow. He shook her shoulder and called her name. When that didn't work, he tried sitting her up. Her eyes opened but then she went right back to sleep.

Thomasson had watched the action from the kitchen door. "I guess I'll get out of here. It looks like she's exhausted."

Byrd nodded. "Man, I appreciate your help. Can I pay you for your time?"

Thomasson laughed. "'Course not. I'll get you back the next time I move."

Byrd watched his friend drive away and then turned to Violet. He could smell the wine on her breath. "Someone over-celebrated," Byrd said.

It took every bit of strength he could muster to get her up and into the bedroom. The bed frame was still in pieces, but he managed to stretch her out on the mattress.

He gave her a last check, her pulse seemed okay, and then threw a blanket over her. He turned off the overhead light and pulled the door closed behind him. Then he went about the business of putting the house into shape.

SATURDAY, NOVEMBER 19, 2005
4:36 P.M.
EL PASO, TEXAS

Clete Petterson walked out of the drugstore with a package in his hands. He wasn't wearing his Western hat or any Western attire. This was truly a day off. He had spent the morning and early afternoon watching the University of Alabama at Birmingham prevail over his University of Texas at El Paso Miners with a score of thirty-five to twenty-three. He and Montana came home for a lunch of leftovers.

Montana had been complaining of a headache most of the morning. Once they ate, she lay on their couch and tried to nap while Clete had spent ten minutes looking for aspirin, only to find an empty bottle.

Montana had finally relented and asked him to run out and buy her some aspirin. He had jumped at the chance to get out of the house.

He glanced at the tall lights around the stadium of Franklin High School, backdropped by the Franklin Mountains. The ranger looked around the parking lot as he came into the sunlight. Off-duty or not, he was cautious. Petterson parked his truck near the door, and he saw a single compact car in the lot. Petterson stuck his hands in the pocket of his jeans to fish out his keys. As he angled toward his truck, he saw the occupants of the compact car get out and head toward the front of the pharmacy. The people were both Asian men. He noticed they both came out of the car at the same instant, almost like a choreographed move.

At that moment, with his right hand in his pocket and his left holding a prescription, Petterson felt a tingle down his spine. He quickened his pace, wanting his truck between him and the men, and took his right hand out of his pocket.

The men passed by without more than a furtive glance at the big Texan. Petterson felt foolish for a moment. He glanced back over his shoulder and saw the pair splitting up, not going into the drugstore. His gun was under his leather jacket, and he started the motion of drawing as he jumped into the bed of the pickup.

He couldn't see which of the men fired first as he rolled into the truck bed and pulled his gun around. He heard the round strike the metal bed of the truck. As he rolled, he popped up and saw one of the men standing in the open. The other used a brick column for cover.

Petterson's first shot from his .45 Colt hit the man standing in the open in the chin. The man's head flew back in a halo of red mist and he dropped to the ground.

Petterson jumped out of the truck on the opposite side, away from the gunmen. He heard rounds hit his truck as he crouched and worked around to the front. A bullet struck the passenger side mirror, just above Petterson's head, as he popped up again. He took two quick shots at the man behind the column. His shots were answered by a volley of rounds striking all around him.

Petterson dived to the ground, stretching out with his front wheel and tire for cover. He shot under the truck as the man broke cover and dashed toward Petterson. His first shot hit the shooter in the left thigh, making the man stagger, and then Petterson's next shot hit the man in the center of the chest.

With a grunt, the assailant dropped to the ground.

Petterson got to his feet and carefully, gun in the low ready position, edged around to the front of his truck. Both men were lying on their backs. Petterson could hear a siren a couple of blocks away steadily coming toward him.

Petterson grabbed his cell phone and dialed 911.

"El Paso Police, what is the nature of your emergency?"

"This is Ranger Clete Petterson. I've been involved in a shooting at the corner of East Redd Road and North Resler Drive. I need EMS and uniformed support."

"What's your radio number and how are you dressed, ranger?"

"I'm DPS 604 and I'm dressed in jeans, a leather jacket, and a red flannel shirt. No official hat or gun belt. I'm standing out front and there are two suspects down." Petterson was breathing hard.

"You okay, ranger?"

"Yes, ma'am. Just had to do a little more running and shooting than I planned for today."

The dispatcher laughed. "I have a unit about thirty seconds out. We got several 911 calls. Have your star out, please, and stay on the line 'till my unit is on scene."

Petterson dug out his badge case and held it in his left hand as the patrol car, a white Expedition with the blue stripes and the sunset badge/logo, pulled up beside his truck.

SATURDAY, NOVEMBER 19, 2005
8:36 P.M.
WESTMINSTER, LONDON, ENGLAND

General Mitch Warren looked over at the Ministry of Defense. His hotel stood adjacent to the Ministry and only a few blocks from MI-5 and MI-6. He would spend the holidays in London but that didn't mean he was on holiday. He planned to work a deal with the "cousins"—the CIA term for the Brits—to leverage his partnership with Rojo. Warren figured a backdoor into a cartel was better than no contact at all.

He had spoken with Omar about his plans and Omar had briefed him on the success of his last two ventures. Warren was pleased with his son's growth.

As Warren neared the hotel, a top hatted doorman pulled the heavy doors open. Warren nodded and passed by into the lobby. With practiced indifference, Warren scanned the desk to his left and the short set of stairs to his right. Between, he noted a well-dressed man sitting in the common area near the desk reading a newspaper. Warren shook off his heavy wool topcoat, draped it over his shoulder, and walked over to the man.

The man didn't look up. "I hope you aren't concealing a handgun with that coat. We frown on that sort of thing in the United Kingdom."

Warren dropped the coat on a seat and sat on the couch beside the man. "You're my contact?"

The man dropped the paper on the floor beside him. "I'm just a go-between. A flunky, as you Yanks would say."

Warren closed his eyes. "Your work name is Steve Loftis. I doubt you can even recall your birth name. You've been with MI-6 for thirty years. You have worked in America on several occasions and are significantly more than a flunky."

Loftis smiled. "We prefer SIS. Secret Intelligence Service. More twenty-first century."

"Are you really acting as a conduit, or is the Secret Intelligence Service interested in a pipeline to Rojo of their own?" Warren asked.

Loftis leaned closer, even though the lobby was empty. "We were told you wanted a safe place to settle down. A place where the DEA and FBI will find a world of red tape if they try to arrest you or your family."

Warren smiled back. "That is a fairly clear picture of the circumstances."

Loftis bunched his eyebrows. "The obvious question for my people is why aren't you going to America? I know you still have the ability to make charges go away. Why come here?"

Warren straightened in his seat. "My son and I are looking for a neutral location to create a new life."

"Cambodia not to your liking?"

Warren chuckled. "Not where I want to spend my declining years. And we have our legal issues with the US Government resolved but the States of Georgia and Texas would give a substantial bounty for my hide. And the same for my son's."

Loftis examined a fingernail. "Anything else?"

Warren shrugged. "I like that you speak English here."

Loftis looked Warren in the eyes. "No plans to smuggle your poison here to our teenage population?"

Warren pressed his lips together. "No. I'm not a fan of drugs; particularly methamphetamine. We got into business with Rojo to provide service vehicles to his group. I convinced myself that the transport side of the drug business wasn't dirty like being an actual dealer. Turns out I was wrong. We did what our government asked, made a little money, but I'm worried about the route my son has taken."

Loftis sat up, as well. "And your route. My associates intercepted a call from America to you. Your attempt on the life of a Texas policeman went awry, I understand."

Warren shrugged. "A misadventure with my Mexican associate, I'm afraid. But I have no intentions of bankrolling another attempt."

Loftis nodded. "What can you do to convince my people of your sincerity?"

"I plan to buy a home for myself and my family. I'm in the process of moving my wife and three daughters here. And I'd like to open a business here, if possible."

"What sort of business? Not something," Loftis coughed, "in the shadows?"

Warren rubbed his chin. "The people in my line, in your line, are always looking for better widgets. All those widgets aren't necessarily deadly. Custom tool belts, warm clothing, rain gear, the sort of thing the military might supply—except this wouldn't be military issue. Right-off-the-shelf stuff for clandestine operators."

Loftis thought it over. "Right. I'll pass this on. I expect we'll reach back out in a few days. Will you be staying here?"

Warren stood. "That's the plan."

Loftis stood and the two men shook. "By the way, it appears your son had several bottles of premium scotch whisky delivered to your room. Next visit we must enjoy a tasting."

Warren nodded and headed for the elevator. *That's my boy*, he thought.

Warren locked the door behind him and dropped his overcoat on the bed. The room seemed small by American standards but was considered spacious by Europeans. He found the bathroom comfortable and the sleeping area had room for meetings. Warren looked over the box situated on the small meeting table. The whisky Omar had chosen happened to be one of his favorite brands. He took the bottle out, pulled the cork, and poured a liberal serving of the honey-colored liquid into a glass.

He held the glass up and examined it. He enjoyed the irony of the two honey-colored liquids his life currently revolved around. The meth oil was making him money and the libation in the glass was costing him money.

Warren was annoyed his two Vietnamese triggermen had failed, but he had been honest when he told the MI-6 man he had no intentions of trying again. He hoped to let Omar sort the matter out after the end of the year. By then, he and Omar should have a sizeable amount of cash put away.

After a moment more of musing, he took a long pull from the glass and savored the flavor. The sharp bite of the neat alcohol was satisfying. He held the glass up again and made a silent toast to the job Omar was doing.

CHAPTER 8
GEAR JAMMING

MONDAY, NOVEMBER 21, 2005
8:25 A.M.
EL PASO, TEXAS

Clete Petterson pushed through the doors of the Texas Rangers' Office in El Paso. Petterson had dressed in his work clothes today. His hand-tooled gun belt and dress belt with the matching Texas Ranger buckles supported the open-top holster that was missing his favorite .45 caliber 1911 pistol. He had his spare gun, virtually identical to the one he had surrendered to the shooting team of rangers out of Austin, in its place.

He poured a cup of coffee and ambled into Major Crosby's office.

Crosby looked up from a document he was reading. "How's my Lieutenant doing? Is this your first officer-involved shooting?"

Petterson sipped his coffee. After a moment he said, "First one where the suspect died. But I'm doing fine. I sure didn't want to sit around the house while Montana was out on patrol."

Crosby grinned. "Well, you look more like a ranger than you did last time I saw you. But I guess we can't expect folks to wear their gear all the time."

Petterson sat in the chair opposite Crosby. "I'm just happy not to be laid out in a box. Thanks for coming out to the scene, by the way."

Crosby dropped his reading glasses on his desk and leaned back in his chair. "What did you do to piss those men off?"

Petterson shook his head. "No idea, Major. Have you heard anything from headquarters yet?"

"Neither man had any ID on their person. We found a room key that we traced back to a motel over in New Mexico. I went with a team over there yesterday to search the room along with the New Mexico State Police. We found a couple of burner phones and some cash. There was nothing to tie them to Rojo but I can't help thinking he had a hand in this."

Petterson sat forward in his chair. "That's as good a guess as any, right now. Will I be suspended pending any kind of investigation?"

Crosby pursed his lips. "I wish we could keep you on the job, but I'll have to give you a couple of days of paid leave. Thanks to the high-quality surveillance video, that pharmacy has some of the best I've seen by the way, you are pretty much in the clear. And the boys who are doing the investigation were very impressed with your tactics. A two-on-one gunfight is tough to escape unscathed."

Petterson sipped the coffee. "I hope this won't impact my working with this new task force."

Crosby chuckled. "If getting shot at got a ranger out of work, we'd end up with nobody to do the job. How did Montana take all this?"

"She told me she wouldn't send me out for aspirin again."

MONDAY, NOVEMBER 21, 2005
5:44 P.M.
WOODSTOCK, GEORGIA

Felisha Gomez waited at the little cafe in downtown Woodstock. She didn't really care for the "foo-foo" style of coffee the shop brewed, having grown accustomed to coffee from the urns in truck stops and service stations around the US. She had grown up an Army brat, moving around the country, with a short detour to Germany, as her father had been transferred around until he retired in Texas. She had a gift for languages and spoke Spanish and German along with her native English.

After registering for a bachelor program at the University of Texas at El Paso, largely funded by her participation in several team and individual athletic programs, she was able to coast through her classes. She had been in her senior year at UTEP when she was approached by a man who offered her a substantial salary to work for the man everyone called Rojo, then a Lieutenant for another drug lord from Mexico City. She had been recruited to smuggle small amounts of drugs across the border aided by her US citizenship and her military dependent ID. This sudden boost in income changed her life completely. Soon, she graduated to moving US currency into Mexico. The quiet girl who studied little, and no longer needed her athletics, began to coast through college.

After graduation, fearful losing her military dependent status would impede her ability to roam back and forth across the border, she married a soldier from Fort Bliss.

The young soldier, smitten with the exotic and athletic young woman, had barely completed the necessary paperwork for Felisha to be listed as his spouse when he had been killed by a hit and run driver. Felisha had then burned the car, gotten her surviving spousal ID card and resumed her cross-border trips.

She had steadily grown her savings and improved her lifestyle over the next ten years. Eight years ago, after another successful border crossing, a fellow smuggler, jealous of her success, tried to rob and rape her. The man grabbed her and stuck a gun in her face, leeringly threatening the things he would do with her when he got her to his home.

Felisha kicked the man like a field goal kicker for the UTEP Miners. She made solid contact with the man's groin. When the man lay on the ground, clutching his injured genitals, she took his pistol and shot him twice through the head.

A week later, she was recruited by Rojo to act as an *asesina*, an assassin, to resolve problems on the US side of Rojo's operations. She had been surprised to find she could kill without remorse. She soon honed those skills to a fine edge. And the financial rewards of her new tasks were more than she could have ever dreamed.

The mission to kill the GBI agent was her twelfth such assignment against an American law enforcement officer in her two years working as an *asesina* for Rojo. It was the first outside the border area for her.

She saw the plain-looking car pull into a parking space outside. The man who got out matched the description she had been given. He dressed in a cheap suit and a bland tie and walked with authority. He had been hired to give her information she could use to stalk Daniel Byrd.

She stood and met the man as he walked into the dark shop. "I think you are looking for me," Felisha said as she extended her right hand.

The man nodded, looking around the inside of the quiet coffee shop, and followed Felisha to her table. He waited for her to sit and then pushed his chair back around, so he had a clear view of the door.

"You're Felisha?"

She nodded. "And you must be Gary Thomasson of the GBI?"

MONDAY, NOVEMBER 21, 2005
5:22 P.M.
EL PASO, TEXAS

Raelynn Michaels nosed her undercover car into a spot beside the little taco stand two blocks from the county courthouse. She had made phone contact with the source of information the sheriff had given her, but the voice on the phone put a face-to-face meeting off until this afternoon.

Even this late, the little stand was busy. Rae climbed out of the minivan and examined the people on the street as she made her way up to the window to order.

Rae didn't recognize any of the faces on the street and hadn't caught anyone watching her with anything more than casual curiosity. She ordered steak tacos with extra jalapeños and a cup of black coffee. She sat down at a table that gave her a good view of the street and took a long sip of the coffee.

A woman who had been in line behind her brought her order over and stood near the table. "You Rae?" she asked.

Raelynn looked her over. The woman looked about five-six and solidly built. Her hair was brown and cut short. Her skin had been aged by years in the high desert sun and wind. Rae guessed her to be in her late forties.

"I am," Rae declared. "Are you Dawn?"

Dawn stuck out her hand and shook. Rae noted her hands were rough from hard work.

"That's what my mama named me." Dawn Lewis laughed sharply. "We talked on the phone."

Rae motioned for her to take a seat. "Pull up a chair."

Dawn dropped into the hard, folding chair and put her food on the table. Dawn took a bite of a taco with eggs and then took a long gulp of hot black coffee. She seemed in no hurry to talk, and Rae let her take her time.

Dawn found a bottle of habanero sauce on an adjoining table and shook the liquid liberally on the rest of the taco. After she took a bite, she took a deep breath. "That ought to wake me up," Dawn remarked.

Rae smiled. "Do you work at night?"

Dawn grunted. "From six yesterday afternoon. Off tonight. I'm dead tired, but that's my regular workday."

Rae leaned forward and lowered her voice. "So, you drive trucks?"

Dawn nodded. "Most of my life. I got tired of being on the road, so I took a job doing local runs. We deliver to mostly food vendors. Lots of fresh produce from Mexico. One of our guys will pick it up and come back to this side of the river, then me and a couple of others sort the produce and drop it off. By the time I'm finished, the sun is usually creeping up on the horizon."

Rae raised her eyebrows. "That's a tough way to make a living."

Dawn shrugged. "I like it better than over-the-road driving. Me and my wife live outside of town, and she works in an all-night diner that caters to truckers. That's how we met. This job lets me stay home with her most of the time."

Rae pursed her lips. "Well, if it works for you, that's what's important." Without thinking, Rae glanced around the area before she asked, "So, how did you come into contact with our friend?"

Dawn seemed puzzled. "Our friend?" Then she connected the dots. "Oh yeah. No need to take a chance by using a name."

Rae nodded.

"One of his gophers talked to me."

Rae frowned. "Gopher?"

Dawn grinned. "Yeah, he goes for this or goes for that. A go-for."

Rae chuckled. "I'll make a note."

Dawn shrugged her shoulders. "Anyway, this dude knew I had my hours cut by the company I drive for. He was a regular at my wife's café. One day he sat down beside me at the diner and struck up a conversation. He started talking to me about how much it costs to live nowadays, wanting to know my financial situation. I was frustrated with the company and told him some stuff I wish I hadn't. About the problems of getting work at a new place at my age and what I paid for a little house I rent over in Sparks. He just listened that first time."

Rae leaned in. "What makes you think he works for Rojo?"

Dawn leaned in too. "He has a reputation around town. He runs with a bunch of rejects from Fort Bliss, but he said he'd be running a special shipment for a certain powerful man from Juárez. There ain't but one man with any power over there, near as I can tell. And it ain't the mayor, I'll tell you."

Rae nodded. "Just stick to the offer you were made."

"They have offered me ten thousand dollars to drive a load from here to Atlanta. They didn't say what the load was, but said it was liquid and there was no way the cops would know what it was."

Rae scowled. "Liquid, huh?

Dawn nodded. "I figured you might know what they're talking about."

Rae shook her head. "I'll do some checking around. When do they want you to do it?"

"I'm supposed to meet the guy heading things up in about a week. Then I take the truck east two weeks from now."

CHAPTER 9
WRONG TURN

TUESDAY, NOVEMBER 22, 2005
7:22 P.M.
DAWSONVILLE, GEORGIA

The city known as the home of moonshine hauling, and by extension the home of NASCAR, was quiet on this winter Tuesday afternoon. Dawsonville residents had gone inside to get out of the cold, it seemed, as Daniel Byrd navigated past the historic courthouse in the center of town, heading toward his new, to him, house in Canton.

Byrd pulled the issued Crown Victoria alongside the gas pumps at a service station and just before he turned off the ignition, his police radio barked to life.

"Thirty-four to eighty-nine. Are you still on the air?" Byrd recognized Doc Farmer's voice.

"I'm still out, Doc. What do you need?" he said into the microphone.

"A student from North Georgia College is missing. She was last seen around noon today. Her family was planning to meet her for dinner, and she didn't show up. The sheriff has asked for our help."

Byrd rubbed his face. "Sure. I'm in Dawsonville getting some gas. I can be there in about forty-five minutes."

Doc came back on the radio. "Can you come up on Highway 9E? They think she went to an antique store and would have used that route on her way."

"Sure. Do you have a vehicle description?" Byrd asked.

"A red 1995 Mustang with Gordon County plates. I should have the plate numbers in a little while. The family is looking for the paperwork on the car right now."

"Got it. I'll see you at the Sheriff's Office."

Byrd climbed out of the car and wrapped his overcoat around him. The wind whipped, the temperature dropping with the sun. He tried to turn his back to the bitter blast as he pumped gas.

Byrd climbed back into the car and retraced his path past the old Dawsonville courthouse. Byrd estimated the fastest route was to take Georgia Highway 53 east to Highway 400. Twenty-eight minutes later, he was exiting 400 onto the back road that had once been the primary route north into Dahlonega.

Highway 400 is a four-lane, limited-access highway built from Atlanta to Dahlonega. Before 400 was completed, Highway 9E had been a busy route frequented by cars loaded with moonshine destined for Georgia's capital. Now, the high-capacity route had replaced the curvy, dangerous two-lane road. Byrd pushed the Ford north, winding along the rough paved road.

Byrd watched the side roads for any sign of the red mustang when he noticed a pair of fresh-looking skid marks across the highway, just north of a sharp curve in the road.

Byrd pulled off to the shoulder of the roadway and activated his blue lights. He grabbed the steel flashlight from his back seat and walked out into the road. There were no cars visible in either direction, so Byrd bent down to examine the marks on the throughfare. The smell of burned rubber was faint but detectable on the lightly traveled road. He stood in the center of the road and used the beam of his flashlight to examine the side of the highway. The tire marks were faint but pointed toward the east shoulder. Byrd trotted toward where the marks ended.

Immediately, in the light, he could see ripped grass and broken bushes. Byrd recognized the location where a car had left the shoulder. He jogged over and looked into the woods. The red Mustang had gone over the embankment and crashed against a giant pine tree. Byrd scrambled down the steep embankment and pushed through thick undergrowth to the driver's door of the crumpled car.

He could see the windshield was shattered and the hood was pushed up and folded. Byrd's heart sank when he saw the lifeless body slumped over toward the console. He pulled on the door and was able to force it open. When he did, he pushed her brown hair aside and put his hand on the young girl's neck. She was cold to the touch and there was no pulse. A life so full of promise, he thought, and ended by a deer running in the road or a moment of inattention. Byrd sighed.

On the way back to his government car, he noted the license plate had a sticker on the bottom indicating it had been issued in Gordon County. He worked his way back up the slope, slower than his trip down. When he got in the warmth of his GBI car, he grabbed the radio microphone and switched channels to the State Patrol radio system.

"GBI eighty-nine to GSP Cumming," he said.

"Cumming, go ahead eighty-nine," came the immediate response.

"Are you familiar with the missing student from Dahlonega?" Byrd asked.

"Ten-four, eighty-nine. My Lumpkin County unit is checking Georgia 400 now."

Byrd felt very tired. "Can you have him meet me on 9E just north of Auraria. The missing vehicle is off an embankment into the woods. The driver will be a fatality."

Byrd heard the radio operator sigh and then say, "I'll have him en route."

After a pause, the radio operator continued. "Cumming to two-eight-nine. GBI eighty-nine has located the missing female just north of Auraria on 9E. Can you meet him? He says it appears to be a ten-fifty F."

Byrd hung up the radio microphone and waited for the trooper to arrive.

Felisha nosed her rental car past the GBI Crown Victoria. She continued slowly around until she could get back in the northbound lane. She'd been following Byrd since he left his office at the State Patrol post in Canton early this morning.

She wanted a chance to close this contract and get back home. She'd never taken so much time for a kill. Nor had she used meth on a regular basis. This job was getting to her.

She couldn't see Byrd due to the flashing lights and the headlights. She gunned the rental car and began to look for a place to turn around. She found a muddy path with a wide entrance a mile from where Byrd sat parked on the road. In the darkness, she would need to be careful not to get stuck.

She cranked the wheel hard to the left and eased off the pavement. The red clay was slick, but she managed to seesaw the car back around. Before she pulled back onto the pavement, she reached into her bag in the backseat. She felt around until she touched her Glock 17. She pulled the gun from its black leather holster and checked the chamber. The gun was loaded as she knew it would be. Felisha laid the handgun on the seat beside her.

She carefully pulled back onto the pavement and then rolled cautiously back toward where she had seen Byrd's car sitting on the highway. She took deep breaths, working to control her breathing, to ensure an accurate shot when the time came. The lonely road would be a good location for her to shoot the annoying GBI agent and then drive directly to the Atlanta Airport.

When Byrd's flashing lights came into view, she rolled the driver's window down. The air blowing in the window was frigid. Felisha squinted as the bright headlights on the GBI car pointed in her eyes. She took her foot off the gas and let the car's momentum take the rental closer to Byrd. She could see him now, dressed in a long black overcoat, standing on the edge of the road on the side away from her. Felisha wasn't happy with the circumstances; she would be shooting a target that would be twenty-five to thirty feet away from a moving car. And she'd need to whip the gun up and shoot on the move.

"I got you now, GBI man," Felisha mumbled to herself. She held the Glock loosely in her lap as she got nearer.

Felisha held the lower half of the steering wheel in her left hand to prevent her own arm from getting in front of the muzzle of the pistol. She took a firmer grip of the Glock, ready to bring the gun up quickly.

The blue lights coming up from behind her caused Felisha's heart to race. Another cop, she thought. *"Mierda!"* Felisha exclaimed out loud.

She gently pressed the gas as she rolled up the window. She tossed the Glock onto her passenger seat and sat back. She knew she'd appear to be just another motorist, curious about what was going on.

She watched a Georgia trooper pull to a stop in front of Byrd's car. Once her car was away from all the flashing lights, she hit the steering wheel with her fist. "*Mierda! Mierda! Mierda!*" she shouted at the roof of her car.

She was so angry she almost hit the ambulance coming her way.

Byrd and the trooper climbed down to the Mustang and were joined by a couple of EMTs who had arrived minutes after the trooper. Each had a flashlight and soon the red car was being inspected by the first responders.

One of the EMTs declared the girl deceased after an examination of her body, but they would need to wait on the coroner to remove her remains from the ruined car. Byrd knew there was nothing more he could do and left the Trooper and medical technicians to their work.

The area was bathed in pulsing blue and red lights as he stumbled up the hillside. When he was back on pavement, he saw two more cars pull up to the scene. He recognized one of them as Doc Farmer's GBI car.

Doc got out and walked over to Byrd. The two men shook hands and watched as the Lumpkin County sheriff helped the mother and father of the dead girl out of his car. The parents were shaking and walking slowly toward the crash scene.

"Doc, what are they doing?" Byrd asked.

Doc hung his head. "The parents insisted on coming to the scene. They said they couldn't live with themselves if they didn't. So, the sheriff said he would drive them down."

Byrd nodded. He hoped they would be able to live with themselves after seeing their daughter dead before she had begun to live. He heard the mother wail and saw her drop to her knees on the side of the road. The father slumped down beside her. The sheriff, a thirty-year law enforcement veteran, tried his best to comfort them.

Byrd looked at Doc. "The sheriff has a tough job."

Doc nodded. "She was their only child."

Byrd sighed. "Damn!"

Doc slumped against Byrd's car and pulled a cigarette out of a pack and lit it. After a long pull, he looked back at Byrd. "Teddy, this part wears an agent down."

Byrd grunted. The two GBI men watched silently as the sheriff herded the mourning mother and father back to his car. When the sheriff pulled out, Byrd walked to the edge of the road and called to the trooper, "Is there anything we can do for you before we pull out?"

The trooper waved up. "I'm good. Thanks for helping out."

Byrd nodded and returned to Doc.

"Have you worked all day?" Doc asked.

Byrd shrugged. "I slept late, so it doesn't seem like I worked all day. What about you?"

Doc nodded. "I got called first thing this morning to an armed robbery up in Rabun County. It turned out to be a teenager with a toy gun. He didn't get much money, and a deputy caught him walking about a mile from the scene. There wasn't much to do by the time I got there."

Byrd rubbed his face with both hands. He stared at the pavement illuminated by the government car's headlights. Byrd looked back at Doc. "I wasted my whole day looking for a witness in a shooting from last week." Byrd rammed his hands in his pockets. "It turned out to be an accident.

The guy shot himself trying to clean his pistol. But his buddy, who saw it all, had a Violation of Probation warrant out for him. I had just dropped him off at the Dawson County jail and was headed home."

Doc met Byrd's eyes. "Teddy, I'm just about worn out. I've been trying to run down leads on whoever shot at Judge Lance but I'm getting nowhere fast."

"What can I do to help, Doc? Nothing I have going on right now is front burner stuff."

Doc sighed heavily. "My doctor says I've got to take it easy till my ticker is healed up. He doesn't have any idea what it's like to be working on a high-profile case like this. Hell, my wife threatened to have my face put on a milk carton," Doc laughed with his whole body.

Byrd struggled for potential clues. "I assume the Judge's secretary has given you the names of the folks he's sentenced lately?"

Doc took a deep draw on the cigarette. "Yep. Nothing jumps out. In spite of his nickname, Lance seems to be a pretty lenient judge. I haven't been able to come up with diddly. And Tina says Governor Franks's office is calling just about every day."

Byrd stared up at the stars. For a moment he wondered why he enjoyed this soul-sucking job. But he did. He glanced over at Doc. "I've got no use for Franks. He's the one who appointed Judge Pelfrey to the bench."

Doc nodded. "Yeah, pretty much an empty suit. But he'll probably get reelected next year."

"Hang in there, buddy. It'll break. Somebody has to know something." Byrd didn't feel as upbeat as he tried to sound.

"How's the personal life? Did you get moved into your house?"

Byrd smiled. "Yep. It needs some work, but I really think I'm going to enjoy living there. You've got to come see it sometime."

"How about that assistant DA? You still seeing her?" Doc tried to sound casual.

Byrd cut his eyes over. "Why?"

"I was in Sheriff Nelson's office over in Cherokee a couple of weeks ago. He told me confidentially that she was on the outs with her boss at the DA's office."

"That's what she tells me. I hate that for her. She'll end up in private practice, I guess."

Doc chuckled. "You think you can date a defense attorney?"

Byrd shrugged his shoulders. "She may not want to date a cop. That might be bad for business."

Doc pointed at the car. He pulled on his right earlobe as he shook his head. "Young folks like her dying from a simple mistake. Makes you wonder what it's all about."

Byrd frowned. "It's hard to understand, that's for sure. She was in the spring of her life."

Doc shook his head. "You look at life like the seasons of a year. When you get to be my age, you realize it's more like the hours of a day. The morning is bright and full of promise. The middle of the day seems so productive and then before you know it, the sunset is coming."

Byrd stood up and faced Doc. "Are you trying to tell me something?"

Doc hung his head. "Life goes pretty fast. I guess almost dying has given me pause." He pointed at the Mustang. "She never made it to lunch. Her life was over so fast she never had a chance to set a course in life. That is hard to understand."

"I don't think we'll understand in this life. Maybe we'll understand in the next."

Doc smiled. "I wonder about all that. Are me and you just learning how to protect people in the next life? I guess that's why they call it the great mystery."

Doc stood up and pointed at his car. "My warm car is calling to me. Let's get home before midnight for a change."

CHAPTER 10
OLD DEBTS

WEDNESDAY, NOVEMBER 23, 2005
4:10 P.M.
GAINESVILLE, GEORGIA

Gary Thomasson was scared. The meeting with the woman had set off alarm bells of every kind. He had hoped he could distance himself from Felisha and her questions about Daniel Byrd.

He was considering his options when the phone on his desk rang.

Machele Stephens, the administrative assistant for the office, told him he had a call on line two.

He pushed the button absentmindedly as he considered his options. "Thomasson," he said into the phone.

"Friend Gary. It's wonderful to talk with you after all this time."

Thomasson felt a wave of nausea. He recognized General Mitch Warren's voice.

"General. What's going on in your world?" Thomasson tried to sound relaxed.

"Just trying to make a buck," Warren remarked. Then he shifted gears. "Did you get my payment from the lady from Texas?"

Thomasson cleared his throat. "I did. And I appreciate it. But about the woman . . ."

"We haven't met. She actually works for a friend of mine. As a matter of fact, I need you to meet her tonight in Jasper. I hope that's not asking too much. She said you were uncomfortable discussing details at the coffee shop. She has arranged a room in Jasper and would like to go over the finer points of Mr. Byrd's life. Can you do that?"

"General, I am pretty busy right now. I was just about to leave the office and follow up on some interviews."

"I can give you ten thousand reasons to meet with her."

Thomasson's mouth was dry. "I can do that. Will the reasons be pictures of dead presidents?"

Warren chuckled. "Technically not. Pictures of Benjamin Franklin. He was never a president."

Thomasson wiped his mouth with his hand. "Where and when?"

"Do you know of the Elite Motel?" Warren asked.

WEDNESDAY, NOVEMBER 23, 2005
7:06 P.M.
JASPER, GEORGIA

Gary Thomasson pulled his government car into a motel parking lot just outside of Jasper. Away from the streetlights, the area was dark as the back side of the moon. Thomasson felt exhausted from the long day he had already put in and hoped this stop off would be quick. He pointed his car toward an empty space near the rear of the back lot. Then he took the list of questions he had been given and got out of the car.

The motel looked old, with outside doors. He looked for the room number he had been given. He picked out the room and noted there were lights on.

Thomasson stood, nervous, as he checked out the surrounding parking lot. He didn't see anything that seemed out of place. Deep down, Thomasson regretted what he was about to do, stabbing a fellow agent in the back. He had gone down this road several years back, as a game warden, when he took a large cash "loan" from General Mitch Warren to help him buy a home. He had believed Warren to be an honorable member of the US military. Within a year, Warren cajoled Thomasson into letting friends hunt Warren's land out of season. Later, he supported Warren's people as they hunted alligators illegally along the Altamaha River. Soon, he was under Warren's thumb.

Thomasson took a deep breath and crossed to the room, looking around as he strode to the front door. He glanced both ways and then tapped lightly on the wooden entrance.

When Felisha opened the motel room door, she peeked around it as she invited Thomasson in. Thomasson checked the room out, looking for anyone else who might be hidden inside, as he cautiously crossed the threshold. He kept his right hand close to his gun, hidden by his sport coat.

Felisha used her body to push the door securely closed. As she leaned her back against the wall, Thomasson realized for the first time she was wearing black lingerie. His eyes widened for a moment and his breathing became shallow.

Felisha walked within a foot of Thomasson. "I hope my sleeping attire doesn't bother you."

Thomasson mumbled, "No, it's fine." His eyes were taking in her caramel-colored skin and her firm stomach and breasts. *Her face has an exotic hint, probably Mayan ancestry*, he thought.

She stepped in closer and leaned into the GBI man. "Before you tell me what I need to know about Daniel Byrd, I thought we could get to know each other. Would you like a drink. I have some excellent tequila."

Thomasson was still cautious. "I've got no love for Danny Byrd." Thomasson stood very still. He cleared his throat. "But I'm doing this for the money your boss offered."

Felisha handed him a drink and sipped one of her own. She stood on tiptoes and put her lips near Thomasson's ear. He felt her hot breath and could feel her breasts press into his chest. "You'll get your money. But first I was hoping you might want to eat a little Mexican."

Felisha watched Gary Thomasson lie on the bed beside her, absent-mindedly twisting his wedding band. Felisha shrugged and then stood up. She grabbed a notepad from her travel case and sat down, naked, in an old, worn chair. "Tell me about Byrd."

Thomasson stood and pulled his pants on, uncomfortably nude after the passion of the moment had passed. "What do you want to know?"

Even with the cash, Thomasson didn't relish the role of Judas. He tried to think of things he'd heard about Byrd around the office. "He lives alone but has a girlfriend who stays at his house sometimes. She's an assistant district attorney. I just helped Byrd move into a new house he inherited from his uncle. The house sits off to itself on some acreage."

Felisha wasn't bothered by her nudity. She began taking notes as Thomasson talked.

"What's he like?" she asked.

"He's the director's boy. He's violated all kinds of Bureau policies and comes out smelling like a rose. I heard he killed several cartel gunmen down in Mexico and then skated because the GBI and the Texas Rangers pulled some strings," Thomasson paused and glanced at Felisha. "Is that true?"

She shrugged. "Could be. I haven't been told why they want him dealt with. It's just a job."

"He is a drinker and was getting a bad reputation when he got out of narcotics. He told me nowadays he keeps it to two drinks. Vodka mostly. He works alone most of the time and can be a cowboy."

"Does he cat around on his girl?" Felisha asked. "You know, pick up girls in bars and such?"

Thomasson glanced down at his ring. "We work together. We don't party together. I can ask around."

"Who might know more about him?"

"Doc Farmer is an agent in the office we're in. He and Byrd are tight. I doubt he'd give up much to me, though. Doc stays pretty close to the vest."

"Older man with gray hair combed back? About five-ten?" Felisha asked.

Thomasson nodded. "How'd you know?"

Felisha smirked. "I do this for a living. This ain't my first rodeo."

Felisha probed with questions and then follow-up questions. She took detailed notes and pressed Thomasson for minutiae. She had him draw a layout of Byrd's house and the area around it. Once she seemed satisfied, she stood up and stretched. Her eyelids were half closed as she twisted and then bent over at the waist. "I'll get your money."

"Thanks."

Felisha counted out $10,000 in $100 bills. Thomasson watched her closely, counting along. She handed him the bundle of cash and then cocked her hip to one side. "You want to count it?"

"I'm good. I trust you." Thomasson split the bills into two stacks and crammed them into his front pants pockets. "Happy Thanksgiving."

Felisha glowered. "Mexicans don't celebrate you gringos coming to this continent."

Thomasson shrugged, unsure if she were joking.

Felisha tossed her dark hair back and stood with her left arm over her head. The posture caused her breasts to jut out. "You want some more of this? It's been a while for me to be with a man."

Thomasson shook his head. His mouth was dry, and he stood to get dressed. "I don't think I can. I've never done this . . . before. I'm a happily married man."

Felisha wrapped her arms around his head and pulled him down to her breasts. "You don't know until you try. Here, take a sip of this. This juice and I will make you even more happy." She handed Thomasson a drink he assumed to be more tequila. He took a sniff and a sip. Suddenly the man's face was bright red, and his eyes were wide. Thomasson was breathing deeply and chewing on imaginary gum. Felisha felt his groin and was pleased that he was becoming engorged.

Felisha took a sip of the meth-laced tequila and felt enveloped by her own scent, a mix of perfume and sweat. Thomasson took off his wedding ring and dropped it onto the nightstand.

CHAPTER 11
THE BEST-LAID PLANS

THURSDAY, NOVEMBER 24, 2005
8:20 P.M.
EL PASO, TEXAS

Omar saw Dawn pause to let her eyes adjust to the bright lights of May's Diner. She probably felt comfortable in the café where her wife worked. Omar and Reyes were the only customers, sitting on the same side of a single booth, which helped Dawn decide he was her contact. The Thanksgiving Day crowd was slim.

She ambled over to the booth where Omar and Reyes sat. Omar had followed her with his eyes from the time she came into the building.

She dressed in a heavy green coat, a red flannel shirt, and a pair of work jeans. Her brown hair, with a hint of gray, had been cut short and parted in the middle of her head.

She slid into the booth with the vinyl seats. "You Bill? I'm here to meet Bill." She looked from one face to the other.

Reyes sat silently watching. Omar pushed back his long, bushy hair and nodded. "That'd be me." Omar watched her size him up. "I guess you're Dawn."

Dawn nodded. "Yep. I'll be one of the drivers. I have a friend who will back me up."

"I understood you are the only driver," Omar said as he slouched back in the booth and nursed a coffee.

Dawn didn't blink. "That Mex who offered me this deal said it was going to be a long haul. And they wanted the goods delivered post haste. You ain't the one putting his ass on the line for this trip. I have a second driver, or you can find somebody else. This trip is probably twenty hours of driving alone. One way. With two of us I can rest while my partner drives."

Omar sat up straight. "My people won't like that. You planning to bring your man with you, huh?"

Dawn smirked. "I don't trust no man to drive with me. They drink or take dope or they're just sorry as hell. I've got another woman in mind who can drive as good as me. This is too long a run to be leaving my butt hanging out in the wind."

Omar thought it over. Two women would certainly be less suspicious than a couple of men, particularly from the pool of drivers the man had to choose from. Most of the men willing to take the trip were ex-cons, and they looked it. Once he had mulled it over, he decided it was a good idea. He planned to tell Rojo he came up with the plan.

"You want extra money for this other driver?" he asked.

"Kid, do you do this shit for free?"

Omar chuckled. "I like your idea of two drivers. I understand you've hauled produce from the border before?"

Dawn scowled. "I've hauled everything under the sun in an eighteen-wheeler. Most of it legal, but not all of it. You want produce hauled? You don't need me for that. Those drivers are a dime a dozen."

Omar nodded. "We have some other product we want delivered. It is obviously something we'll pay a premium for. We just need you to drive a forty-eight-foot trailer from the border to Atlanta."

Dawn scowled again. "Weed?"

Omar shook his head. "It will be some barrels of liquid. Nothing that smells bad for the dogs to hit on. As a matter of fact, most of the trailer will be taken up by real produce."

"How much does this 'product' weigh in at?" Dawn asked.

Reyes spoke up for the first time. "Maybe ten thousand pounds in fifty-five-gallon drums."

Dawn thought the information over. "Lots of hassle and risk for such a small load. A driver's gonna have to be stopping at every weigh station across the southeast operating a big rig with a forty-eight-foot trailer. And if your team is as disorganized as most of the crews on the border, the produce will be going bad by the time we get the trailer rolling. On the other end, we're stuck with ten or twelve thousand pounds of stinking lettuce or whatever you use for cover. Is that a fair calculation?"

Reyes leaned forward. "We have done this thing many times. You have no track record. Do you want the job or not?"

Dawn started to stand up.

Omar reached across the table and grabbed her arm. "If you were running the show, what would you do?"

Dawn sat back down and sniffed. "I'd run a box truck. The biggest box trucks can handle five tons, easy. No need to stop for weights or inspections. Make it look like we're moving. Maybe throw some furniture on the back to make it look good. We drive across the country, and nobody will even notice."

Omar looked at Reyes. "That makes sense. No phony bills of lading and paperwork to deal with. And we are still hauling more than double the last load. Where do you get the truck? I don't want to have to deal with a rental agency for this. As you mentioned, our timetable has to be flexible."

Dawn pursed her lips. "I can get a twenty-six-foot box truck from a friend. We'll call it a short-term lease. That'll be ten thousand up front for the truck. I'll want our expenses covered. Sounds like it would be worth thirty thousand each for me and my copilot."

Omar laughed. "I'll pay for the truck 'lease' like you asked. For you and your copilot, I'll make it fifty thousand for the trip. You divide it any way you want to. That's up to you and your partner."

Dawn exhaled a deep breath. "Okay. One other thing. We get paid up front."

"Fifteen thousand up front; ten for the truck and five for set up expenses. The rest upon delivery. That's the best I can do."

"What size load are we talking about again?" Dawn asked.

Omar glanced around before he answered. "Seven pallets of fifty-five-gallon drums."

Dawn shook her head. "A twenty-six-foot truck can haul about five tons. A load that size would be closer to six tons. It'll work, but we'll have to take a little bit more time. Keep a close check on the tires and brakes."

Omar nodded. "You do know your stuff."

Dawn shook her head. "No matter what kind of drugs you're having me haul, that weight should amount to between fifty and a hundred million dollars if my calculations are close."

Omar smiled. "You really do know your business. Let's say we pay you around seventy-five thousand if you get the load to Atlanta safe and sound. That'll cover the cost of the truck and we'll add a couple of grand each for fuel and food. You pay your copilot whatever you think is fair."

Dawn did some calculations. "That sounds more like it. But let's make it around eighty thousand."

Omar chuckled. "I like you." He shook her hand. "Eighty, it is."

Dawn slid out of the booth and stood. "Sounds good. Do we load in El Paso or where? I need to do some planning to figure out routes and the best times to be on the road, amigo."

Omar looked up at her. "I'll be in touch about the details." Omar pushed a burner phone across the table toward Dawn. "Keep this phone handy. I'll give you plenty of notice. Any questions?"

Dawn shook her head. Then she remembered to say, "No."

Omar hunched over his coffee. "You just better not fuck this up."

Dawn scowled. "I thought you liked me."

Omar nodded. "And we both like living. I want to keep on doing that."

Dawn turned and strolled out of the café.

Omar turned to Reyes. "This is going to cost Rojo half a million, plus expenses. Let's call it six hundred thousand. I expect cash on hand in Georgia. Can that happen?"

Reyes thought it over. "With such a large shipment, I think the amount is reasonable. I will let you know on Monday."

Dawn felt as though her whole body was soaked in

sweat and her knees were going to buckle. She tried her best to look calm as she left the meeting with the two smugglers. She determined she wouldn't be intimidated by some kid who'd probably never seen the inside of a jail or had a gun pointed at him. But Rojo's cousin was a different matter. He had a direct link to Rojo and could have Dawn killed with a flick of a finger.

She leaned on the aluminum and glass door as she took a breath. Then she pushed the door open and aimed for her car. Her only hope was to keep moving.

As she passed through the door and made her way to the parking lot, she leaned down and whispered into the microphone. "I hope you got all of that."

Raelynn clicked off the recorder. She couldn't wait to call Adeline Riley and tell her they had a hook in Reyes Hernandez. The members of the task force knew him to be Rojo's US fixer and was directly connected, by family, to Rojo.

She watched Dawn climb in her Jeep and leave the parking lot. Rae followed her away and kept her car in sight as she headed toward the University of Texas at El Paso campus. They planned to meet in the university parking lot near the stadium. Once there, Raelynn would get the tiny recorder Dawn had worn and Raelynn would do a debriefing. Even though Raelynn had heard every bit of the conversations, she wanted Dawn's interpretation of the meeting. Dawn may have seen something that Raelynn missed.

As she tried to stay focused on following Dawn, to make sure she wasn't under counter-surveillance, Rae's mind raced through the variations this case could undergo. She also wondered if she could keep Dawn under control. The feisty truck driver was bold and brassy. But she had demonstrated that she liked to be in control. Raelynn would have to reign her in at some point. Or she could blow the whole operation sky-high.

Fun times, she thought.

THURSDAY, NOVEMBER 24, 2005
12:05 A.M.
CANTON, GEORGIA

He had organized most of the furniture and had a working TV. What more could a man ask for?

Byrd hung his swearing-in documents from the GBI in his bedroom, along with a couple of photos taken with other agents. He did it more to please Violet than for himself.

When he had hung all of himself he cared to, he poured a vodka and cranberry juice, for the vitamins it offered, and then headed for the bedroom. He began undressing when his Bureau phone rang.

He saw the number calling was a Texas number. "Byrd."

"Daniel Byrd, what the hell are you up to this fine Thanksgiving evening?" Byrd recognized the voice of Clete Petterson.

"Had some turkey at my parents' house, came home and did some fixing up, and am now getting ready for bed. What the hell are you doing calling at this late hour? Usually, when this phone rings, someone has been murdered in Georgia. Do you have a murder you need help with out there in the Lone Star State?"

Petterson chuckled. "Nothing so sinister, or so simple I'm afraid."

"Omar Warren has turned up dead?" Byrd joked.

"Nope, he's turned up alive."

"What?" Byrd asked.

"Do you remember Raelynn Michaels?"

"Sure. El Paso County Narcotics. Blond curly hair with a sweet smile." Byrd hadn't dealt as closely with Raelynn as he had Adeline, Montana, and Clete but she had earned his respect when he was in Texas last.

"She just watched a cooperator meet with a couple of folks she was told worked for Rojo. One was Omar Warren, and the other was Rojo's fixer on this side of the Rio."

"Rae was sure it was Omar?" Byrd asked.

"She was sure. And she got some still pictures of Omar during the meeting." Petterson told Byrd about a truck driver who had been approached to drive a load of drugs to Georgia. He explained Raelynn Michaels would be doing the undercover for the operation. Petterson went on to explain they had a plan to drive the load from the Texas border to a place in Georgia.

"Do you think you can help out?" Petterson asked as the story concluded.

Byrd tried to leave the drug cases to the GBI drug unit. "Maybe, or I can connect you with someone to run things on this end. Is it a lot of dope?"

"I think our director will be calling yours on Monday. We really would like for you to help on this, Danny. They want her to drive six tons of liquid meth."

Byrd coughed. "Did you say six tons?"

"Yep!"

"Are the feds involved?" Byrd asked.

"The federal agencies here in El Paso have decided they don't want to waste any time or money on Rojo. It's all a state and local game."

Byrd put the glass of vodka on the end table by his bed and started making notes. "Do I need to come out there and get myself up to speed?"

"Will the GBI pay for a trip? It sure would help."

Byrd thought about the answer. "Maybe. But I bet I can get Arlow to fly me out there. He'd love to get involved."

"That's a great idea. Having a surveillance plane that can help out as we cross the country would make life easier."

"I'll let you know tomorrow afternoon," Byrd declared. When he hung up, he decided to brief his chain of command tomorrow. He picked up the vodka glass and sipped it.

"Omar is more ballsy than I gave him credit for," Byrd remarked out loud. Then he took a long drink. "Damn it. I'm talking to myself again!"

THURSDAY, NOVEMBER 24, 2005
2:48 P.M.
CANTON, GEORGIA

Daniel Byrd and Jackson "Doc" Farmer were in the field behind Byrd's new home. Byrd was walking Doc around the property. "Son, you have hit the jackpot. This place is more than you'll ever need."

Byrd chewed on his lower lip. "What do you mean?"

"Single agent living alone. You got a place to shoot, a place to eat, and a place to lie your head. What else would you want?"

Byrd looked around. "It'd be nice to have a garage to put my car in and a place to park the G-ride." He shrugged his shoulders. "I guess I have plenty of time to build something like that."

Doc stopped. "You good with your hands? *Can* you build something like that?"

Byrd grinned. "Hell, no. But I'm awesome with a pen and a checkbook. I'll just have to save up."

They walked around the field until they came to the wood line. Then Byrd led the way toward the creek. As they twisted and turned through the naked underbrush, Doc asked, "What do you think about the new guy; Gary?"

Byrd stopped. "Thomasson? I haven't been around him a lot. He's spent most of his adult life in South Georgia. I guess he seems a little odd to the folks in the mountains." Byrd resumed blazing his way through the undergrowth. "Why, is there something going on?"

They had come to the creek. "Tina has been having him ride with me. It might be that we haven't hit it off," Doc offered.

Byrd pursed his lips. "Okay." He waved his hand at the creek in front of them. It was ten feet wide and probably a couple of feet deep and the constant gurgle of the water was soothing. "What do you think of this, Doc?"

"I love that sound. Can you hear it from your bed-room?"

Byrd nodded. "If the rain is really coming down, I can hear it with the window open."

Doc shook his head. "Why would you want to sleep with your windows open during a downpour? Son, you ain't right."

Byrd chuckled. "You're just saying that because you love me." Byrd shifted gears. "Anything new on the attempt on 'No-Chance Lance'?"

Doc fished out a cigarette. He took a moment to light it and then inhaled deeply. "It's an odd case, I'll give you that. We've gone through every sentencing from the last year, checked on anybody he sentenced who's been paroled lately, and run down anyone who lost their child custody by one of Lance's orders. So far, nobody pops out."

Byrd raised an eyebrow. "I thought your doctor told you to quit smoking?"

Doc looked at his shoes. "He said I *needed* to quit. But he also said, once he put those stents in, I was as good as ever."

"Doc, you need to take care of yourself. I don't want a new guy like Thomasson working the case if I were to get shot."

"Hell, Teddy. What makes you think I could do any better? Between people you've locked up, men and women you've pissed off for one reason or another, and the occasional case of road rage, I wouldn't know where to start."

Byrd led the way back up the hill. "Should I be watching out for Gary Thomasson?" Byrd asked.

Doc was getting winded walking up the steep incline back to the gravel drive. "All that's on the down low. Tina says she is worried he's not catching on to the GBI paperwork. But there's something about him that ain't right."

Then Doc looked around him. Even in the woods, he was cautious. He lowered his voice. "I think he's cheating on his wife, among other things. He's been keeping odd hours and comes in looking like hammered dammit." Doc looked Byrd in the eyes. "Kind of like you when you're not on a good case."

Byrd cocked an eyebrow. "I'll quit when you quit."

Doc looked away. "I don't drink."

"You know what I mean."

Doc changed the subject. "I hear you're headed back to Texas next week. Have they got anything out there other than scorpions and rattlesnakes?"

"Tequila. Lots of tequila."

"You mean to-kill-ya," Doc corrected him.

They walked the rest of the way to Doc's GBI car. "Son, you sleep with one eye open. I'm not so sure that bullet was meant for the Judge. Whoever it was could just have easily been gunning for you."

Byrd shook his hand. "I'll do it, Doc. Let me know if you get anything on that."

"And you keep the info about Thomasson under your hat. Just pay attention whenever you're around him."

The two men stopped by the door of Doc's issued Crown Vic. "Son, you listen to me and keep your head on a swivel for a while. At least 'till we get someone on this shooting." Doc knitted his brows. "I still think you're a better target than the Judge."

Byrd wasn't buying it. He shook his head. "I guess it comes with the job."

Doc chuckled, "It doesn't pay much, but we have a lot of fun."

Doc slapped Byrd on the back before he climbed into his car.

Byrd watched him drive away.

MONDAY, NOVEMBER 28, 2005
9:22 A.M.
CANTON, GEORGIA

Daniel Byrd and Violet Childs walked along the old roadbed that passed in front of Byrd's new home. The path, still easily discernable, led to the creek that marked Byrd's property line. Byrd wrapped his arm around Violet's shoulder to warm her as they walked.

The burble of the water in the creek was peaceful and Byrd pulled Violet close and kissed her hard. "I really like this piece of land. It's got everything I could ask for."

Violet grinned up at him. "You seem really happy. I'm glad for you."

Byrd hugged her close against the cold close to the water. "You don't think you'd be interested in this as your home too?"

Violet turned away. "Danny, I just got out of one serious relationship. I'm not ready to get into another. I'm still working through my life, my relationships, my medical issues. You name it, I need to work on it."

"Your back seems to bother you more lately," Byrd observed.

"You're just around me more. It never goes away completely. I just need to keep enough pain medication in me to feel normal."

Byrd watched her. "You concern me sometimes. I know your back is a problem, but you need to be careful self-medicating. You'll end up in deep trouble. You get drug tested, just like I do."

Violet's face reddened. "Oh yeah? You drink till you

pass out and nobody gives a damn. I try to feel like a normal person and not be crippled by pain and everyone thinks I'm a druggie. How the hell is that fair?"

Byrd shook his head and tried to reach out to her. Violet wasn't having it. "Don't you touch me!" Violet exclaimed. "Cops are all alike. I'm hurting most of the time and your only concern is whether I might get in trouble. Fuck you!"

Byrd held his tongue.

After a moment, Violet looked back at him. "I'm sorry, Danny. I know you care about me; I just don't know what comes first with you. Is it your job or me?"

Byrd offered his arm. "Let's head back to the house. You have to be in court soon and I need to pack for Texas."

"Texas?"

Byrd nodded. "I told you last night when you got here. We have a big load of meth we're helping some friends of mine from Texas with. I got a call from my boss saying it had been approved for me to help on this case. I'll be gone a few days."

Byrd could tell by the look on her face she didn't remember. Violet started off ahead of him. "That'll give both of us time to think."

"Will you stay here while I'm gone? You're welcome to do that."

Violet shook her head. "I've moved all my stuff, what my husband let me have, into my cousin's place in Roswell. She's letting me live with her till I figure out what I want to do."

"I just wanted to offer. My house is closer to your work than Roswell would be." The idea seemed rational to Byrd.

"Don't push it with me, Danny." Then Violet turned and trudged up the steep hill back to Byrd's house. Byrd followed behind her.

Byrd realized the walk back was going to be longer than the walk down had been. And much colder.

Byrd rolled his GBI car into a parking spot at the Cherokee County Airport. He had arranged with Arlow Turner, of the DEA Air Wing, to meet there to begin the flight to El Paso.

Arlow stood beside the DEA Aero Commander that served as his office. He was running through his pre-flight safety check. Byrd watched him go down the list and examine every part of the plane.

"How long will the flight take?" Byrd asked.

Arlow looked at his flight chart. "Less than seven hours flight time, but we'll need to refuel somewhere along the way."

Byrd sighed. "I guess it's too far for one hop."

Arlow pointed at the chart. "The range on this baby is 1,480 miles on a full tank of fuel. The distance to El Paso is 1,420 miles. Do you really want to bet your life on my calculations?"

Byrd shook his head. "Nope. Let's keep plenty of fuel in this thing. No need to tempt fate."

Arlow nodded. "We break the law every time we take off."

Byrd raised an eyebrow. "You don't have a pilot's license?"

Arlow looked over the control surfaces on the turbo-prop aircraft. "We break the law of gravity. And gravity can be a heartless bitch."

Byrd stopped in his tracks. "You sound like you've dated her."

Arlow stopped what he was doing. "Kid, you fly long enough, you'll end up having an emergency. It's not if; it's when. The trick is to survive."

Byrd frowned. "You've had midair emergencies?"

Arlow kept his thumb on the list as he talked to Byrd. He didn't want to lose his place. "I've crashed a few times. I always walked away, though."

Byrd was suddenly concerned. "What's a few times?"

"Eight."

"Shit, Arlow. Eight times?"

Arlow shrugged. "Well, those are the ones that got reported. There were a couple of times I was able to repair the plane and get it back in the air. What DEA doesn't know won't hurt them."

"This plane?"

"No, my first agency plane was a seized 182. It was tough, but landing on dirt roads and unimproved runways took a toll. That and an oak tree I clipped."

"Are you kidding me?" Byrd asked.

"I don't kid about that."

Byrd let Arlow finish his inspection. He idly wondered if his state health insurance would cover him in a plane crash. Then he guessed that would be the least of his problems.

The two lawmen climbed into the white and red twin-engine plane, a high-wing aircraft which makes ground surveillance easier, and strapped into the seats. Arlow took his time warming up the engines and running through the instrument checks, steps as vital to a safe flight as the examination of the airframe.

Once Arlow was satisfied with the gauges, he rolled the airplane forward as he called out on the radio. "Aero Commander 23 Alpha, departing Cherokee County Regional Airport on runway twenty-three," Arlow said as he rechecked the area for any other traffic.

The sleek airplane rolled to the end of the taxiway. "You ready?" Arlow asked.

Byrd nodded and double-clicked the intercom microphone.

Arlow pointed the plane south and gunned the engines. "Here we go! Breaking the law again."

Byrd felt tempted to close his eyes.

The flight halfway across the country took twelve hours. Bad weather over Mississippi had cost time, and near Dallas, they had been ordered to divert to clear a route for Air Force One. Even with the two-hour time difference, the sun was behind the mountains when the Aero Commander rolled to a halt at Biggs Army Airfield northeast of El Paso.

Byrd climbed out of the airplane to stretch. Arlow went about the business of tying the airplane down on the ramp and checking in with the operations officer. Once they were finished, the men ordered a taxi to a motel near the ranger offices.

"Arlow, how did you get into this screwed-up business?" Byrd asked as they sat in the motel lounge.

Arlow chuckled. "It can be crazy, at times. That's for sure." Arlow shook the ice in his drink. "I was crop-dusting in Arkansas. A town called Cabot. I had a degree from Florida State, but wasn't doing much more than flying a few hours a day. One day, a guy from the DEA approached me about a pilot who'd landed at the airport I used. He was a big smuggler. I didn't know anything, but I asked the DEA agent if they were hiring. I guess I was looking for adventure."

Byrd nodded. "I guess you got it."

"I did," Arlow continued. "I did some undercover work in Nicaragua, and I kept myself current as a pilot.

When the DEA began the airwing I was in the right place at the right time. What about you?"

Byrd sipped his drink. "I had wanted to be a cop since I was a kid. I read detective novels and watched all the shows on TV. My dad took me to see a movie called *Manhunter*, about an FBI profiler. I thought I wanted to be a G-Man. I got out of college and applied, but they said I wasn't qualified."

"Because your parents were married?" Arlow asked.

Byrd laughed. "No, I was too young. I got a job as a cop with Canton PD when I was still nineteen. Worked there till the Georgia State Patrol hired me as a radio operator. Went to work with the GBI two months after I turned twenty-three. I could have gone back to the FBI, twenty-three is their hiring age, but I decided I liked the agency. I discovered over the last few years I made the right decision."

"Yeah. The DEA and the FBI don't play well together. Really the FBI doesn't play well with anyone." Arlow finished his drink. "Have you ever thought about working for the DEA?"

Byrd shook his head. "I got in the GBI to be a coat-and-tie agent, working big homicides. I wanted nothing to do with drug cases. Then one day, I got the HOG treatment."

Arlow grimaced. "The what?"

Byrd smiled. "In the GBI, you get moved because you have demonstrated proficiency in the agency and ask to be relocated. That's the best way. The other way is the HOG. The 'hand of God' comes down, picks you up and reassigns you to some job they can't get a volunteer for. I got HOGed into my first undercover job."

"You didn't like it?"

"Let's say, I was never as glib as some others. I did it,

and I survived it, but I wasn't good. Now, I'm happy not being good at being a regional agent working homicides."

Arlow leaned back in the booth. "Don't underestimate yourself. By the way, what are you doing on this case? Is it a HOG?"

"More a request from one director to another. The Texans think I did a good job when I was out here last."

Arlow winked. "Maybe by Texas standards you do a good job. They might not have much to compare you to."

"On that note," Byrd commented dryly. "Let's have another drink. No flying tomorrow, no driving tomorrow, just meetings with bosses."

Arlow shook his glass. "Sure. We're on travel status."

"DEA pays for alcohol when you're on travel status?"

"We call drinks umbrellas," Arlow remarked.

Byrd shook his head. "I don't get it."

"A few years back, an agent was in Seattle to testify in court. He was getting soaked in the rain when he got there, so he bought an umbrella. When he submitted his travel voucher with the umbrella on it, it got kicked back. The DEA refused to pay for the umbrella; said it was a personal item. So, the agent reworked the voucher."

Byrd was still not connecting the dots. "Yeah?"

"His boss took the paper, looked at it and said, 'I'm glad I don't see that umbrella on here.' The guy looked at his boss and said, 'It's on there, you'll just have to find it.'"

Byrd laughed. "Time for another umbrella."

CHAPTER 12
GETTING IT TOGETHER

WEDNESDAY, NOVEMBER 30, 2005
8:22 A.M.
EL PASO, TEXAS

The conference room at the El Paso County Sheriff's Office was full of cops. Sheriff Jim Hallman sat at the head of the table, with Major Crosby of the Texas Rangers on his left. The rest of the Texas Rojo Task Force was in attendance. Byrd leaned against a wall at the back of the room. He'd spent the last day working out a basic idea of how to run the load of meth to Georgia. Now the bosses would have to work out the fine details.

Ranger Addy Riley and Deputy Rae Michaels stood near Byrd and watched the faces. The case was moving quickly, more quickly than government agencies could respond to under normal circumstances. Both were aware they were getting pushback from the states along I-20 on the way to Atlanta. They were hoping the Texas Rangers could exercise some influence with their sister agencies in Louisiana, Mississippi, and Alabama, but that didn't seem to work.

Hallman called the meeting to order. "I hate to get things off on a sour note, but I've been on the phone with some of my contacts across the route we'll be taking. Nobody wants any part of this operation. I tried to explain to some of the sheriffs along the way how important this case was, but I got nothing but static back." Hallman looked to Major Crosby. "I damned sure hope we don't have to go down to the Feds with our hats in our hands," Hallman continued.

Major Crosby tipped his hat back. "I'm afraid I'm running into the same problems on the state level. They think having that much meth on the loose is just too risky."

Hallman wasn't ready to give up. "Suppose we lock the back of the truck. Assign some SWAT deputies to ride shotgun. We can send as many cover cars as we can muster. We can just do the operation on our own."

Crosby shook his head. "Sheriff, we can't break the law to get the drugs to Georgia. It would sink any prosecution. And without the help of an agency in each state, I'm afraid we're out of luck. We need to find a way that is legal."

Byrd stepped out of the room.

Sheriff Hallman watched Byrd sneak out. "Any chance the GBI would have more luck calling in favors?"

Crosby looked back to where Byrd had stood. "We can sure give it a try. We also have to deal with some of the logistical issues."

Hallman turned to Crosby. "Like what, Major?"

"Ranger Riley will be in charge of the operation for the state. I'm sending Lieutenant Petterson along, too. He's got a lot of experience dealing with Rojo and his people."

"I'm good with that. Clete's good people. And it'll get Clete out of Dodge until we know more about these hitmen. Will you need any manpower from my agency? I'm not crazy about sending my deputies to Georgia, but we'll do what we need to do," Hallman declared.

"Thanks, but I think we'll use the members of the Rojo task force. They're sworn in as state officers. They can cover the undercover and the cooperator along the way. I am working to get the Director of DPS to allow Trooper Montana Petterson to be a part of this."

"To keep Clete company or to keep him safe?" Hallman quipped.

Crosby smiled. "Both, but she is also still a certified peace officer in Georgia. I spoke with the GBI Director this morning and he's willing to swear her in when she gets there."

"That can't hurt," Hallman opined.

Crosby looked at a list he'd made. "We'll need the crime lab to test the dope on both ends. We'll have to mark the barrels they send it in. That part should be easy enough, just another step in the process. And we probably need to get a small tracker to put on the truck, just to be on the safe side. You can bet your hat these folks will run countersurveillance on the truck while it's on the road."

Hallman looked to Lenny Estrada, his commander of investigations. "Lenny, can we pull a rabbit out of our hats? I'll get approval to buy whatever we need to keep Deputy Michaels safe."

Rae flushed at the mention of her name. "And our cooperator would probably expect us to go above and beyond to keep them safe," she remarked under her breath.

Lenny stood and headed for the door. "There is a guy we've used for special video and audio equipment in the past. Name's James Costner, from South Florida. Runs a business building specialized surveillance vehicles."

Hallman scowled. "That's a long way from here. You think he can pull something off."

"I'll make a call right now," Lenny offered.

Lenny pushed the door open as Byrd came back into the room.

"Will this load be under forty-two thousand pounds?" Byrd asked.

Rae nodded. "Yep. Something like fifteen thousand at the most. They claim it's less, but I figure they'll try to dump more on us at the last minute."

"I think I've arranged for a plane from the Georgia Air National Guard to pick the dope up here in Texas and haul it to Georgia. They can't get the truck in, I don't think, though."

Major Crosby nodded. "We figure the truck will be followed by some of Rojo's men. But running an empty truck from here to Georgia is perfectly legal!"

"I'm working on a C-130H from a group in Savannah. We can load at Fort Bliss and drop the barrels off at Dobbins Air Reserve Base in Marietta. That's only a few miles north of Atlanta. I'd guess that would be where they plan to warehouse the load."

"How'd you pull that off so quickly?" Major Crosby asked.

"One of the agents in my office still has connections with the Guard. He got tentative approval. Their boss will make a phone call and put this together. Our agent is named Gary Thomasson."

Hallman slapped the table. "Now that's what I call a plan. Hell, we can have the drugs under our control until we pass them off to your folks in Georgia. Won't even touch any soil in Louisiana or Mississippi."

Byrd spoke up. "Don't forget Alabama."

Hallman laughed. "I like you, boy. When the GBI fires you over this, I'll have a job for you out here."

Byrd swallowed hard.

WEDNESDAY, NOVEMBER 30, 2005
11:29 A.M.
GAINESVILLE, GEORGIA

Gary Thomasson hung up the phone. His contact with the Georgia Air National Guard said they had done something similar in the '90s for the DEA. He didn't think it would be a problem to fly the load of barrels across the country. For the C-130H, he was told, fourteen thousand pounds was a piece of cake.

Thomasson called Byrd's cell phone and passed the word that the Guard would be on standby to move the load. They would need about eight hours' notice, he reminded Byrd.

"That won't be an issue," Byrd remarked. "We should have about twelve hours for them to get to El Paso."

"All right. Just let me know if you need anything else." Thomasson held the line open. He felt a deep sense of guilt over his betrayal of Byrd but the intense feelings he was having from the drug-fueled sex with Felisha was controlling him.

"Thanks, Gary."

The words tumbled out. "When are you coming back?"

Byrd hesitated. "I'm not sure. Dope deals are always on their own timetable. Why, do you need something?"

"I just wanted to offer my help if you still had things to move," Thomasson offered.

"Nope. You saw my apartment that last time when we left. Nothing left behind but dust."

"Right," Thomasson mumbled. "Well, let me know if I can help on this case."

Once he hung up the phone, Thomasson slumped at his desk. He knew he should call Felisha and pass the information on, but he wanted to see her again. To be wrapped in the aroma, the feel, the raw sexuality of her. He knew intellectually the act of using methamphetamine was a risk to his job and his family. But damn, she set him on fire.

He had been honest when he told Felisha he'd never done that before. But the one single transgression had been like a dam bursting. And his soul seemed to have washed away with it.

He grabbed his padfolio from his desk and started for the office door. "Machelle, I'm going over to Jasper for a while."

"Are you going to be helping Doc on the shooting case?" Machelle asked. She noted his departure time in her logbook.

"The Judge thing? No, I'm catching up on interviews in an older case."

He'd forgotten that Machelle typed every interview and every report on all the cases in the office. Her expression told him she wasn't buying his story.

Thomasson hoped Felisha would get her job done soon and get back to Mexico; or wherever she came from. But in the meantime, he needed to be with her.

WEDNESDAY, NOVEMBER 30, 2005
1:35 P.M.
WOODSTOCK, GEORGIA

Felisha Gomez had left her favorite deodorant back at the motel room in Jasper. She had started calling it her

131

"love shack." She and Thomasson were meeting every other day. *I'm pumping him for information on Byrd while he pumps me,* she thought with a laugh.

Thomasson had been helpful, but the GBI men often worked alone. Thomasson seldom knew for sure where Byrd would be the next day. She had spent too much time in Georgia already and was not close to putting a bullet in the *pájaro*, the bird.

She showered after spending two hours walking over the area near Byrd's home. She climbed near the house but had chosen not to examine the house itself for fear of security cameras. She took a tumble on a slippery hill and had almost been injured as she rolled across the tree-strewn landscape. She had caught herself by grasping a small oak tree just before she rolled off a ledge.

She toweled off and lay on the bed in her motel room in Woodstock where she kept her "work tools." She had her firearms in a locked case stored in the little clothes cupboard in that room. She had decided she could probably get around to the rear of the GBI man's house and take another long shot with her rifle. This time, she wouldn't use the bulky silencer, which she felt had affected her aim last time.

She went over her recollections of the way she thought would be best to access the house. There was a church just up the street from Byrd's house where she could stash her car while she made her way through the woods. It would be a long shot, but she felt confident she could put the *pájaro* down.

She had stretched and decided to take a quick nap. Then she might call Thomasson and meet for a little meth sex. She had been careful not to overdo her use of the drug, but once a week had turned into four times a week.

Or she had been careful not to overindulge—and she knew five times this week was a lot, but she knew people who used way more! They were the ones with a problem, not her.

She considered her options for the afternoon when her work phone vibrated. She shook her head. It had to be Rojo. No one else would call that number.

"Yes?" she asked when the connection was made.

"The men the American spy hired have been killed. Are you making progress? It has been some time that you have been in Georgia."

She sighed. "Yes, but this man is elusive. He covers many counties and is constantly on the go. I've been following him but have had trouble getting him in a situation where I could get to him. I have a plan to take him at his home, but there is a problem with that—for the time being."

"And what might that be?"

Felisha hated to be the bearer of bad news. "He is in El Paso."

"Now?"

"Right now. On a big case, according to the *el soplón*, the snitch."

There was silence on the line. Felisha waited.

"Can he be looking into my business again?"

"That would be a likely explanation," Felisha remarked. "If the Byrd is looking into one of your operations, do you think the ranger might come back here with him?" Felisha wondered.

"I wish that were the case, but I doubt it. The American police are very protective of their turf. I want him dead as soon as he is back in Georgia."

"Me, too!" Felisha declared.

"If the ranger should show up, I will double your pay if you put him in the ground as well."

"I will let you know when the Byrd is done. Can you have someone send me a photo of the ranger? If he should show up here, I will take him as well." Then she broke the connection.

She immediately used her cell to call Thomasson. She wanted to pressure him to meet for more information. He was way ahead of her.

CHAPTER 13
PRESIDIO OR BUST

MONDAY, DECEMBER 5, 2005
5:22 A.M.
EL PASO, TEXAS

Rae's stomach was tight. She had done undercover operations before, but never for these stakes. They would be operating with minimal cover and largely on their own. At best, an agent undercover had to be constantly alert to danger. Even running into someone from your personal life who called you by your real name in front of your target could get an agent hurt or killed. Rae was no coward, far from it, but the reality of being undercover in such a remote location for several days would be exhausting.

The cover of "truck driver" didn't fit her, either. The truck they were in stood over ten feet tall and thirty feet long. Dawn had tried to work with Rae to get her comfortable with the monster, but to no avail. The bosses had decided, after conferring with Dawn privately, the operation would go on as planned. Dawn would simply do all the driving.

She glanced over at Dawn as the trucker casually wove through morning traffic and skirted the border. Dawn looked comfortable in the big gray driver's seat, the most comfortable aspect of an otherwise spartan cab. Raelynn was relegated to a vinyl-covered, gray bench that sat like a witness chair. The only splashes of color in the gray and black cab were the red fire extinguisher under the dash and the yellow parking brake handle.

Atlanta's going to be a long ride, Rae reflected.

The sun would be staring into their windshield soon enough. They'd meet its glare head-on for the first few hours of the trip.

Dawn kept the truck exactly on the speed limit as they put El Paso behind them. In Van Horn, they exited the interstate and pointed south toward Presidio. In just over two hours the truck rumbled through Valentine, a little town with a part-time bar, a catholic mission, and a post office. The area had been settled when the Southern Pacific railroad pushed through the basin between the Davis Mountains and the Sierra Vieja Mountains. US 90 ran parallel to the railroad tracks still running the same route pioneered in 1882. Rae checked the GPS and guessed they were still a couple of hours out of Presidio.

The scenery was beautiful, Rae thought, but seemed to be more miles of the same view. They passed a Border Patrol checkpoint on the northbound side of the highway. Rae noted it for future reference. A break came when they passed through Shafter, a ghost town near the US highway, with a large catholic church looming over the little burg. Rae rechecked the GPS and was relieved to see they were less than thirty minutes from their destination.

"Showtime, girl. Are you still locked and loaded?" Rae asked.

Dawn smiled wryly. "Have I got another choice at this point?'

Rae shook her head. "I think we're both committed at this point."

Dawn pulled the truck into the lot at the first motel they came to. Rae climbed from the truck and went to the front desk to book rooms.

Rae was surprised to see Omar sitting in the lobby with Reyes. They wouldn't recognize her but as soon as Dawn dismounted and came, there would be conversation for sure.

Dawn stopped in her tracks when she saw Omar. "Well, small world. What are you doing here, kid?"

Omar walked over to join them. "Don't call me that. And just how many motels do you think there are in this little wide spot in the road?"

Dawn chuckled. "I guess you're right about that." She pointed to Rae. "This is my other driver, Stacey Carter."

Rae stuck out her hand. Omar reciprocated, and then he said, "Nice to meet you, Stacey. I hope y'all brought some extra clothes. It looks like things are still being arranged on this side of the border. It may be a couple of days before we're ready to move."

Dawn groaned. "Fuck! I thought you had a well-oiled machine."

Omar shrugged. "Our people have to float the barrels across the river one at a time. Shit happens."

Dawn sighed. "I should have asked for more money."

Omar smiled. "I hope this isn't a one-time thing. I got us a couple of rooms. You and Stacey in one and me and Reyes in the other."

Dawn shook her head. "We need separate rooms. She likes boys, I don't."

Omar didn't blink. "Get over it. It's over sixty miles to the next hotel cause it's in Marfa. We don't have many options here. They have Border Patrol cops on temporary duty who've got every other room in town booked. We'll have to tough it out."

Dawn tried to protest. "She won't like it."

Omar turned to walk away. Over his shoulder, he remarked, "I'm rooming with Reyes and he may like boys for all I know. It never came up. Be grownups and work it out."

Dawn didn't take the dressing down lightly. "Kid, I got shoes older than you!" Dawn turned on her heel and headed outside to park the big truck in a corner of the crowded parking lot.

Rae knew her life was suddenly infinitely more complicated. Living and eating with the two targets of the investigation would mean any little slip by Dawn, or Rae for that matter, could result in their deaths. And Dawn seemed to be intent on pissing Omar off.

Rae checked into the motel room using her undercover name and credit card. She grabbed the room keys from the clerk as Dawn came through the door from parking the truck.

MONDAY, DECEMBER 5, 2005
5:22 P.M.
EL PASO, TEXAS

FBI Assistant Special Agent in Charge Ben Brown was a native of Seattle, Washington, and hated the arid posting to El Paso. At forty-five, he knew he had to get promoted to special agent in charge very soon or he would be left here to rot. He had gotten into the Bureau late, having earned a law degree after serving six years in the navy submarine service. Brown had joined the FBI with the plan to move up the food chain to a prestigious job in Washington, DC, but his late start and poor people skills had hampered his rise. Now he saw a chance to make a move.

Brown sat behind his desk in the Federal Justice Center reviewing paperwork when the secure phone buzzed. "Brown."

Brown recognized the voice of the duty agent. "Sir, you have a call from Jameson Dagget of the Department of Justice's Office of Intelligence Policy Review."

Brown had met Dagget at a training session at Quantico where the big barrister taught a class on the Patriot Act. After the class concluded, Brown made a point to seek out the apparently well-connected lawyer. They lunched together in the cafeteria and Dagget told Brown he would reach out if he ever needed help in the West Texas area.

Brown had heard rumors about the debacle that Dagget had been involved in earlier in the year. Some kind of spook operation the DEA and the Texas Rangers had managed to foul up completely. Brown was thankful he hadn't known anything about the mess. The Bureau had a way of punishing people for just being aware of a failed operation.

Brown knew, on the other hand, Dagget had influence within the Bureau and could help him break out of El Paso.

"Assistant Special Agent in Charge Brown here," he announced into the phone. His secretary had told him the caller's name, and he thought the full title sounded more impressive.

"Ben, this is Jameson Dagget with the DOJ. Is it okay if I call you Ben?"

"Of course, Mr. Dagget. How can the El Paso office of the Bureau be of assistance?"

"Ben, call me Dag. That's what my friends call me."

Brown grinned broadly and leaned back in his office chair. "Well, thanks, Dag. So, how can I help you out? I still remember things you talked about in that training class. You're a phenomenal instructor."

"Thanks, Ben. I appreciate that."

Brown waited.

Dagget didn't make him wait long. "Ben, I'll be direct. I need some help from the Bureau in keeping some of our friends from running off the rails. I have been made aware of a rogue CIA operation that's running both in Mexico and Texas."

Ben sat back up. This could be the break he was looking for. "You bet, Dag. What can we do for you?"

"The operation I'm talking about is being run by a former operative of your cousins. They plan to engineer the shipment of a substantial amount of drugs from down on the border to a place near Atlanta. The truck, a standard-size box truck, will be driven by two women who are a part of this organization. I want you put the word out that the truck must be stopped and the drugs seized. Can you do that?"

Brown felt excited to be read into a covert operation. "Of course. I'll call Headquarters and have a Special Operations team down here from DC. We can wrap this up in a pretty bow. Anything special I need to know?"

Dagget had given the answer some thought before he dialed the phone. "No federal charges. I just want you make sure the El Paso County Sheriff and the local DPS are not alerted to the matter. That may not be the way you'd hoped to resolve this, but I want this case kept out of federal court. These are my marching orders," Dagget said with more venom than he felt. "I personally think we should prosecute them under the Patriot Act."

Brown saw some potential for political fallout. "Both those parties are good friends of the Bureau. But so are the Louisiana State Police. I'll pass the ball to them and keep an eye out to make sure they do what needs to be done."

"This favor is being requested from the highest authority. Your help won't go unnoticed."

Brown smiled. "No worries, Dag. I'll handle the details myself."

CHAPTER 14
WAITING GAME

TUESDAY, DECEMBER 6, 2005
8:14 A.M.
DECATUR, GEORGIA

Quinan "Buster" Hicks was at his desk. He'd been in Savannah the day before, speaking to a group of businessmen about the GBI's commitment to investigating truck hijackings, and wanted to get an early start.

When the direct phone line on his desk rang, Hicks was startled. He picked up the receiver and held it to his ear. It could be a wrong number, he considered. "Hicks."

"Director, how are you? This is Director Davis with the Texas DPS."

Hicks sat back in his chair. "Good, thanks. How are things in Texas?"

"Busy, Buster. I just wanted to pass some information on to you."

Hicks prepared to make notes. "Go ahead with it."

"We had an attempt on a Texas Ranger a few days ago. It seems that a fellow from Georgia has put out a hit on our ranger over a case from early this year."

Hicks leaned forward. "Let me guess. You think the Georgian is a blind for Rojo. Is your man okay?"

"Yes, sir. He took the two shooters out. Real cowboy stuff."

"Good!" Hicks declared emphatically.

"Our folks were able to crack the phones of the hired gunmen. It looks like they were hired by a man from Georgia. Mitchell Warren. Does that name ring a bell to you?"

"It does, for sure. We are under the impression he is out of the country. We understand he's in Cambodia. No extradition," Hicks sounded disgusted.

"That's what we hear too. I'm sure your Attorney General is trying as hard as ours to get him back. But that's not why I called."

"Hmm?" Hicks asked.

"Our sources say that Rojo and Warren are working together to put our ranger and your Agent Byrd in the ground."

"There are more shooters? What can you tell me about the others?" Hicks asked.

"Not much. Except the shooter sent to Georgia is a woman. She's a US citizen but of Mexican descent. A very seasoned killer. And she's already there."

Hicks took a deep breath. "That's more than we had."

Once he hung up the phone, Hicks dialed SAC Tina Blackwell's cell phone.

"Blackwell."

"Hello, Tina. This is Buster Hicks. How are you this morning?"

"Headed to a meeting with the Pickens County Sheriff. Our office is still pressing on the attempt on Judge Lance."

"Good." Hicks leapt right into the new problem. "I just got a call from Texas DPS. They have credible information that there is a female hitman, or hit person I guess, in

Georgia looking to kill our friend Agent Byrd. How would you like to proceed?"

"I'll put him on alert, boss." Blackwell couldn't help a snicker. "The jokes on her. Byrd's in Texas."

Hicks nodded to himself. "When's he coming back?"

"Director, they're on doper time. We won't know until they move."

"Okay, Tina," Hicks said. "Please keep me in the loop."

FRIDAY, DECEMBER 9, 2005
8:22 P.M.
PRESIDIO, TEXAS

Omar walked into the little metal building near the heart of Presidio. As soon as his eyes adjusted, he could see over two dozen black metal barrels lined up near the wall. He walked over to one and sniffed. He couldn't detect any smell that might give the shipment away once it had been loaded.

Reyes Hernadez materialized from the shadows. "I like how you think, but there is no odor to give us away. We do have one barrel that was damaged during the crossing. We are keeping it outside this building."

Omar scowled. "Not as many barrels here as I'd hoped."

Reyes nodded. "I, too, am frustrated. I had hoped the load would be on the road now. We could all be much richer by Christmas. Now, I fear we may be delayed even longer if a good rain raises the river."

"We might just have to go with what we have," Omar observed.

Reyes sighed. "You may be right. We have two more in a shed near the river, waiting to be moved up here. If things go well, we can have another four within a few days." Then Reyes smiled at Omar. "But then, thirty is a lucky number where I come from. Are there any other problems you can see?"

Omar met Reyes's eyes. "One."

"What's that, my friend? The ladies complaining about their accommodations again?"

"No. In the past, the drivers have taken the load to Rojo's people in Georgia. This time we are using our new people. And that presents a problem for me."

Reyes shook his head. "What is the issue?"

"I don't speak any Spanish, and neither do either of the women. I can't negotiate the offload point by phone, which is a pretty big security issue, if I can't talk to your people. And none of them speak English."

Reyes rubbed his face. "I don't like getting out of this part of the world." He considered his options. "But I am afraid you are right. I'll make preparations to accompany you to Atlanta. We'll want to shadow the truck at any rate."

"Right. Our part will be to connect the truck with the warehouse in Woodstock. We won't be doing any loading or handling any product."

Reyes examined his fingernails. "I certainly hope not. These hands weren't made for common labor."

Omar slapped him on the back. "You'll be making enough off this operation to pay for manicures for the rest of your life."

Omar started for the door. "I guess I'll go break the news to the drivers." He looked back and grinned, "Unless you want to do it."

Reyes was quick to respond. "No, thank you!"

Rae sat on the bed watching cable TV. Most of the channels were Spanish language TV and her language skills were limited. She was waiting to call Addy Riley, hoping she'd have something to report. Dawn slept on the other twin bed, seemingly oblivious to the TV.

Rae started at the knock on the door.

She felt for her pistol, tucked into her jeans and covered by her sweatshirt, before she cautiously opened the door.

Omar stood outside, looking almost guilty. "How's it going, Stacey? I just wanted to keep y'all in the loop. We are still delayed getting all the product across the river. It's going to be a couple of more days."

Dawn sat up on the bed. "This is horseshit. How much longer do we have to wait? I got Christmas presents to buy for my wife and her kid. We need to get on the road."

Omar ducked his head. He was actually afraid of the little truck driver. "I'll make sure you get compensated for all this downtime. That's all I can do right now."

Dawn lay back on the bed. "Make yourself useful and bring us another bottle of tequila. The good stuff this time."

Omar mumbled, "Sure. See you, Stacey." He pulled the door closed.

Rae turned back to the TV. "I don't know how much more I can drink," she remarked to Dawn's back.

Dawn didn't move. Rae heard her muffled response. "I can handle it if you're not up to it. And it sounds like Omar's sweet on you."

Rae shook her head, ignoring the jibe. "It's not just the drinking. We've been lucky to dodge Omar and Reyes for this long. We can't afford to get in any casual conversation with them and accidentally let something slip. My cover is pretty thin."

Dawn rolled over on her back. "That's why I've been such an asshole to them. I figure they'll think twice before inviting us out to eat, you know what I mean?"

Rae watched Dawn stretch in the bed. "Where are you from originally?" Rae asked.

Dawn stifled a yawn. "A little place north of Memphis, Tennessee. A wide spot in the road, like this place. We was poor as church mice but we didn't know it. You ever eat collard greens or poke salad?"

"Can't say I have. I'm not even sure what pork salad is."

Dawn chuckled. "Poke salad. They're basically weeds. You have to boil 'em twice, cause it's poisonous. You boil it then change the water and boil it again. Then you drain it and add some lard."

Rae sat down at the little table they had been using for meals. She stretched her feet out and stared at the ceiling. "My folks never had much. My daddy was in the army, and we traveled all the time, it seemed like."

"Army brat. I've heard the term. What made you get into the police?" Dawn asked.

Rae laughed. "I thought I wanted to help people. But it turns out, you don't do as much of that as you'd think. It's more refereeing family disputes and taking reports on stolen property. Then I got a chance to get into our drug unit. When you lock up a dealer, you make an impact on a neighborhood. At least for a little while."

Dawn shook her head. "I got family that's hooked on meth. They're crazy as a shit house rat. I wish we could wipe it all out."

"Is that why you agreed to do this job for us?" Rae asked. She kept her eyes on the ceiling.

Dawn rolled over on the bed. "It wasn't me being a saint or anything. Yeah, I'd like to see meth gone from this country, but it won't happen because of me. I just thought it might be something I could be proud of. And maybe a story I can tell my grandkids, if I ever have any."

Dawn turned the volume up on the TV. "Besides that, that Mex' who recruited me called me a lesbian in Mexican."

Rae scowled at her. "You are a lesbian, aren't you?"

"Yeah, but he did it like he was saying it behind my back. Saying it in another language he figured I didn't understand."

Rae appreciated the honest answer. "The adrenaline rush of this job can be addictive."

Dawn's voice was muffled as she rolled onto her face. "I ain't seen nothing that heart racing yet."

Rae got up and stretched out on her bed. "This is the boring part. The waiting game. When the shit hits the fan, things will change. Have you given any thought to what you'll do once this all goes down? It'll be hard to live in El Paso."

Dawn nodded. "Your Sheriff told me he'd help me relocate my family back up toward Memphis. Said I'd get a cut of any money seized, if that was to happen. Mainly, I just want to get away from this border. Back to a place with pine trees and grass that's green instead of brown."

"He's a man of his word," Rae reassured her.

"He better be!" Dawn mumbled as she rolled over on her bed.

Rae rolled over and tried to nap. *Rest when you can*, she thought.

Across the way, in a room on the second floor that offered an unimpeded view of the room Rae and Dawn called home, Adeline Riley sat back from the window. She sat far enough back to be hard to see from outside. With the powerful binoculars she held in her lap, she could almost see into their room.

She was wearing jeans, a cotton shirt, and wore her long hair down on her back. Boots were replaced with tennis shoes and her favorite white western hat hung on a rack back at home. Far from the image of a Texas Ranger.

She would skip breakfast, grab a double order of take-out for lunch, and then have what was left for dinner. The maids had stopped asking her if she needed directions to any of the local attractions. There really weren't any on this side of the border.

There was a DPS narcotics investigator a couple of doors down who was available to relieve Adeline when necessary. Adeline was too close to Rae to be away from her post for long. The motel was small and the area too confined to have any more officers in the area.

When she saw Omar leave the room, she called Rae on her cell. When she was briefed, she called Clete. Clete tried to be upbeat during the call.

"How are the ladies holding out?" Clete asked.

"Watching a lot of TV and drinking a little tequila," Adeline remarked.

"Make sure it doesn't end up the other way around," Clete cautioned before he broke the connection. It would have been nice if Clete had asked how she and the surveillance team were doing, she thought.

Adeline continued to keep an eye on the room as she dialed her husband. He answered on the first ring. "Are you keeping the house clean while I'm gone?" She asked the voice on the other end.

"I thought you told me rangers don't work drugs." She thought he sounded cheerful as he joked with her.

"Rangers range. That's what we do."

"Any chance you'll be home before Christmas? Or should I hold off on buying you a present?"

Adeline laughed. "You'd better already have me something. I've had you a present since September."

"It's good to hear you laugh. I wish I could hold you too."

Adeline tried not to sound sad. "They never said this job would be easy. I miss you too. If this goes on much longer, how would you feel about a rendezvous in Presidio?"

"A four-hour sex-drive doesn't sound that long. When can I be there?"

Adeline was tempted to plan something immediately. Then that oath she took kicked in. "I'll let you know. I sure do love you. I can't wait for this to be over!"

"Me too. Call again when you have a free minute."

She closed the phone and wiped her eyes. The waiting was beginning to wear on everyone.

MONDAY, DECEMBER 12, 2005
4:01 P.M.
PRESIDIO, TEXAS

Omar stood at the door of the room shared by Raelynn and Dawn. The door stood open to allow fresh air in. Rae saw Omar standing awkwardly, waiting to be acknowledged.

"You ladies care for a drink?" Omar asked.

Dawn ignored the question and went back to watching the evening news on the room TV. Rae decided it was time to have a long talk with Omar. Ignoring her own warnings to Dawn about being alone with Omar and Reyes, she decided to go for the ride. Maybe he would give up something that would be useful.

"Close the door after I'm gone. The sun is going down and it'll be colder than an Eskimo village soon." Rae directed as she grabbed her jacket. She flipped her blond curls up, so they hung over her collar.

Dawn mumbled something through her pillow.

Rae followed Omar down to his rented truck. He tried to open the door for her, but she beat him to the punch. She climbed in and buckled up. "Where are we headed?" she asked.

"The closest place I've found to get alcohol is a liquor store in Marfa," Omar replied.

Rae scowled. "That's an hour away."

"You got anything better to do, Stacey?" Omar asked as he started the truck.

"Not really."

Omar pointed the truck north on the aptly named Texas Mountain Trail. The two were soon winding through the Chinati Mountains.

"How'd you get into this business?" Rae asked casually.

Omar kept his eyes on the road. "My dad got me into it. But I was ready to do something."

"Your dad?" Rae was incredulous.

Omar nodded. "My dad. He had dabbled in the smuggling business for most of his life. Some for the government and some against the government."

"How do you mean 'for the government'?"

"He started smuggling guns into South and Central America. He'd trade them for marijuana and cocaine. The US government wanted the guns getting in the right hands but wanted their own hands clean if anything went wrong. Dad sold the dope and that's how he was paid."

"He didn't worry about getting caught?" Rae asked.

Omar glanced over. "He has connections."

"Wow. Some connections!"

"How long have you been driving a truck?"

Rae knew she was getting into a dangerous area. She knew next to nothing about the job.

"I fell into it right after high school," she lied. "I guess your dad was rich?"

It was Omar's turn to dodge a topic.

"What made you want to do this?" Omar asked.

Rae shrugged. "Money. I need more of it."

Rae heard the classic popping sounds of a dry mouth. Omar seemed nervous about something. Rae pushed a little harder. "I guess your family's loaded with all the money you've made off of this dope business?"

Omar nodded. "The load you're taking will put us all in the money. And I think we can do a load a month if the market can absorb it."

"How old are you, Bill?" she asked.

"My real name is Omar. But I've used a lot of names the last year. You can call me either one."

"So, how old are you, Omar?"

Omar looked uncomfortable. "Old enough."

"For what? This is a mighty harsh game you're playing, with some ruthless people."

Omar kept his eyes on the road. "Old enough for you, I guess."

Rae had feared this moment. She didn't want to throw up a wall between them but she couldn't let there be any relationship either. She stared through the windshield.

"That's not a good idea. I'm along for a little cash and then I plan to move my kids and me to a little town outside of Kansas City."

"You have kids? Where are they?"

"I have two," she lied. "They're staying with my mama."

The truck got quiet. They rolled along in silence until they came to the Border Patrol checkpoint on the highway. The officers in their green uniforms gave the truck a glance and then waved them on. Less than ten miles later, they crossed the city limits of Marfa. Omar pulled the truck in beside a white square building with black letters. The cactus growing around the door promoted the name, Cactus Liquors.

Omar found a bottle of aged scotch whisky and Rae picked out a bottle of bourbon and a pack of plastic cups. Omar offered to pay and Rae let him.

By the time they started back toward Presidio, the sun was setting behind the mountains. Rae opened the pack of cups and poured herself a small taste. After a sip, she remarked, "It's been a while since I've had good whisky."

"Pour me some, then."

Rae opened the bottle of scotch. The scotch had been expensive, so she poured it carefully. "Here you go."

Omar held the cup and took a sip. A few miles past the Border Patrol station he turned to the left onto a sandy road used to service a cellphone tower. Once he cleared the pavement, he put the truck in park and shut it off. Omar climbed out and stood in the dark.

Rae stepped out and walked around to join him. "What's up?"

Omar looked up at the stars. "I can't get over the view out here away from the city lights."

Rae looked up and saw what he meant. The cold air and the lack of ambient lighting to interfere made the stars seem especially bright. "You do this a lot?" she asked.

Omar looked over at her in the dark. "Not much else to do since we've been here."

Rae stood still, enjoying the silence for a moment. Omar stepped over to her and pulled her close. Before she could stop him, he kissed her on the mouth. Or maybe, she thought she didn't want to stop him. They kissed softly, but not passionately, for a moment. Then she broke it off.

"Dude, you're a cute guy . . ."

Omar stepped back. "But . . ."

Rae finished her sentence. "But it can't work."

Once the moment had passed, they climbed back in the truck.

"Stacey, I sure hope I didn't piss you off being too forward," Omar said sheepishly.

Rae didn't say anything. She wished she had turned off the recorder before they'd stopped. *Too late now*, she thought.

"No harm, no foul," she declared.

She wondered, as they crossed the high desert highway, if any of the surveillance teams had seen them on the side of the road.

Adeline Riley parked in the motel parking lot and waited for Rae and Omar to go to their respective rooms. Once the coast was clear she climbed the stairs to her own room.

She dialed Rae's number and waited.

"Were you on us?" Rae asked.

"Girl, what were you thinking?" Adeline asked.

"That I might get him to talk. And I did get some admissions from him. He talked about his dad getting him involved in drug smuggling."

"You know what I mean."

Rae knew what she meant. "It just happened. He's a kid and he has a crush, I guess."

"That's not going in my surveillance log. But you need to be careful. That kid is still working with one of the most dangerous drug organizations in this hemisphere." Adeline's frustration with her friend showed.

Rae seemed contrite. "I know. It won't happen again."

"Good," Adeline declared.

"He's a good kisser, though."

"Not funny," Adeline said as she hung up the phone.

Adeline began to undress. Her husband was asleep on the motel bed. She was happy he hadn't left. She climbed into bed beside him. A part of her wanted to let him sleep. That part was completely overwhelmed by the part of her that wanted him. She rolled on top of her husband as his eyes fluttered.

"I didn't ask for room service," he said.

"Funny." She grabbed his face and kissed him deeply.

SATURDAY, DECEMBER 17, 2005
8:22 A.M.
PRESIDIO, TEXAS

Omar banged on their room door. The women hadn't seen him for several days.

"Wake up, ladies. It's time to wrap our Christmas presents and get on the road."

Rae and Dawn had been drinking coffee when they heard the pounding. For the last week, they had passed their time drinking coffee in the morning and tequila in the evenings. Rae was hungry to get the case moving.

Rae stood and opened the door. As soon as she did, Omar passed her a piece of paper with an address scribbled on it. The address was on Simon Gonzales Street, just a couple of blocks away.

Omar wasn't in the mood for small talk. "Load 'em up, girls. Time to get this show on the road."

"Suits the hell out of me," Dawn shouted as the door closed.

Twenty minutes later, Dawn pulled the truck into a dust lot with a worn metal building with a single roll-up door. Rae dropped to the ground and walked up to the roll-up door. She saw it was locked with a rusty padlock.

A small, stocky man walked out of the shadows and approached as Dawn joined Rae. He was dressed in jeans and a worn work shirt. His cowboy hat was worn and stained, as were his teeth.

"You back your truck up to the roll-up door of the building. Your truck will be here about three hours." The man turned and put a key in the padlock.

"You ain't about to fuck my rented truck up, are you?" Dawn asked, standing with her hands on her hips.

The man pulled his cowboy hat off and wiped sweat from his head. "No, it just takes a while to load the product. Why don't you go back the way you came? There's a Mexican restaurant right around the corner."

Dawn climbed up into the truck. "This is Presidio. There ain't nothin' but Mexican restaurants!"

The man laughed and pulled his hat back on. The man pulled up the door and then he and Rae watched as Dawn parked the big box beside the metal building.

"We going to be done while we still have daylight?" Rae asked.

The man grunted but said nothing. He opened the

metal door with the street numbers and a second man drove a forklift out and loaded a wooden pallet onto the truck. Rae noted the pallet held four blue drums.

As they turned to walk away from the truck, Rae got a whiff of a strong chemical smell. She wrinkled her nose. *Methamphetamine oil,* she thought. Cooks called it "the honey," the amber-colored liquid they processed with acid to produce meth crystals. She saw a discarded drum with a hole in its side. She hoped the other drums weren't leaking.

Rae nudged Dawn. "How much did you say this truck hauls?"

Dawn looked around. She raised her eyebrows. "About ten thousand gallons. How much dope will that make?"

Rae shrugged. "I'm guessing each gallon is about a kilo of meth."

Dawn whistled. "Damn!"

CHAPTER 15
TIME TO GO

SATURDAY, DECEMBER 17, 2005
3:22 P.M.
PRESIDIO, TEXAS

As Rae had predicted, the loading process had taken twice as long as it should have. The truck rolled out of the dusty lot with Dawn at the wheel. She pulled the truck out onto Simon Gonzales Street, a pitted, barely paved street devoid of stripes or markings. "Let's get Presidio in our rearview mirror," Dawn remarked.

Raelynn Michaels nodded in agreement. "Yep, I'm ready to get this show on the road."

The two bounced along on the rough street until they reached US 67, the route would take them to the interstate. The highway leading out of the little Texas border town was lined with palm trees and single-story buildings as far as the two women could see.

Dawn guided the truck along US 67 toward Marfa. She shifted effortlessly, her years of experience on full display, as they headed toward the heart of the Trans Pecos region of Texas.

Rae had adjusted her side mirror so she could watch for surveillance behind them. She noticed Omar's pickup truck on their tail almost immediately. Omar and Reyes weren't trying to hide.

The drive from Presidio to Marfa was slow. They stopped for the Border Patrol checkpoint and were waved through after they assured the agents they were US citizens. Once in Marfa, Dawn turned onto US 90, a chunk of asphalt shared with US 67, for the short ride through Alpine. As the truck neared Alpine, Dawn pointed out Cathedral Mountain off to the east. Rae kept her eyes on Omar's truck in the rearview mirror.

Rae's nerves were getting the best of her, and she kept checking and rechecking their position on the dash-mounted GPS. As they put Alpine behind them, she knew the tension would only mount.

They turned north on schedule. Now Rae would cycle between the GPS, the rearview mirror, and the horizon. They had been driving for twenty minutes when the radio on the floor squawked. "Air support to the undercover."

Rae pulled the portable radio to her face. "Arlow, is that you?"

"It is. I'm flying overwatch as long as I can. Then I'm meeting Clete in El Paso. We'll be tagging along all the way to Georgia."

Rae was relieved she now had close cover and it was someone she trusted.

"Do you have an eye on us?" Rae asked.

"Yes, ma'am. And I see the pickup truck right behind you. Is that the bogie?"

Rae nodded unconsciously. "Right. The road has been pretty open since we left Presidio. We haven't had a chance to get ahead of them much."

"It's almost showtime. You should have a lot of company in just a few minutes. The chase has started."

Rae looked over at Dawn. "You clear on what we need to do?"

Dawn nodded. "As soon as we have some space, we hit the gas."

"That's it," Rae said. She saw the windmill up ahead on the left side of the road. It was a landmark she'd been given by Addy Riley last night when they spoke. "There's the windmill."

Almost on cue, Rae saw the red and blue lights coming from behind them. "Here they come!" Rae exclaimed.

Rae saw Dawn was watching the mirror also. Now they both could see the line of Texas Highway Patrol cars rushing their way from the south. Rae noted Omar's truck appeared to be slowing down. Omar must have seen the cars with flashing lights and screaming sirens headed their way. The troopers were still too far out for Omar to tell what was going on.

Dawn pushed down on the gas pedal. She carefully pulled ahead of the pickup on her tail. The flashing red and blue lights were advancing steadily toward them. Omar appeared to be watching too, as he slowed his truck.

Rae watched anxiously as the procession got closer. The car the troopers were chasing came into sight. She saw the little compact car swerving from one side of the pavement to the other, probably trying to avoid a PIT maneuver. The Precision Immobilization Technique, or just PIT, was a way to draw dangerous police pursuits to a close. The officer would pull up beside the rear of the suspect and nudge the rear of the fleeing vehicle. If performed correctly, the PIT would spin the offender around and end the pursuit. At higher speeds, the PIT could even cause the suspect to overturn.

As the cars got closer, Rae watched the fleeing driver

swerve left to avoid Omar's truck. Dawn saw it too and floored the big truck she was piloting.

The little car swerved back to the right, cutting off Omar's truck, and the lead THP patrol car moved alongside. Without hesitation, the THP car nudged the little sedan and caused it to spin like a top. The little car ran off the side of the pavement in a cloud of dust and skidded to rest against a fence post.

The rest of the black and white patrol cars blocked the roadway as Rae and Dawn continued out of sight. The pickup, with no other options, stopped in the middle of the road and watched the highway patrol troopers drag the driver out of the once-speeding car.

Omar slammed the dash of his truck with his fist. They were surrounded by Texas trooper cars and a helicopter landed on the highway, further blocking the roadway. They watched as the driver of the fleeing car was pulled out of the crash and dragged to a trooper Tahoe. The troopers were so efficient, Omar barely got a glimpse of the driver before he was secured.

Omar looked over at Reyes. "Well, this wasn't part of the plan."

Omar pulled the phone from his pocket and dialed the number of the phone he had given Dawn. The call went directly to voicemail.

Omar shook his head. "Damn it!"

Omar fumed as he put the truck in park. He wasn't going anywhere for a while.

Daniel Byrd sat in the back of the black and white Tahoe. His hands were cuffed behind his back, and he sat slumped over. He didn't want to take a chance Omar might recognize him. His face and chest were covered with corn starch, fallout from the airbag in the little car going off in his face.

Trooper Montana Petterson pulled the driver's door of the highway patrol cruiser open and leaned in to talk to Byrd. "Are you okay?"

Byrd sighed. "The chase was fun. I had a ball right up until your PIT."

Montana took her uniform hat off and laid it in the seat. "I told you not to get too fast. I was as gentle as I could be. And don't forget, this was your plan."

Byrd nodded. "It seemed like a good idea at the time."

Montana looked him over. "I don't see any bleeding."

Byrd shrugged. "That was good advice to take off my watch and empty my pockets. The airbags going off was the worst part. That rattled my cage."

"I told everyone to be careful getting you out, but to make it look as real as they could."

Byrd shook his head. "I'm just glad I've got a little time to get myself back together. How long do we have to stay here?"

Montana laughed. "I'm going to get you transported, but we'll keep the road blocked as long as we can."

Byrd nodded gingerly. His head throbbed, but otherwise he felt okay. "Can I get the cuffs off too?"

Montana closed the front door and came around to where he sat. She used her cuff key to release his shackles.

"The highway patrol helicopter is taking off and the pickup truck is moving," Arlow's voice sounded very near on the radio.

"Great," Rae responded. "We're just about to turn west on Interstate 10 and should be well clear before they can catch up."

"I'll fly overwatch. I should be able to see them turn east on 10."

Rae thumbed the button. "They should hit 10 just long enough to hit highway 18 toward I-20. The plan is for us to take I-20 all the way into Atlanta."

Through the ether, Rae heard Arlow say, "I'll keep an eye on them, then. You guys meet the tech team."

Dawn gave Rae a thumbs up, pressed the gas pedal, and pointed the big box truck toward the setting sun. They went a single exit toward El Paso before they pulled off on an industrial street. They saw the other box truck, almost identical to the one they were in, pulled off to the side.

"I hope they brought a forklift. Otherwise, we're in for a long day," Dawn observed.

Rae eyed the other truck. "They'll need to get us back on the road as soon as possible. We've got some miles to make up!"

Several people started swarming the two trucks. A team began unloading the truck Dawn drove and transferring the load to the other truck. A couple of specialists Raelynn had worked with before, members of the task force who focused on hidden cameras and transmitters, escorted another man out. The trio started examining the frame of Dawn's rig and taking photos of the entire truck from top to bottom.

Dawn looked annoyed. "What are them boys doing?"

Rae climbed down. "I'll find out. I'd like to know too."

Rae walked back to where the men stood. "What's up, guys?"

One of the task force techs pointed at the third man. "This is James Costner. He runs a specialty company in Palm Beach, Florida. He's going to check the truck for bad guy trackers and then install one he designed."

Costner paused to stick out a hand. "Nice to meet you." Rae noted he had a central European accent. "I see a simple transmitter under the frame. They probably won't have much range on it. I'm going to damage the antenna connection so they'll have to be on your bumper to receive anything."

"Are they able to listen to us over that thing?" Rae asked.

Costner shook his head. "Not with this. I'm going to check the cab for listening devices."

Rae wondered, while the loading was going on, what other surprises Omar's boys might have added.

SATURDAY, DECEMBER 17, 2005
11:02 A.M.
MIDLAND, TEXAS

Dawn had pushed the truck as hard as she could, but it appeared to everyone involved she couldn't make their first overnight stop. Omar had insisted they spend the night in Weatherford, Texas, a city just west of Fort Worth. The delays unloading the truck and rigging the electronic equipment had put them well behind the curve.

Rae had been doing calculations with the map. After calculating drive time and distance, they had come up with a plan. The surveillance team from Texas, members of the Rojo Task Force assigned to follow the box truck, would speed ahead and get off at the first exit. The team leader would call Rae when they got checked into a motel.

Rae opened the burner phone Omar had given Dawn. She powered the device up and waited for it to connect. She dialed the only number programmed in.

"Dawn, where the hell are you?" Omar shouted into the device.

"This is Stacey. We've had a couple of problems. Nothing too big, but we ran over a damned mattress on the interstate."

"Wait. What?" Omar asked.

"A damned mattress. It got hung up under the truck and we didn't realize it. Then a few miles down the road, Dawn saw smoke coming out from underneath our rig. We took an exit in Midland and found a shop that could look underneath. Turns out it was nothing, just the mattress dragging on the highway got hot. I guess it could have caught fire, but it didn't. So, we're running behind."

"Where are you now, Stacey?" Omar asked.

Rae sighed loudly. "We just left Midland. But we got everything checked out and should be good."

"Can you make Weatherford tonight?" Omar asked. Rae could hear Reyes in the background asking where they were.

"We'll be doing good to make Abilene. Dawn and I both are worn out and your people took forever to get us loaded. We'll find somewhere in Abilene to crash and get rolling early tomorrow."

Rae heard the tension in Omar's voice. "Well, why haven't I been able to reach you on this phone? I've called you about fifty times since we got split up."

Rae sounded shocked. "That was you following us?"

Omar fumed. "Of course, it was me. You didn't recognize the truck?"

"Hell no! We went back toward El Paso for a ways trying to lose whoever was on our tail. That's the other reason we're running behind."

There was silence for several seconds.

"And the phone, did it get damaged by the mattress too?" Omar's voice dripped with sarcasm.

"It died. Dawn had left it on, and the battery crapped out. We bought a charging cable where we had the truck fixed. You sound like you don't believe me." Rae listened intently.

She heard Reyes tell Omar, "You should have known better than to hire two women for the job."

Omar finally asked Rae, "Okay. Where do you plan to stay?"

"The first place we see off the interstate. And we plan to hit the road by six in the a.m.," Rae replied. "And tell your riding partner that he needs to use his inside voice when he talks shit about us. No man could have done any better. Hell, it was probably a man that didn't tie the mattress down to begin with."

Omar clicked off the call.

SATURDAY, DECEMBER 17, 2005
11:55 P.M.
BIGGS ARMY AIRFIELD, FORT BLISS, EL PASO, TEXAS

The big C-130H airplane from the Georgia National Guard stood in a corner of the Biggs Army Airfield on the Fort Bliss Army reservation. A scientist from the Texas DPS Crime Laboratory stood next to the uniformed aircrew as the white truck pulled onto the ramp and parked near the rear of the transport plane.

Clete Petterson's truck pulled in and parked behind the box truck. Petterson, Addy Riley, Montana Petterson, and Daniel Byrd climbed down and shook hands with the aircrew and the crime lab technician.

Petterson spoke to the scientist. "We don't see lab rats out this late very often."

Mark Burns ignored the jibe. "Clete, I understand we have several barrels. Do you want samples from all of them or just a couple?"

Petterson looked to Addy for an answer. She would be the case ranger for the investigation. Addy screwed up her face. "I guess we can go with a single sample. We're just planning to use it for probable cause, anyway."

Burns nodded. "One sample will take me about thirty minutes. I heard you might have as many as thirty barrels. You can count on that taking me till lunchtime tomorrow."

Addy shook her head. "We don't have that kind of time. We need to be in the air by daylight. Just loading the drums and getting in the air will push us for time. Do you agree with that, Danny?"

Byrd shrugged. "If we have to prosecute in Georgia, that should be enough for a trafficking charge. And then we'll have the whole package to use if things go according to plan."

Burns pulled on a pair of latex gloves and grabbed his sample kit. "Point me to them. I'll get my samples, mark the barrels on the side with a number for identification, then I'll get out of your way as quickly as I can."

Petterson turned to the aircrew and approached a man wearing the wings of a full colonel. "Are you the man in charge of this beast?" Petterson asked as he gestured toward the big gray airplane.

The man stuck out his hand. "That's me. Colonel John Flynn of the Georgia Air National Guard. We're part of the 158th Airlift Squadron out of Savannah, Georgia. You can call me 'Birddog.'"

"Clete Petterson. Texas Rangers Company E. And you

can call me Clete. The other ranger is Adeline Riley, also of Company E. That ugly-looking guy without a cowboy hat is GBI Agent Daniel Byrd. And the last member of our little band is Trooper Montana Petterson."

The Colonel's right eyebrow went up. "Any relation to you and the trooper?"

Petterson shook his head. "Just by marriage. She's my wife."

The Colonel nodded. "Well, I'm happy to welcome the whole family on board our little heavy lifter."

Byrd stepped forward to shake the Colonel's hand. "Daniel Byrd, sir. I'm with the GBI. Thanks for your help, Colonel. It'll just be Ranger Riley, Trooper Petterson, and me on your plane," Byrd turned and looked up at the tail thirty-eight feet above them. "She sure is impressive. How much can she haul, Birddog?"

"This bird is rated at forty-two thousand pounds. Plenty of room for what you have planned." Birddog turned to point at the hulking plane. "We've had C-130s in service for the US military since 1956. And this baby, along with about two thousand of her sisters, was built in Marietta, Georgia."

Petterson nodded. "I've seen them at a distance, but never up close. It's an impressive airplane."

The colonel motioned for Byrd to come with him to a side door. "Come on. I'll show you where you'll be riding. It's not especially comfortable, but we make up for the discomfort with the noise and vibrations." Both men laughed.

"How long will the torture last?" Byrd asked.

Birddog did some quick mental calculations. "If we don't have any weather, about five hours door to door."

Byrd looked up at the wings. "What if we hit weather?"

Birddog shrugged. "It might add an hour, but no more. We'll probably dodge around it. We have plenty of range on this ship."

Petterson looked serious. "Good to know. You'll have some important cargo on this bird in more ways than one."

Birddog pointed at the box truck. "I'll get my loadmaster, Sergeant Gunning, to start loading the barrels. He'll have to certify the load is properly secured and then give me the thumbs up. His crew shouldn't take more than an hour. Once we're buttoned up, we have a priority departure from the tower. We can be in the air and out of Texas by about three a.m. Georgia time. That should put us on the ground about the time the sun comes up."

Petterson nodded. "Thanks, Colonel. We appreciate all your help."

Petterson turned and gave Montana a hug. "I guess I'll see you in Georgia. Get some rest once you're there. I'm afraid we'll have some long days coming up."

Montana returned the hug. "You be careful, cowboy! You've got some catching up to do."

Petterson nodded. "Arlow says he can catch the truck by daylight. Then comes the tough part. Keeping eyes on them halfway across the county."

Byrd and Montana stood by the Colonel as Petterson drove away. Byrd glanced at Montana. "His part in all this is scary as hell."

Montana gave him a quizzical look. "He's flying with Arlow. What's so scary about that?" Then Montana gave it some thought. "Oh, yeah. He's flying with Arlow."

CHAPTER 16
HIDE AND SEEK

SUNDAY, DECEMBER 18, 2005
12:18 A.M.
JASPER, GEORGIA

Gary Thomasson needed to get home, he knew, but his desire for Felisha had become an obsession. They were naked in the motel bed, gasping for post-coital oxygen.

"I got to quit doing this. My wife is starting to ask questions," Thomasson said.

Felisha heaved up from the bed and scrapped some meth under her fingernail. She stuck her finger up Thomasson's nose. "Go home in a little while. Right now, let's make the most of our time."

He sniffed and then she stuck the finger into her own nose. She took a deep breath of air, sucking the meth from under her nail.

Thomasson began to stroke himself as Felisha danced around the room. Her feet were sticking to the worn carpet as she imitated a belly dancer.

"You leaving as soon as this thing with Byrd is done?" Thomasson asked as he ran a hand through his hair and gently tugged.

Felisha stopped dancing for a moment. "I guess. Why?"

Thomasson stood and began to dance with her, gyrating his hips and waving his hands. "Byrd's coming back to Georgia tomorrow. Well, I guess it's technically today that he's coming in. I'm picking him up in Marietta early this morning."

Felisha pushed Thomasson onto the bed and climbed up his prone body. She leaned in and bit his ear with her sharp teeth. She breathed into his ear. "Good. You still got time to make me happy again."

Thomasson rolled her around and climbed on top of her. "I'm about to make one of us happy."

SUNDAY, DECEMBER 18, 2005
2:46 A.M.
ABILENE, TEXAS

Omar had planned to circle the parking lot of all the motels near the interstate. He found the box truck on his second try. The lot at the Best Interstate Extended Stay Motel and Suites was hardly full. The truck occupied four slots in the front parking lot. *At least they had made a point to park it under a light,* Omar thought.

Omar had Reyes stay with his rented pickup truck while he strolled toward the box truck. When he felt comfortable no one was watching, Omar slid underneath the white box truck and felt around for the tracker he'd placed on the frame. Lying on his back on the cold concrete, with the sound of big trucks zooming past on the interstate. He reached up into the frame and felt around in the dark.

Omar took several minutes to find the waterproof box

with the magnets that tracked the box truck. When he finally found the electronic gizmo, he took a penlight out of his pocket to examine it. Omar was surprised to see the antenna wire which would broadcast the truck's location had been torn and frayed.

After trying to reconnect the wire, with no luck, Omar crawled out and checked the heavy pad lock on the truck's roll-up door. It seemed fine, but the ladies had a key in case they were checked by a suspicious cop.

Omar stood looking at the truck for several minutes. He had to admit, even with the glitches, the load was going pretty well. He walked over to where Reyes sat waiting.

"We might as well get a room here and get a little rest. This next leg will be a bear," Omar told Reyes.

Reyes didn't argue.

SUNDAY, DECEMBER 18, 2005
2:46 A.M.
ABILENE, TEXAS

Sergeant Helen Saenz, of the Texas Highway Patrol, sat in the dark motel room. She had drawn the short straw. She was to watch the box truck while it was parked at the motel and then, when the truck got on the road, get some rest and head back to El Paso. Her Lieutenant had been resistant to her helping at all but, when Texas Ranger Major Crosby called and asked for help, she got the green light.

She saw the shadowy figure creeping toward the box truck. She pulled up the expensive camera she had been loaned for the night. The clicking noise as the shutter opened and closed was annoying but she knew the skulker couldn't hear it.

When she zoomed in, Omar Warren's face was clear under the powerful security light in the motel parking lot.

"Got you!" she exclaimed as she watched him rolling under the truck.

Her long night wasn't wasted.

CHAPTER 17
ROAD TRIP

The C-130H worked its way through airspace shared with the world's busiest airport, Hartsfield-Jackson Atlanta International. The big transport plane landed at Dobbins Air Reserve Base on the primary runway. The enormous tarmac had been the testing field for the Lockheed C-5A and was ten thousand feet long and three hundred feet wide. The skilled aircrew brought the big plane, loaded with over a hundred million dollars' worth of drugs, to a rest on the east ramp of the field.

Byrd and the two Texans had been strapped into red jump seats, little more than a steel frame with a mesh back. The inside of the aircraft was a bare metal box forty feet long and almost ten feet wide. The distinctive smell of military electronics created by the various materials such as glue, flame retardants, protective coatings, and plasticizers used to manufacture each piece of avionics, permeated the space.

Byrd stood to stretch and flex his back. Addy and Montana took their belongings and stood, as well. Once the engines had stopped and they could finally hear each other, Byrd turned to the Texas Ranger. "Welcome to Georgia, Addy."

Addy didn't seem impressed. She lugged her gear up and headed toward the rear hatch as it lowered to the pavement. "I'm not sure I will be able to see Georgia, or anything else, until we get some sleep."

Montana grunted. "That flight sure wasn't conducive to getting shut-eye."

Byrd headed for the ramp. A team of agents and crime lab scientists were waiting for them. Byrd headed for Mario Ortega, a GBI agent assigned to the Major Violators Squad. "Is the duplicate truck here?" Byrd asked Ortega.

Ortega pointed toward the rear of the plane. "Jill Leonard is driving it. Here she comes."

"And we have troopers to guard the truck 'till tomorrow?" Byrd was anxious.

"Two troopers around the clock. As soon as you tell us where to park it, we'll lock her down for the night."

Byrd rubbed his chin. "Can you work it out with GSP to park it at the patrol post in Villa Rica?" Byrd wondered.

Ortega nodded. "You got it. The post commander is a friend of mine. He'll love to be a part of this."

Byrd shook Ortega's hand and picked up his bag.

"We might as well get the paperwork out of the way, and then let these folks who slept in their own bed last night get everything in order," Byrd commented over his shoulder.

Ortega took the evidence receipts for the barrels and pointed to one of the waiting crime lab personnel. "We'll get everything sorted out and under lock and key," Ortega said. "You guys get out of here. You look whooped."

Byrd nodded. "Gary Thomasson is here somewhere waiting to take us to Canton. He'll take us to my place, and we all get some rest and freshen up."

Montana shook her head. "That little cracker box of an apartment you live in? No thanks!"

Byrd was defensive. "I live in a three-bedroom house now. I'm using one of the rooms as an office, but I can make room for all of us to have some rest and some privacy."

"You have a house! I'm shocked. Does this mean you're finally growing up?" Montana laughed.

Byrd shook his head. "Let's not go too far."

They walked down the ramp together, arms loaded with luggage and equipment. Byrd saw Gary Thomasson walking over to meet them. Byrd thought he looked gaunt and tired. "Were you up all night waiting on us?"

"Putting in lots of hours, too many probably, trying to learn this job," Thomasson grumbled.

Byrd made the introductions and then they piled everything into the back of the GBI car. Once they were on their way north, Thomasson glanced over at Byrd. "This must be a big operation to call out all these resources," Thomasson observed.

Byrd nodded. "You weren't in the Region 8 office when I was involved in an investigation over in Texas, where this ex-CIA spook named Mitch Warren was trying to run meth by airplane to Georgia. This is another piece of that case."

Thomasson jerked the steering wheel sharply but quickly corrected himself.

SUNDAY, DECEMBER 18, 2005
1:55 P.M.
RUSTON, LOUISIANA

Rae watched the Louisiana State Police patrol car tagging along behind them. She had seen the car pull onto the interstate just west of Shreveport and it stayed about the same distance back. She wondered if Omar was aware of it.

Rae looked over at Dawn. "You doing okay over there?"

Dawn looked at the side mirror. "What's going on? That LSP car has been behind us since the state line, or there abouts. Are we about to get put on the shoulder?"

Rae didn't mention to Dawn the blue unmarked car in front of them. She had seen it earlier, with two middle-aged guys in blue windbreakers, pacing them as they steadily crossed the Sportsman's Paradise.

Rae stared back at the state police car. It was getting closer. "Let's get off at the next exit up here. Cooktown Road. There's a Waffle House at this exit. We can stop and get some grub."

Dawn grinned. "I like your style."

"Be sure to signal early."

Dawn's forehead furrowed. "Okay."

Rae noted the blue car slowed as soon as Dawn hit the turn signals. A second brown sedan forced its way over to follow the blue car. Rae shook her head. The poor surveillance technique screamed "Feds."

As the truck ascended the ramp to the cross street, Rae noted a small caravan on their tail. Two other marked LSP cars had joined the first.

"We might not get food as soon as I thought," Rae observed.

FBI ASAC Ben Brown's pulse was pounding. Today would be his first time in the field in over a year. He had been anticipating the moment when the LSP K-9 unit would be in position to make the stop safely. They had been on the tail of the box truck since it passed through a natural choke point on Interstate-20 in Marshall, Texas.

Brown took control of the arrests. "Brown to all units. The FBI cars will box the truck in at the top of the ramp. Are you clear on that LSP?"

He heard a mumbled affirmative response. "Okay, we'll try to be as low-key as possible until we have an eye on the drugs."

Brown leaned down and activated his blue lights. He stopped the blue sedan short of the stop sign ahead. The brown sedan did the same. Brown could see two LSP units blocking the big white truck in from the rear.

Once he was sure the truck had stopped, Brown and a second agent in blue windbreakers, with the letters FBI emblazoned in gold, took positions on either side of the truck cab.

A uniformed LSP trooper approached the driver's door while a trooper in tactical gear, being tugged along by a dog, came up to the passenger door.

Brown watched as the female driver rolled down her window. "Is there a problem, officers?" she asked innocently.

The trooper at the driver's door took the lead. "Trooper Montgomery with the Louisiana State Police out of the Bossier City post. We stopped you because you failed to maintain your lane back in Shreveport."

Brown watched the trooper as he climbed up on the side of the truck so he could see both occupants. "My partner, Trooper Ramey, is going to run his dog around the truck while I check your paperwork. Could I see your license and proof of insurance, please?"

Brown saw the driver hand her license and a piece of paper to the trooper. "Well, since you said please . . ." she answered.

Petterson radioed the other surveillance units. "I've got an eye on Omar Warren. He rolled on down the interstate and got off at the next exit."

Arlow caused the airplane to climb as he rolled into an orbit above the little city of Ruston. "It looks like he's staying put. They are pulling up at a gas station."

Petterson nodded. "Yeah. They may be making this into a pee stop."

Arlow pulled the plane into a tight turn. "Can you tell what they are doing?"

Petterson put his hands on the cowling as he fought to keep his last meal down. "Buddy, you're going to need to back off on this turn. I may have to embarrass myself."

Arlow looked over at Petterson, surprised at the sudden change. The ranger was pale. "Sorry. I'm used to it. I'll level the plane out."

Petterson took deep breaths as the airplane came level. "Sorry, Arlow," Petterson apologized. "I guess I'm tired."

Arlow let the plane drift as he turned in his seat to check on the target. "I see them standing by their car. I think we're okay. Does anybody on the ground have contact with the locals?"

Petterson cleared his throat. "No. They aren't hauling anything illegal, so we didn't bother to set up contacts along the route."

As the airplane drifted west, Arlow sat up high in his seat. "Hang on. I think there are FBI raid jackets on some of the guys down there."

Petterson sat up in the seat and tried to get a view. "I can't see them. Let me check with the ground units."

Petterson switched over to the police radio. "Six-oh-four to eighty-one forty-four, can you see what's going on with the truck?"

"Clete, I just looped around. I'm pulling onto the ramp. You ain't gonna believe what I see."

Petterson glanced over at Arlow. "Try me."

"There's a bunch of FBI agents around the truck. They're looking all kinds of pissed. And our cooperator is giving them down the country!"

Dawn stood with her fists on her hips. She stared at the trooper who had approached her window. "You boys can look in my truck all you want. I gave your buddy from the FBI the key to the back. There ain't a damned thing back there. Now is there something else you need from us? I've tried to be a lady about all this, but I'm hungry and cold and tired of this horseshit. So, who's in charge of this goat roping?"

The trooper inclined his head toward the FBI contingent. "Those gentlemen in the suits are the folks in charge. They are FBI El Paso."

A man in an FBI windbreaker came up to Dawn. "Is there anything other than furniture in this truck? We'd hate to have to unload it here on the side of the interstate."

Dawn stood her ground. "You unload it; you can reload it." She stuck her finger in the agent's face. "Who's in charge of this three-ring circus?"

The chagrined agent pointed at an older man standing near the blue sedan.

Dawn marched over to the senior-looking FBI official. "Can I go now? Or do you want to check my immigration status? You ain't found a thing in my truck, and we were stopping to get something to eat."

"My name is Ben Brown. I'm with the FBI office in Baton Rouge."

Dawn cut him off. "That trooper there says you're from El Paso. That's a long way from here. What kind of federal horseshit is this you're pulling?"

The man who called himself Brown glowered at the trooper. "We are involved in a national security matter. That's all I can tell you, ma'am."

"Are you from El Paso or Baton Rouge, then?"

Brown smirked. "El Paso, if it makes any difference to you."

Rae spoke up. She had recognized Brown. "Well, it seems like I did some moving job for the new SAC with the FBI in El Paso," Rae said. "I got the phone number saved right here. Said if I ever needed help to call."

The man called Brown was visibly shaken. "No need to call her. I can assure you that this was all a mistake. We are going to lock up your truck and let you go on your way."

It was Dawn's turn to smirk. "Yeah. Well, you boys get back in your warm cars and we'll see you later."

Dawn walked purposely up to the front and climbed into the cab. She put the truck into gear as the FBI cars cleared the way.

Dawn waited until they were at the top of the ramp. "You know the FBI SAC in El Paso?"

Rae grinned. "I know they've got one. And I know they move them folks around a lot."

Dawn leaned back and laughed. "You're something,

you are!" Dawn's burner phone rang. She glanced at Rae before answering. "Yeah?"

"What was all that about?" Omar asked.

"Some troopers looking for drugs," Dawn responded.

"Did they find anything?" Omar sounded worried.

"Just what we wanted them to find. A couple of damsels in distress moving to greener pastures."

She could hear the relief in Omar's voice. "Great."

"That's what you're paying us for," Dawn declared. Then she shut the phone and dropped it back in her pocket.

ASAC Ben Brown doubled over in the passenger seat of the Bureau car as he sat on the side of Interstate 20. His abdomen was in knots as the acid released by his panic state caused his bowels to rumble. *Dagget set me up*, he thought.

If his SAC realized he'd led an assault on the wrong truck in a state outside of their purview, his career would be over. *If I were lucky,* he considered, *I'll be assigned to the Fairbanks, Alaska, post of duty.* His wife, very conscious of her husband's status within the Bureau, would leave him in a minute.

Brown needed to find a bathroom, quickly. Then he'd have to make the thirteen-hour drive back to El Paso without rest. He hoped the cover story he'd given the two agents from Baton Rouge would protect him until he could get Dagget to make all of this right.

Brown pushed his way into a stall in a large truck stop bathroom and took a seat. As soon as he felt able, he dialed Dagget's number. The high-powered DOJ official would have to get him out of trouble. Brown's stomach convulsed again when a recording stated in a dull monotone the phone number for Dagget had been disconnected.

CHAPTER 18
ARE WE THERE YET?

SUNDAY, DECEMBER 18, 2005
9:38 P.M.
ANNISTON, ALABAMA

Dawn watched the mirrors as she moved over to exit the interstate in Anniston. Her eyes were tired, and a gentle rain had started outside of Birmingham, causing every light to glare on the windshield. Dawn glanced over at Rae. "We're gonna need fuel before we can get a room. We're down to a quarter of a tank."

Rae shook her head vigorously. "Can we make another sixty or seventy miles on what we have left?"

Dawn's foot came off the gas as she considered the question. "Yeah. We'll for sure need diesel by the time we do that. Do I need to stay on the big highway?"

Rae watched for Omar's truck in her mirror. "Yes, we have to give the GBI a little more time. Bryd is working on some kind of smoke and mirrors to get us reloaded by tomorrow."

Dawn shrugged as she pressed the gas pedal. "One more hour won't kill me."

As soon as the box truck had picked up speed, the burner phone rang. Rae grabbed it and answered. "What?"

"Stacey, I thought you were stopping at that last exit?" Omar asked.

"We're trying to squeeze everything we can out of this tank. I figure we get a full load in the morning and don't stop again till we're ready to unload. You haven't told us where in Georgia we're headed but it's a big state."

"Pick a place to stay then. We'll get back on the road around four in the morning. I want to get through Atlanta early."

Rae glanced over at Dawn who was nodding. "Beat the rush-hour traffic, then?"

Dawn pursed her lips. "About as bad as LA or Washington, DC. Ask him if we're going around or through."

Omar had heard the question. "We'll take I-285 around to the north."

"How far do we go tomorrow?" Dawn asked.

"One hundred miles from the state line."

Rae leaned back in the seat. "Okay! Payday before lunch tomorrow!"

"Just be sure we're rolling by four. I have people waiting to meet us. I don't want to be late," Omar ordered as he disconnected.

SUNDAY, DECEMBER 18, 2005
11:38 P.M.
CANTON, GEORGIA

Adeline Riley's phone rang. "Ranger Riley."

"You answer the phone 'Ranger Riley'?" Raelynne Micheals asked.

"You're calling me to ask me that?"

"Nope, I'm calling to let you know we just got stopped by the Louisiana State Police and the FBI," Raelynn remarked.

Adeline Riley waved at Daniel Byrd to get his attention and then motioned him over. "So, the FBI was involved in a traffic stop?" Riley continued.

"Not just the FBI. The FBI agents, at least the one in charge, were from El Paso."

Adeline Riley shook her head. "That beats all. I guess the Feds don't bother to deconflict when they're working on drug cases."

Raelynn chuckled. "They are the FBI."

"Well," Riley continued. "I'm glad you called. I've been working with Danny to come up with a plan to switch out the trucks. We're going to stash a duplicate truck with the meth on board at the Georgia State Patrol barracks in a place called Villa Rica. It's a few miles over the Georgia line."

"How do we shake Omar and Reyes long enough to do the switch?" Rae asked.

"We're working on it. We'd hoped to get you into Georgia and do it while everyone was sleeping. But it looks like you'll not make Georgia tonight. Do you have any ideas?"

"I guess we can't do the switch in Alabama?" Rae asked.

Adeline glanced over at Byrd, who was listening to the call. Byrd shook his head. "Not legally. We could lose everything in court if we do that."

"I heard him, and I understand. Omar wants us on the road early. We're getting up at three in the morning. I hope you have a way to pull a rabbit out of your hat by then."

"We're working on it. I'll let you know in the morning." Riley broke the connection.

Adeline Riley and Byrd looked at each other. "We've got to come up with something fast."

MONDAY, DECEMBER 19, 2005
3:44 A.M.
ANNISTON, ALABAMA

Rae swung her arms against the cold air as Dawn fueled the box truck. The lights in the truck stop were brutal and the one cup of coffee Rae had swallowed in a gulp wasn't enough to wipe away the spider webs in her head. She paced near the passenger door, watching her breath turn into condensation, as she waited for Dawn to finish.

Dawn finished pumping the diesel and then the two women walked into the truck stop. The big shopping area stood empty except for the tired looking clerk who was propped on a fist as she sat behind the counter. Dawn squinted in the lights that seemed even brighter than the ones on the outside.

"Hey, Rae," Dawn said. "I'm gonna hit the little girl's room before we get on the road. Get me a cup of coffee, if you don't mind."

Rae nodded. "Black as usual?"

Dawn smiled. "I like my coffee like I like my women. Dark and bitter."

Rae shook her head. "You're something else, girl. How are you holding up?"

Dawn shrugged. "I'm good. But I ain't gonna lie, I'll be happy when this is over."

Rae nodded. "Me, too. I'm getting 'road weary,' I guess."

Dawn laughed. "We call it the 'asphalt blues.' Getting tired of that blacktop rolling under your wheels."

Rae arched her eyebrows. "I've got to remember that one."

As Dawn started for the hallway with the toilets, the burner phone rang. She stopped and turned back toward Rae. Rae hustled over and leaned in. Dawn answered the phone. "What?"

"There's been a problem," Omar grumbled. He sounded frustrated.

Dawn was genuinely angry. "What now?"

"It's on us. The boys in Woodstock are saying they can't take the load until this afternoon. We need you to find a place to eat and wait 'till you hear back from me."

Dawn slammed the phone shut without responding. "Fuck me!"

The clerk behind the counter sat up for a moment. She eyed the two women and then went back into her position.

Rae pulled her work phone out of her pocket and dialed Daniel Byrd. He answered on the fourth ring.

"Is there a problem?" Byrd asked without preliminaries.

"Where the hell is Woodstock? I thought that was some rock concert my granny went to."

"Why?" Byrd asked.

"That's where we're headed," Rae said. "But we're circling the field again. Some problem on the Georgia end. They want us to find a place to eat and wait on them."

Byrd was quiet for a moment. "We need to get the box

truck in Georgia where I have jurisdiction," Byrd sounded like he was moving.

He gave them directions to an eatery located on the first exit off I-20 in Georgia. "We've got to make the switch. Do you know where Omar and Reyes are?"

"His rental was still at the motel when we left to fuel up. The Texas team was on him."

Byrd was breathing hard. "I'll call you right back. For now, call Omar and tell him you're looking for food and will call him when you pick a spot."

Rae motioned for Dawn. "Go handle your business and then meet me at the truck."

Rae waited until she was outside to call Omar. "Dawn says she remembers a good place to eat right on the interstate. Once we find it, I'll call you with directions."

Omar seemed preoccupied. "Sounds good. Let me know where you end up. We might join you."

They climbed into the truck and Dawn fired it up. "Where to?" Dawn asked.

Rae winced. "Have you ever heard of Tallapoosa?"

Dawn nodded. "Yeah. There's a diner at the exit. When I was driving long haul, I stopped there a couple of times."

Rae sat back in the seat. "Head that away. We're doin' the truck switch there."

"I thought we were doing that in Villa Rica?"

Rae wiggled, trying to get comfortable in the seat. "I guess the plan has changed."

Dawn put the truck into gear and swung around the parking lot. She nosed the truck toward the interstate highway. The traffic was light and she gunned the engine up the ramp and merged with the eastbound early morning traffic.

Rae watched the traffic ahead when her phone rang.

Byrd was almost shouting into the phone. She could hear traffic noise in the background. "Get that truck rolling. I need you to get to the diner I gave you directions to and I need it now. We're going to make the swap in the parking lot."

"Now? What about Omar and Reyes?"

"They're about to be tied up. We have about thirty minutes. Let's go!"

Omar sat in the motel parking lot, engine running, as Reyes spoke to the crew who were supposed to meet this morning in Woodstock. He was animated as he shouted at the man on the other end of the call. Omar understood the words "Rojo" and the Spanish word for "asshole" but not much more. Both men were concentrating on the call when Omar saw the blue lights behind him.

Omar was caught completely off guard. He watched a man step from the police car behind him. "Get off the phone, Reyes," Omar instructed his passenger.

Reyes looked pale as he closed the phone and dropped it into the console of the truck. Omar rolled his window down.

The cop was huge, Omar noted, as he filled the window of the truck. "Gentlemen, I'm Trooper Augustus Milton. My daughter happens to work the night shift at this little motel. I may be a touch overprotective but I try to keep an eye on this particular parking lot. Could I see some identification, please?"

Omar nodded as he fished out the Texas driver's license. Omar had hoped Bill Kleinman of Midland, Texas, would be able to avoid any encounters with the law. That ship had sailed.

MONDAY, DECEMBER 19, 2005
6:02 A.M.
TALLAPOOSA, GEORGIA

It felt to Rae as if Dawn would take the corner on two wheels. She turned right and made a beeline for the little diner.

Byrd was waiting in the parking lot.

Rae climbed down from the cab of the truck and almost gave Byrd a hug. "Damned glad to be in Georgia, buddy!" she said instead.

Byrd was all business. "Get in there and get a seat." He turned to Dawn. "Give me the keys to that thing. We'll make the switch now, I hope."

"You hope?" Dawn asked.

Byrd nodded. "The place we planned to do the switch is about forty miles up the road. I've got an agent driving the replacement like a bat out of hell." Byrd turned to the highway, willing the other box truck to appear. "But we may be cutting it close."

"What about Omar and Reyes?" Rae asked.

"They've just been introduced to an old friend of mine who is an Alabama trooper. He's as big as this box truck. They'll be tied up for a little while."

As if on cue, the burner phone rang. "This is Omar. Where are y'all at?"

Dawn gave Omar directions. "Hell," Omar remarked. "You're probably thirty minutes ahead of us."

"We'll keep the coffee warm," Dawn remarked into the phone. Once the connection was broken, she turned to Byrd. "I'd say you've got less than thirty minutes."

Rae and Dawn were on their first cup of coffee and started their meal when the other box truck came rolling into the parking lot. Rae checked her wristwatch. "Twenty minutes left. Good job, Danny."

Rae, seated with her back to the wall, watched Byrd rushing around the two trucks. There were more officers helping now. Rae assumed they were GBI agents. She watched as Byrd personally switched the license plates and then walked around the two trucks looking for any differences.

Rae saw Byrd answer his cell and then started waving his arms.

When he was satisfied, Byrd slapped the fender of the truck Dawn had driven. GBI agent Jill Leonard was in the driver's seat. She gunned the engine and backed up.

Omar was being cautious after the talk he'd gotten from the giant trooper in Alabama. He came to a full stop at the end of the exit ramp. He signaled his turn.

Reyes pointed at a white box truck turning in front of them. "Hey, there they go."

Omar looked where he was pointing. "Who?"

"Those two crazy women," Reyes grumbled angrily. "I wanted to get food."

Omar shook his head. "Nope. That truck has a Georgia tag on it. Ours has a Texas plate." Omar watched the other box truck head east on the Interstate followed by several other vehicles.

Reyes shrugged. "I guess all those trucks look the same."

Rae watched Omar park his rented pickup truck beside the box truck. The two men climbed out and stretched. Omar walked around to the box truck and looked it over.

Rae's head was pounding as he checked the tires and then checked the padlock on the back. She watched as he walked around to the front and looked at the headlights and the grill. *What the hell is he up to,* she wondered.

Omar and Reyes came into the diner. Omar sat beside Rae and Reyes slid into the booth beside Dawn. Dawn scooted closer to the wall.

"What's good here?" Omar asked.

Dawn took a gulp of coffee. "The coffee is damned good," she observed as she sat the cup down. She motioned for the waitress to refill her mug.

Rae tried to sound casual. "Something wrong with the truck? I saw you scoping it out."

Omar shook his head. "I was wondering if you'd mind adding a box or a duffle bag in with your luggage. We have some items we need to get back to Texas and I figured you'd be heading that way."

Dawn looked over at Omar. "You asking for a free haul?"

Omar smiled. "No, but we have a good bit of money to get back. We can pay you. No point in deadheading."

Dawn glanced over at Rae as she shrugged her shoulders. "You're right. We're going back anyhow. Might as well make a couple more dollars."

MONDAY, DECEMBER 19, 2005
8:02 A.M.
CANTON, GEORGIA

The phone on Wally Demopolis's table started to vibrate. Wally Demopolis was the commander of the Cherokee

Multi-Agency Narcotics Squad, locally known as CMANS, and he preferred to sleep light when the unit had been out late. He felt around with his hand and grabbed the cell phone. *Who the hell could be calling me at this hour,* he wondered.

"Hello?"

"Wally, this is Daniel Byrd with the GBI."

Demopolis sat up in his bed. "I know who you're with. What the hell are you doing calling a narc at this hour? The sun's barely up."

"It's after eight thirty," Byrd countered. "I was calling to help your stats for the year. How much meth have you seized this year?"

Demopolis became defensive. "I don't know. Maybe a hundred pounds or so. Why?"

"I'm following a load from Texas that is headed to Woodstock. Do you and your unit want to come out and play?" Byrd asked.

Demopolis fell back into the bed. "I'm guessing we are looking at several kilos? That's probably enough for me to get up early for." He scrubbed his face and the top of his head with his bare hands in an effort to wake up.

"This load is probably a little bigger than most."

Demopolis smelled a rat. "How much bigger?"

Byrd paused for effect, then he said, "Six tons."

Demopolis groaned. "Did you say six kilos?"

"Tons, Wally. About twelve thousand pounds."

Demopolis sat upright. "You got my attention. Where in Woodstock?"

"We're not sure yet, but as soon as I know I'll give you a shout. I expect we'll know where by lunchtime. Can you get your people together by then?"

Demopolis got out of bed. He headed to the bathroom and turned on his shower. "I'm on it."

"I guess we should get out of here before they throw us out," Reyes remarked. He picked up the ticket and dug in his pocket for cash. "Once I get outside, I'll call the warehouse and see how much longer it will be."

Omar held the door for the women as they filed outside. "Dawn, do you know of a place y'all can hide out until we get the word?" Omar asked.

Raelynn spoke first. Byrd had briefed her on this question. "There's a place a few miles from Woodstock, a mall that would give us plenty of room to park and wait."

Omar nodded. "That'll work. How long will it take you to get there?"

Dawn checked her watch. "Less than two hours, depending on traffic. Better to get on that side of Atlanta now rather than waiting 'till traffic picks up."

"Great!" Omar exclaimed. "Call me when you get there. Maybe by then, I'll have an idea about when we can unload."

The women climbed into the cab of the truck as Omar joined Reyes standing near the door to the diner. Reyes was deep in conversation on his phone.

Dawn clicked the switch and waited for the diesel engine to prime. Then she fired it up and negotiated the parking lot to get them back on the highway.

As Dawn waited for a chance to jump into traffic, she glanced over at Rae. "I hope they don't look this rig over too close."

"Why?"

"The rig we were driving was a 2000 model. This is a 2003," Dawn observed.

"Will they notice, you think?"

"I sure hope not," Dawn said as she accelerated into traffic.

CHAPTER 19
URINE A LOT OF TROUBLE

MONDAY, DECEMBER 19, 2005
8:59 A.M.
CANTON, GEORGIA

Gary Thomasson had to stop and make a phone call. He didn't want the call listed on his home phone or cell phone records. He found a good prospect in Dawsonville. The pay phone was in front of a convenience store on the edge of town.

Thomasson dug through his change and, once convinced he had enough loose cash to make the call, dialed Mitch Warren's cell number. He quickly fed change into the machine until the call was connected.

Thomasson wasn't surprised when he got a voicemail. Warren was notorious for not answering his phone. After waiting for the beep, he spoke quickly. "This is Gary. The GBI is fixin' to grab the load of dope you're bringing to Georgia. Get out!"

Thomasson hung the phone up, looked around to make sure he wasn't being watched, and then climbed back into his GBI car. He had to be in his office in Gainesville to take care of some overdue paperwork.

When Thomasson walked into the Gainesville Region

Office of the GBI, he was worried about an overdue case report. He had forgotten to dictate the required reports which would have made the case eligible to be closed. Now he would have to admit to Tina Blackwell he had messed up. He dreaded the meeting. He had always felt overwhelmed by the GBI machine's hunger for reports; lengthy, detailed, and prepared within a short time period.

He nodded at Machelle Stevens as he glumly turned into the hall leading to SAC Blackwell's office.

Tina looked up at the agent with a worried face. "What's going on, Gary? Your face reminds me of how my son looked when he wrecked my car." She examined his expression. "You didn't hit my car, did you?"

Thomasson dropped into a chair opposite her desk. "No, nothing that bad."

He leaned forward and put his elbows on his knees. He propped his head on his hands and struggled for words. "I'm having a hard time with the paperwork since I came over to GBI. I'm knee-deep in paper and can't seem to keep it all between the ditches, if you know what I mean. I'm working all the time to make all the deadlines."

Tina leaned back in her chair and crossed her arms. "Sure, we've talked about it. What's the problem now?"

Thomasson shook his head. "We tried that arson case in Dawson County a couple of months ago. He was convicted by the way."

Tina looked over the top of her reading glasses. "I heard the case was closed. But now that you bring it up, I don't remember seeing the disposition paperwork coming across my inbox."

He hung his head. "It didn't. I forgot it."

Tina nodded slowly. "Well, that's not the end of the

world. I know we've talked a lot about paperwork since you got here. It's an important part of this job, as you're seeing, and we expect everyone to do reports in a timely manner."

Thomasson could only hang his head. "I know that. And I'm trying hard to keep up. This job is harder than I thought it would be."

Tina laughed. "It looks easy from the outside. Like anybody can do it."

Thomasson nodded and tried to smile. "That's the gospel truth."

Tina rubbed her chin. "I can't ignore this, and it'll go on your annual evaluation report, but I think you need to learn from this."

Thomasson nodded again. "I sure do appreciate your attitude. I was worried I might get sent back to DNR." He stood and shuffled his feet. "I sure do appreciate this, Miss Tina."

Tina opened a drawer in her desk. She took out a form and put it in front of her. "While you're in here, there is one more thing I need to handle. I got an email this morning from the personnel office. Your name came up for a random drug screen. Once I sign this form, I'll need you to run over to the hospital and pee in a cup. You can catch that paperwork up as soon as you get back." Tina signed the form with a flourish. "You had these at DNR. Every state employee is subject to the random screens. And every agency gets their list of names the same day. You'll have to submit to the test this morning or you'll be subject to termination with cause." She held the form out toward Thomasson. "Just don't forget to come right back and do that paperwork."

Tina saw Thomasson's face turn ashen. His mouth was

moving, but nothing was coming out. Tina asked, "Gary, are you all right?"

Thomasson slumped into the chair he'd just left. He felt like he might throw up in his boss's office.

When the phone on GBI Director Quinin "Buddy" Hicks's desk rang, he didn't bother to look away from the computer. He scooped up the handset with his left hand and brought it to his ear. "Yes?"

"Director, this is Bob. We have a problem." Hicks recognized the voice of Inspector Robert Sullivan, a seasoned leader in the GBI. The tone of his voice told Hicks this call was going to be trouble. Hicks turned his chair to face his office window.

"What can I do for you, Bob?" Hicks asked.

"I have Tina Blackwell on the phone with me. She just called. Tina, can you brief the Director?"

Hicks heard Blackwell clear her throat. "Director, do you remember the attempted shooting in Jasper a couple of months ago? We operated under the assumption the shooter was trying to kill the Superior Court Judge."

"Of course. Judge Lance. Do we have a break?"

Hicks heard a long sigh on the line. He wasn't sure if it was Blackwell or Sullivan.

Tina continued. "We just got a name. And the target wasn't the Judge."

Hicks waited for the other shoe to drop.

"The shooter was after Danny Byrd. It relates back to the case out of Texas."

Hicks sat forward in his chair. "How good is the information?"

"Pretty good, sir. It came from Agent Gary Thomasson. We have taken Agent Thomasson into custody. Doc Farmer is talking to him now."

"What?" Hicks asked.

"Gary's name came up for a drug test this morning. When I gave him the form he collapsed in my office. Said he knew he would piss hot because of doing meth with this woman, the hired gun, and having sex with her. He's been taking money from General Warren, the CIA spook Danny tangled with earlier this year. Warren has been paying Thomasson to feed information to a hitman, or rather hitwoman, working for one of the Mexican cartels. She has been paid to kill Byrd for the death of one of Warren's men."

"The man who died in Canada?" Hicks asked.

"Yes, sir. Thomasson had been taking money under the table when he worked for DNR. Warren had tipped him for favors and then, a little bit at a time, he'd led Thomasson to the dark side. When this woman came to town, Thomasson was her local eyes and ears. It seems she lured Gary into a physical relationship—if you know what I mean."

Hicks grunted. "They had sex?"

"More than the once. She was squeezing him for information on Danny."

"We think she's the shooter, not just someone sent to compromise Thomasson?"

"Right, sir. She admitted to Gary that she missed the shot in Jasper. And she fed Gary some meth mixed in a drink to"—she coughed—"enhance his abilities. They've been meeting and having sex for the last couple of weeks, as near as we can tell."

"Was he using meth the entire time?" Hicks asked.

"Yes, sir."

"Has he compromised Byrd's investigation in Texas?"

Tina didn't answer.

Hicks sighed. "What do we need to do?"

"I sent agents to Jasper, to the motel where he's been meeting her. She's in the wind. We're taking a full statement from Thomasson and trying to work with Intelligence to see if we can track her. The motel has a photocopy of her Texas license, but it could be bogus. We're on it hard."

"Does Byrd know?"

"He's in Woodstock, trying to set up the arrests on this load he helped arrange out of Texas," Tina remarked. She added, "When it rains it pours."

Hicks squinted out the window. "Good work. Bob, see to it I'm kept up to date."

Hicks heard the two "Yes, sir" in unison. He dropped the handset onto the receiver and slumped at his desk. He wiped his face with both hands and shook his head.

"Today sure is a Monday," Hicks mumbled to himself.

MONDAY, DECEMBER 19, 2005
11:21 A.M.
CANTON, GEORGIA

Violet Childs left the courthouse with a form in her hand. She looked over her shoulder at the big white marble building. She wondered if it would be for the last time. It would certainly be her last time to work here.

Her boss had called her into his office this morning as soon as she arrived. He passed the form over to her without comment. She had looked at it and realized she had been chosen for a random drug screen.

She walked out of her office on wooden legs. Her ears were ringing on the elevator ride down to the main floor.

She found her car and climbed in. She sat for a moment, examining the form, before she started the engine.

Her options were limited. If she didn't show up at the Medical Center to pee in the cup, she would be dismissed with cause. If she took the test, she felt confident the painkillers she took would show up. She had a prescription for at least one of the pills but the two others she was taking were street buys.

She backed her little car out of the reserved parking spot and pulled around to the exit onto North Street. As she waited for a pause in traffic, she slammed her hand on the steering wheel. "Fuck!" she shouted.

She turned out of the parking lot and pointed her car toward Byrd's new home. As long as she didn't take the test, she wasn't at risk of being fired for using the painkillers she had bought on the street, she reasoned. She had until the end of the workday to submit for the test. But if she resigned by email as quickly as she could after she left her office, she could preserve her bar privileges and any retirement funds she might have accumulated. Violet knew the law was full of loopholes. She hoped she'd found the one that would retain her ability to earn as a lawyer, even if it meant becoming a lawyer on the dark side.

She made the short drive to Danny's house, hoping he wouldn't be there. She was elated to find he was working and she'd have privacy. She sat down at his home computer and sent an email to the district attorney. She carefully composed the memorandum, writing and re-writing some sections.

The body read: "*My ongoing medical issues with my back, exacerbated by long hours in the courtroom, have forced me to seek other employment. My resignation is effective upon the date and hour on the heading. I appreciate the opportunity to work in your office, but my immediate supervisor has recently made comments and gestures that tend to make me believe I am in a hostile work environment. I have no intentions of making an issue of this, for I think you are a great prosecutor. I do believe you should consider reassigning said supervisor. Best wishes, Violet Childs."*

She hit 'send' as she finished her first cigarette in a couple of years. Then she started calling lawyers in her hometown, looking for a position. She had an offer within fifteen minutes.

Her last act in Canton was to write a note to Danny. Violet took a piece of paper from Danny's little desk and began to write to him. She wanted to be kind in the note but her bitterness at the system seeped through.

She needed to pack as many of her clothes as she could get in her car, then head for her friend's apartment in Roswell.

CHAPTER 20
GEORGIA ON MY MIND

MONDAY, DECEMBER 19, 2005
5:22 P.M.
WOODSTOCK, GEORGIA

Omar had figured the cash he would receive would weigh about twelve pounds. He had prepped a large bag he would check when he flew back to Texas. The money would be surrounded by dirty clothes and souvenirs.

Reyes and Omar sat in the truck they had driven from Texas. Reyes was nervous, out of his element.

"As soon as the truck pulls in, I'll send you on your way. I'll walk down to the building from here and make sure the product is passed to our friends and then catch a cab to the Atlanta airport."

Omar nodded. "That works for me. And you'll be paying the ladies?"

"Of course." Reyes was ready to be finished with this venture.

Omar was startled by the vibration of his personal cell phone. He'd been using the burner phone since before he left Cambodia. When he looked at the phone, he recognized his father's number.

"Yes, sir."

"Are you alone?" Mitch Warren asked.

Omar glanced at Reyes. "Reyes, this is my dad. I'm going to get out and talk to him. He has some family business to discuss."

Reyes gave a quick nod. "Of course."

Omar was puzzled. "What's going on?"

"I got a call this morning but didn't listen to the message until just now. The caller was Gary Thomasson, do you remember him?"

"Sure. The game warden who went to work for the GBI."

"Right. He called to warn me that the GBI is onto this load you're shepherding."

"Damn!" Omar exclaimed.

"What stage are you at?" Warren asked.

"The load should be pulling up any minute."

"Hmm. The leak was probably on the Texas end. I recommend you not accompany the barrels into their stash house in Georgia. Will that be a problem?"

"We're getting paid as soon as the truck pulls in. Reyes will be tied up organizing the unloading. Unless we're already boxed in, I should be able to slip off then."

"Do you have the bust-out kit that came with your other IDs?"

"Of course. What should I do? Head back to Cambodia?"

Warren was thinking. "No, I'm afraid we can't get the cash past immigration at the airport in Phenom Phen. I suggest the first flight to Heathrow. I'll meet you at customs there and walk you through."

As his father was speaking, Omar saw the familiar box truck coming toward him. They would turn off Highway

92 into the industrial park where he and Reyes were parked.

"They're here," Omar observed.

"Wait on the money if you can," Warrens offered before he clicked off.

Reyes stepped from the truck and motioned for Omar. "I see them," Omar said.

Omar and Reyes climbed back into the pickup truck and pulled in behind the box truck. They followed the taillights along the asphalt path to a plain-looking, single-story building with a loading dock and a single roll-up door.

As they watched Dawn swing the truck around, Omar parked his truck in the parking lot of broken concrete. Reyes dropped to the ground. "I'll be right back," he remarked over his shoulder.

Omar tried to remain calm. He knew the police would be on them in seconds.

Arlow described the building the box truck had backed up to. "Looks like we kicked an ant hill. People moving all around the truck. I see a forklift coming out on the loading dock. Do we have an ETA on getting people in here?"

Byrd keyed his radio microphone. "The surveillance cars just passed the address and description of the warehouse to our guy at the courthouse. He should be able to get a search warrant signed in about thirty minutes. The judge is on standby."

Arlow sounded concerned. "A lot can happen in thirty minutes."

As soon as Byrd had gotten the address for the business, Wally Demopolis had deployed his agents in the area. "This is CMANS 601. We've got some ground units that should be closing the area off within the next five minutes," Demopolis announced over the radio. "I had one of my teams drop an agent off in the woods with a walkie-talkie. We should have 'eyes on' in the next couple of minutes."

Byrd tried to think of contingencies as he waited to hear from the ground surveillance. Then his radio came alive. "CMANS 618 to GBI 89. I've got eyes on. I'm working my way around to the side of the building where the unload is taking place."

"How many at the site?" Byrd asked.

"I see a truck up front with a driver in it. Looks like he's waiting for something. There are a couple of trucks over here by the loading dock. They might be able to get four or five guys in them. Then a flatbed truck is off in the corner. I'm guessing the flatbed is what the load will be transferred onto. There's no way I can find a spot to watch all of them."

Byrd considered the options. "Okay, 618. Get as close to the flatbed as you can and hold what you have."

Byrd heard the double-click of the microphone in answer.

Byrd called for Arlow. "Flint, what can you see?"

"Sorry, Danny. I had to move out of position. I'm in the path of air traffic at McCollom airport here in Kennesaw. I'm working with their tower to get the area over the building cleared up for me, but it's taking a minute."

Byrd groaned. He hadn't counted on losing the eye in the sky. "Do your best."

Arlow's frustration was obvious in his voice. "They reminded me they get over four hundred takeoffs and landings a day. I reminded them I was an Omaha flight and needed priority. They said they were working on it."

Reyes approached the truck with a bag in his hand. He was smiling broadly. "Here you go, my friend. Have a safe trip back to Texas."

Omar hefted the bag of cash. "I'll see you soon, Reyes. Next trip, I'll hire an interpreter for this end of the job. You can stay at home with your family."

Reyes seemed relieved. "I like that idea."

Omar was tense as he started the engine and drove out of the parking lot. He watched Reyes walking back to the building in his rearview mirror. Omar followed the narrow street back out to highway 92, expecting to see blue lights in his mirrors at any time.

"Flint 355 to GBI 89, go ahead."

"What have you got Arlow?" Byrd asked.

"I'm back over the target location. I'm hoping I can stay here until the cavalry arrives. Any update?"

Byrd thumbed his radio mike. "The eyes on the ground say the bad guys are working on unloading the truck. We know that'll take about an hour of back and forth. I got a call from the agent at the courthouse a minute or two ago. The judge is reading the affidavit for the search warrant. I expect it to be signed within the next ten minutes."

"Great," Arlow came back. "By the way, did one of the trucks leave? It looks like the one in front of the building is gone."

One of the CMANS agents keyed his radio. "Six eighteen to GBI eighty-nine. I can't see from back here. It was a big white rig."

"Is that Omar's rental? It's not there anymore," Arlow observed.

"Shit!" came Byrd's reply. Byrd keyed the mike again.

"Wally, can you put out a lookout on the main sheriff's office channel? We need to grab the people in that truck."

Byrd got a double click in acknowledgment.

Byrd flipped his phone open as soon as it rang. "Byrd. Give me good news!"

It was Wally Demopolis. "My agent just called from the courthouse. The warrant is signed and the tactical team is ready. They should be pulling into the lot within the next five minutes."

"Good job. I'll put it out on the radio," Byrd said. He grabbed the radio microphone and pressed the button. "Eighty-nine to all units on the surveillance. The search warrant is signed. The tactical team is moving up and should have a five-minute ETA. Get your raid vests on and be ready to provide perimeter cover."

Against his better judgment, Byrd had added Adeline Riley and Montana Petterson to the tactical team. He wanted people on the team who knew Raelynn and Dawn by sight. The situation would have been less complex if Byrd had been able to get Montana sworn in, but there hadn't been time.

The team, in a plain Sprinter van, rolled into the parking lot quietly. The driver of the van, one of the CMANS agents, pulled the van as near as he could to the roll-up door.

CMANS agents in tactical gear, accompanied by a Texas Ranger and a Texas Trooper, ran into the building. Wally Demopolis, not one to lead from the rear, shoved his M4 rifle into the face of the man driving the forklift. Other agents rounded up the offload crew. Addy Riley and Montana Petterson handcuffed Raelynn Michaels and Dawn Lewis.

The raid went down precisely as planned. Reyes Hernandez tried to run and was tackled by CMANS agent Freddie Torres. Reyes struggled with Freddie, who was twice his size, until handcuffs were locked around his wrists. Once everyone was in custody, Addy Riley checked her watch.

"Damn, guys. From the time the van door opened to the time everyone was in cuffs was less than two minutes. Reminds me of my bull roping days."

Daniel Byrd parked by the raid van and joined the tactical team. He grabbed Raelynn and Dawn and escorted them to his car. Raelynn twisted around, looking behind her. "Where is Omar?"

Byrd scowled. "That's the million-dollar question."

Rae shook her head. "Don't tell me he got away!"

"Okay," Byrd said. "I won't tell you."

10:27 P.M.
WOODSTOCK, GEORGIA

The search had been going on for over two hours when Wally Demopolis approached Byrd with a big grin on his face. "You sure have made my day."

"A lot of dope on the table, that's for sure," Byrd replied.

Demopolis motioned Byrd to follow. They joined an agent standing beside a six-foot-tall gray metal locker. It was the type manufacturing plants provided their employees for their personal effects.

The agent swung the door open. Byrd was shocked at the stacks of cash in the cubbyhole. He looked at Demopolis. "How much?"

Demopolis shrugged his shoulders. "We're guessing about five million."

"It just gets better," Byrd declared.

"Any word on the one that got away?" Demopolis asked.

Byrd shook his head. "You're a buzz kill, Wally."

TUESDAY, DECEMBER 20, 2005
6:19 A.M.
WOODSTOCK, GEORGIA

Byrd sat in the raid van, now being used as a mobile evidence processing unit, and rubbed his face. He was on his fourth cup of coffee. His stomach was complaining and his eyes felt like they were being pierced by needles. Uniformed officers from the Woodstock Police Department and the Cherokee Sheriff's Office had taken those people arrested to the Cherokee County Adult Detention Center, otherwise known as the county jail, to be processed and booked.

Byrd had put a lookout on Omar's rental truck almost twelve hours ago, but the truck hadn't been located. Byrd wasn't surprised.

Montana and Adeline climbed into the back of the van. Both were able to stand up without crouching. Something Byrd couldn't do.

"Where are we in the evidence process?" Byrd asked.

"The crime lab guys are getting ready to take the box truck, as is, to the lab in Atlanta. They're getting a contingent of troopers and deputies to escort them. All the paperwork on this end is done. And two agents escorted by a couple more troopers are headed to the bank with the cash." Adeline ran her fingers through her hair. "A good day's work, I'd say."

Byrd was elated. "That went better than I was afraid it would. We can grab some breakfast and then head over to the courthouse to take warrants."

"Breakfast sounds good," Adeline said.

"Where did Raelynn and the cooperator end up?" Byrd asked.

"A motel down the street. I told them to sleep in and then we'll work on getting them back to Texas," Montana offered. "Arlow and my wayward husband will probably want to meet us for breakfast."

"What happened to them?" Byrd asked.

"They'd been flying a long time without much of a break. They landed in Kennesaw and got a motel. Clete just called me to check in."

Adeline hung her head. "I'm glad someone got some rest. I'm dead on my feet."

Byrd smiled. "All that speed and we can't take advantage of it."

Adeline stepped down from the van. "Not funny," she remarked over her shoulder.

As the Texans walked away from the van, Byrd tried Violet Child's cell phone again. He had tried her a few times before midnight. He still got no answer.

3:22 P.M.
CANTON, GEORGIA

Byrd signed the last arrest warrant at 3:15 p.m., which he duly noted in his notepad. The copies of the last warrants were shooting out of the copy machine. Byrd tucked the copies into his padfolio and joined Montana and Adeline in the atrium of the courthouse. His last cup of coffee was running out. Byrd's eyelids felt like lead. He blinked a couple of times and took a deep breath.

"What say we grab some steaks and sides and retire to my new house? I've got a grill on the back porch and we can wrap this thing up with a meal." Byrd headed for the doors without waiting for an answer.

"Just keep it to a quick meal. I'm exhausted," Montana declared.

"Great. Call Clete and Rae and tell them the plan," Byrd said.

"Rae and Dawn caught a flight home this afternoon. One of the GSP troopers took them to the airport. I think Rae was ready to get home again. She's been away too long," Adeline commented.

"What about you?" Montana asked. "Aren't you ready to get back home? You have a husband waiting, don't you?"

Adeline sighed. "I sure am. But I couldn't begin to get on a plane till I get a shower and some sleep. I'm beat."

Montana nodded in agreement. "A shower sounds pretty good right now, but if I get in a hot shower, I'll crash and burn. I need to keep moving."

"Amen," Byrd got in his car and fired it up. "Let's get some groceries and get this show on the road."

As he backed out of the parking space, he tried Violet's cell phone again. There was still no answer.

CHAPTER 21
A BULLET FOR BYRD

Felisha had spent the early morning hours reconnoitering Daniel Byrd's house and property. The piney woods and rough terrain were foreign to her and she took her time looking the area over. The time had been well spent, she believed. She had found a place where she could wait for Byrd to return home. She was still jumpy from the last meth she had snorted.

She had never used meth so casually; nor had she spent so much time on the road to accomplish a job. She justified her use of the powerful stimulant by rationalizing that her solitary life in Georgia had been boring and dreary.

Her plan for today was simple. Shoot Byrd, make sure he was dead, hope the Texas Ranger was with him, finish him too, and then get out of the area. Her payday for one would be substantial, but killing both could set her up for the year.

Felisha opened her knapsack and pulled out a sandwich and chips she had packed that morning. She opened a thermos of coffee and then made herself comfortable. She had found a hiding spot near the creek which served as the boundary line for Byrd's property, according to Thomasson. Now she would settle down to wait for Byrd to return.

The area was protected from the worst of the weather that was moving into the area. She had watched a local weatherwoman on the TV in her motel room before striking out. A storm had been predicted to move into the area with high winds and rain. The winds were already whipping through the big oaks that surrounded Byrd's home. The rain was holding off, for now.

She decided she would wait in the spot until the sun was down. If Byrd and his friends hadn't come home by then, she would make her way back to her car. She could be back on the property by sunrise if needed.

She was finishing her sandwich and chips when she heard a car on the gravel driveway. She scrambled to gather up her trash. She crammed the sandwich wrapper and the bag of chips into her knapsack. As she turned to check for any other evidence of her presence, she kicked over her thermos of coffee.

TUESDAY, DECEMBER 20, 2005
4:22 P.M.
CANTON, GEORGIA

Byrd organized the supplies the group had bought on the way to his house. He put the steaks and the salad ingredients in the fridge and laid several potatoes in the sink to wash. He was surprised when he didn't see any of Violet's clothes or personal effects as he tossed his coat into the bedroom.

Then he saw the note on the center of the bed.

Byrd sat on the side of the bed and read the note. He could hear the Texas crowd working in his kitchen. Once he read the note through, he slumped over and considered what the note intended to say. He wasn't shocked, but he also wasn't clear on what had precipitated the rift.

He used his cell phone to call Sheriff Willie Nelson, a former DNR Ranger and current Sheriff of Cherokee County. "Sheriff, I need some information."

"What do you need, buddy?"

"Has something happened to Violet Childs?" Byrd asked.

The phone was silent. "Are you there?" Byrd thought he'd lost the connection.

"I forgot you and her were friendly," Nelson responded. "At least, that's been the courthouse gossip."

"You could say that," Byrd acknowledged. "What's going on?"

Sheriff Nelson told Byrd about her sudden resignation and the circumstances surrounding it. Nelson sensed Byrd was hurting. "I'm sorry to be the one to have to tell you all this, Danny."

Byrd had no desire to tell everyone about his problems. He stood up and wiped his face. His eyes had been red before, from lack of sleep, and he wasn't concerned about them as he walked into the kitchen.

It was Montana who, among the Texas officers, knew Byrd best and realized something was wrong. She poked Petterson in the ribs and leaned into his ear.

"Something's up with Danny. Why don't you get him outside and see what we can do to help."

Petterson glanced over at the Georgia cop. "Are you sure?"

Montana scowled at Petterson. "Just get him out on the back deck and give him a chance to talk to you, you big lug."

Petterson sidled over to where Byrd stood, looking like a lost puppy. "Show me the view from the deck. You've got a great place here."

Byrd mumbled something Petterson couldn't understand. They walked out onto the back deck and Petterson stood by the railing, examining the tall oak trees that surrounded Byrd's new home.

"We don't have trees this tall in West Texas," Petterson observed.

Byrd glanced around, avoiding eye contact with Petterson. "Yeah, I love all these hardwoods. They make this place special to me."

"How much land do you own?" Petterson asked.

Byrd started down the back stairs. "Come on. I'll show you the creek that's my property line. I ended up with about ten acres out of this deal."

Byrd's house sat on the highest spot on the property. The front yard was less than six feet across before the ground fell off sharply to the broad gorge that had been carved by the creek. An old roadbed, now little more than a wide path, led from the gravel drive down the hill to the burbling freshwater rivulet.

They walked along the old roadbed, surrounded by trees with a handful of golden dead leaves. Once the two men were close to the water, Byrd stopped and looked all around. "This place is so peaceful," Byrd observed. "I wish the house was closer to the water."

Petterson nodded. "I understand that. The sound of the water running over these big flat rocks just feeds your soul, doesn't it?"

Byrd turned to face Petterson. He noticed Byrd was chewing his lower lip. "I guess you figured out that something was wrong?"

"Montana did. She took one look at your face and sent me to talk to you. I'm not trying to pry. I'm just here for you."

Byrd wiped his face with both hands. "Thanks, buddy. I guess I could stand to talk about what's going on."

Byrd explained about the note and his relationship with Violet. He held himself together, more pragmatic than he expected, as he talked about the most recent issues.

"She ducked out to save her ability to practice law, even if she lost her job as a prosecutor. I guess she'll be moving to her hometown in South Georgia." Byrd observed as he walked deeper into the woods.

Petterson walked along, not commenting, as his friend seemed to relax. Talking things out always helped, Petterson believed.

Suddenly, Byrd stopped short. "Clete, do you smell anything?"

Petterson sniffed the air, but the wind was whipping through the forest of broadleaved trees and tall pines, and he couldn't smell anything.

Byrd looked all around, crouching to examine the earth near them intently. He found a moist spot near the trail. He rubbed his fingers on the ground and then sniffed them.

He looked up at Petterson. "I thought I smelled something. This is fresh coffee," Byrd pointed to the ground.

Felisha walked in a crouch as she tried to get a look in the windows of the little house. Every sound in the forest made her stop and look around. She realized intellectually that the paranoia was from the meth but that knowledge didn't change the adrenaline dump or its effects. She hoped the brewing storm would muffle her steps. She crept up beside the propane tank used to service Byrd's home. She could see people moving in the kitchen but couldn't distinguish anyone.

Time to put the rifle together and get ready, she thought.

She pulled the end cap off the stock of the AR-7 rifle. The little rifle had been developed for pilots during the Vietnam War. With the receiver, barrel, and magazines fitted into the stock, the gun could be carried easily. It should have taken her less than thirty seconds to attach the barrel to the receiver and the receiver to the stock, but her hands were shaking. She drove a magazine home and charged the little rifle. The last job was to attach the scope to the rifle, and despite her twitching fingers, Felisha finally turned the knob that held the scope in place. She was sweating and the salty liquid was getting in her eyes. As she finished the construction of the sniper weapon, a cold, gentle rain began to fall.

Petterson speed-dialed Montana. He held his hand cupped around the phone as he whispered. "Get away from the windows and arm yourselves. We think that Mexican hitman is in the woods behind Danny's house."

"Ask Danny if there are any guns here in his house," Montana demanded. "We'll make sure she doesn't get inside."

Petterson relayed the question.

"In the bedroom closet," Byrd replied. "There's a couple of rifles behind my clothes and extra magazines on the top shelf. And have someone dial 911."

Once he'd conveyed the answer, Petterson pointed toward the front of the house. "You go up the hill toward the front door. I'll work around the lower side and try to get eyes on the back of the house."

Byrd nodded, pulling his Glock and running up the long path back to his gravel driveway. His heart was pounding as he doubled back along the precipice in front of his home.

The Cherokee Sheriff's dispatcher hit the alert tone three times; the universal signal of a hot call to follow. Her voice was calm but tinged with urgency. "Any unit in the vicinity of 17955 Scott Road. Officers need help. There is an armed suspect on scene. Described as a Hispanic female dressed with no further description. Be advised there are undercover officers on site who will be armed. Use caution upon approach."

The uniform shift supervisor responded, "Dispatch, be advised that's the home of GBI agent Byrd. Delta 1 is responding Code 1."

More deputies responded in the same way.

Byrd worked his way around the red clay ledge in front of his house. The ledge had been formed by the water many years ago when a river ran through the low ground. He glanced at the edge of the hillock and realized he was thirty feet above the trail. Byrd's feet moved silently on the bed of pine needles and dead leaves that covered the ground, but the discarded foliage had grown slippery from the cold raindrops.

Byrd crouched as he moved from tree to tree for cover when he saw a movement near the side of his house. Byrd stopped and tried to get a look at the figure but he had no doubt it was the Mexican assassin. He considered calling Petterson on his cell phone. He decided there was no way to communicate with him without alerting the woman looking into his home with a rifle scope.

Byrd kept his eyes on the woman as he stole closer to her. She was too far away to try a pistol shot in this light. He needed to move nearer.

Byrd knew the bed of leaves would be slick from the rain but he couldn't risk taking his eyes off the woman. As he worked away from the edge, he lost his footing and tumbled over backward, banging into an old oak tree and bouncing off. He felt the wind knocked out of him as he slumped over and the wet leaves took him to the ground. He was sliding toward the ledge, head first. The bed of damp pine needles and leaves was like a sheet of glass and Byrd couldn't get hold of anything to slow his progress.

Just as Byrd's head slid off the ledge, he lay on his back as gravity worked against him. He flailed his arms and managed to hook a sapling in the crook of his right elbow, halting his descent, and succeeded in keeping a grip on his pistol.

Byrd tried to get to his feet, crunching his body and using the sapling for leverage. He got to his knees, breathing deeply, when he felt the rifle barrel on his neck.

"El pájaro," Felisha hissed. "Drop the gun, please."

"Since you said please." Byrd dropped the gun at his feet hoping it wouldn't slide off the hill.

"Where is your friend, the ranger?"

Byrd shook his head. "I guess he's headed back to Texas. Who are you?"

"Don't bother to lie to me. I saw you both go in your house." Felisha leaned against a tree to keep from sliding herself.

Byrd raised his hands to ear level. He stood up painfully. He planned to try to hit Felisha with his elbows.

"Stop moving, pajarito. I am your angel of death. But don't worry, I will make it quick."

Byrd hunched his shoulders. "You're no angel, darling."

Byrd twisted around hard. Felisha had expected him to try something. She whipped the rifle barrel out of his reach and laughed harshly.

Felisha moved her feet, working backward up the incline, when the rifle was suddenly snatched from her hands.

Petterson threw the scoped rifle into the woods as he grabbed Felisha's sweatshirt from behind. "Here I am, lady. What did you have in mind?"

Petterson yanked Felisha hard and spun her around, using the momentum to keep her off balance. She fought like a wildcat, swinging her arms and kicking her feet. Clete stuck his pistol in her face.

"You okay, Danny?" Petterson asked without looking away from Felisha.

"I'll live. For now!" Byrd grumbled through clenched teeth. "But I think I'll be sore tomorrow."

Byrd grimaced as he found his gun and holstered it.

"You look like you're hurt," Petterson commented.

Byrd groaned again. "My back and right shoulder are going to be sore as hell."

The two men, each holding an arm, shoved Felisha to the top of the hill and toward Byrd's front door. Adeline and Montana were positioned on Byrd's front porch with

Byrd's rifles propped on their hips. They could hear sirens in the distance.

Doc Farmer sat in Byrd's kitchen taking notes as Clete Petterson explained how Byrd had realized the Mexican assassin was near his home. Farmer led the team of agents investigating the attempt on the two lawmen.

The doors to the house were standing open as GBI agents and deputy sheriffs came in and out. Darkness had fallen and the rhythmic flash of blue and red lights punctuated the activity at the scene.

While the investigators were in the house and examining the grounds, Montana had taken Byrd's car and gone for take-out burgers. The steaks and fixings were abandoned for the night.

Byrd lay on his couch as a Cherokee County EMT examined him for injuries.

"You boys were lucky tonight. If you and Danny hadn't gone for that walk, things could have gone a lot differently," Doc said as he laid his pen down.

Petterson nodded. "Yep. If Danny hadn't picked up on that coffee smell, we might have been lying in this house with chalk lines around us."

Doc smiled. "We don't do the chalk thing in Georgia."

Petterson chuckled. "We don't do it in Texas either. I just thought it made for a good visual."

Doc sat back and crossed his arms. "Well, for a paid assassin, our girl is talking her head off. Says she was paid by a character she calls Rojo. Acts like I should know who that is. Says she got the order to kill you after some other boys dropped the ball."

Petterson scowled. "I never knew of Rojo using any Asians. That came from left field."

"She says those boys were working for some spook living in Cambodia. I'm assuming that would be Danny's old friend Mitchell Warren."

Petterson sighed deeply. "That would explain some things. Some kind of killer exchange program."

Doc stood and stretched his back. "When do you guys head back to Texas?"

"We have a flight out around noon tomorrow. I'm hoping we can get some rest tonight, but I'm not too hopeful."

"What's your rush?" Doc asked.

"We got folks to track down and arrest back in Texas. We can't let the GBI do all the work."

Once the exam was over, Byrd walked gingerly into the kitchen. "Well, this celebration is shot to hell."

Doc looked Byrd up and down. "Only fitting. You look shot to hell too."

Byrd attempted a grin. "Damn, my head hurts. But the 'ditch doctors' said I didn't have any major damage. Just that I'd be sore for a few days."

Doc closed his notepad. "Those EMTs, or 'ditch doctors' as you call them, saved you a trip to the ER. And I'm still not sure it would hurt for you to have some X-rays."

Byrd opened a cabinet and took out a bottle of vodka. "Tina's not coming here, is she?"

Doc shook his head. "Don't get too deep in that stuff. We'll need to be in court tomorrow afternoon for the lady's first appearance hearing."

Byrd poured a generous serving and took a gulp.

"Doc, I thought it was folks your age who fell and got hurt."

"Son," Doc replied. "You better hope you live to be my age. At the rate you're going, you'll beat me to the grave."

Byrd turned to Petterson. "Clete, I'm a poor host. Would you like some vodka to go with your burger?" Byrd motioned to the grease-stained sack on his kitchen counter.

"You got any bourbon?" Petterson asked.

Byrd opened the cabinet again. "I got a couple of brands. You pick."

Petterson found a bottle he liked and poured himself a glass. "I think I'm due."

Montana Petterson and Adeline Riley came into the kitchen as Clete Petterson took a long drink. Montana shook her head. "You boys don't act like we've been up a couple of days without any rest."

Clete Petterson held his glass up to Byrd's as they toasted. "To a job well done. And wishing our steaks could have been." Clete paused. "Or medium rare at least."

Byrd winked. "Those burgers are cooked just like you ordered. Burned and greasy."

Doc headed for the door. "Y'all have a safe trip home. I'll do my best to take care of Teddy after you're gone."

Byrd raised his glass to Doc Farmer. "Thanks again, Doc. Sorry you had to come out tonight, though. Did I keep you from your last-minute Christmas shopping?"

"Putting cuffs on this girl," Doc checked his notes. "Felisha Gomez. Putting cuffs on her is my present from you."

Byrd walked Doc out the door and onto the front porch. "Seriously. Thanks, Doc." Doc noticed he was limping.

"You bet. And don't get wasted tonight. I'm saying that as a friend."

The two men stood for a moment looking at the dark sky as the light rain from earlier continued. Byrd put his left arm around Doc's shoulder. "You're a good friend, Doc."

Doc Farmer stepped off the porch and jogged to his GBI car to get out of the rain. Byrd watched his friend start his car and drive away.

He came back in to find Addy and Montana eating the burgers they had picked up. Montana pointed at the bag. "Get something to eat or you'll crash and burn. You know that vodka is not good for you."

Byrd sat down at the table and dug in the brown paper bag. "You ladies think these burgers are good for me?"

Addy pushed back her baseball cap. She glanced over at Montana. "He might have a point. Are you up for sleeping on the floor? We'll get into his liquor stash and make it a night." Addy stood and poured her cup of sweet tea into the sink. "I guess it's time for some brown liquor. Something from Kentucky or Tennessee."

Montana shook her head. "Nothing for me. It would make me feel worse!"

"It won't be the first time we've slept in the same house," Byrd offered.

Addy looked over her shoulder as she poured a cup for herself. "I'd like to hear that story."

Byrd looked at Montana. "You can tell her what happened. The version I tell makes me sound better."

Montana cocked her head to one side. "You were a caring lover."

Byrd sat up to protest. "Clete, things never went . . ."

Petterson shook his head. "She's just screwing with you. She told me the whole story, tightie whities and all."

"Did she mention that she didn't sleep in my room?" Byrd asked.

"Uh-huh."

"Good, 'cause there won't be anybody else sleeping in there tonight either."

"Damned straight!" Montana exclaimed. "I talked to one of the Georgia troopers outside. They have kindly offered to drive your drunk asses to a motel after we are finished here."

Clete poured a strong bourbon and then held his glass high. "God bless the Georgia State Patrol."

WEDNESDAY, DECEMBER 21, 2005
10:50 A.M.
CANTON, GEORGIA

Byrd recruited another agent to help ferry Ranger Adeline Riley to the Atlanta Airport. Clete and Montana Petterson had ridden with him. He pulled up to the curb, cars jammed in all around, and got out to help them with their luggage. They lugged all their tactical gear and clothes out and stood together. The Texans had gotten a few hours' sleep and looked like it. Red eyes all around.

"I could have slept another day, but it'll be good to get home," Montana remarked as they stood on the curb. There were people all around, going and coming, who had no idea who the little group was or what they had just been through.

"I owe y'all. If it hadn't been for Clete, I'd be getting prepped for an autopsy about now." Byrd was glib. He moved slowly as he helped get the heavy bags on a cart. The strained muscles and the bruising were catching up with him, he thought.

"I already owed *you* my life. Me and Addy both. Just don't be a stranger," Clete seemed to be choking up.

A second GBI car pulled to the curb and Adeline Riley climbed out. She joined the group under the big metal and glass awning over the airport entrance. "You ladies ready to go?" Adeline asked Clete and Montana.

Clete nodded before he turned back to Byrd.

"Come to Texas sometime for a visit, instead of waiting on us to get a case going." Montana stepped up and gave Byrd a long hug. "And thanks for everything. You're the best!"

Byrd was rigid for a moment. When she stepped back Montana pointed to Clete. "He has something to tell you."

Clete's face was red. "Montana is pregnant. She didn't want anyone to know for fear they wouldn't let her come out here on this case."

Byrd stood still. "Congratulations! That's great. When will you find out if it's yours?"

Clete laughed. "Very funny."

"Come to see us!" Montana said. Before she turned to leave, she added, "And we're not naming the baby Daniel or Danielle. Just so you know." She was giggling as she prodded Clete.

Clete was already pulling his bags toward the door. "Come on, Montana. With any luck we can catch the UTEP football game when we get home."

"What is a you-tep?" Bird asked.

Clete rolled his eyes. "College football, son. UTEP is in the GMAC Bowl!"

"What's a GMAC?" Byrd called to the back of his head.

Byrd watched as they took the heavy bags into the airport. Then he got back into his government car for the long ride home.

CHAPTER 22
PRESENTS UNDER THE TREE

THURSDAY, DECEMBER 22, 2005
11:48 P.M.
WOODSTOCK, GEORGIA

"I gave up my lunch for you." Anne Kuykendall wasn't angry; she just wanted the information out there.

Daniel Byrd felt uncomfortable in the office he had frequented so many times just a year ago. "I thought you loved me," Byrd tried to make light of the situation.

The counseling office situated on Main Street in Woodstock was quiet the week before Christmas. Anne pushed the heavy door closed and pointed to a plush chair for Byrd.

The therapist sat across from Byrd, dropping her shoes and tucking her feet under her as she settled in. "Tell me what's happened in your life to bring you here right before Christmas."

Byrd's voice was muted, almost a whisper, as he told Kuykendall the story of his relationship with Violet Childs. He didn't bother to try to hide any of the details. He thought Kuykendall knew him too well to be able to keep anything from her.

When Byrd stopped, she asked, "And your drinking. Is that worse?"

Byrd chuckled. "I won't lie. I had too much to drink the other night. My friends from Texas finally made me go to bed. The next day, I killed a couple of bottles of vodka."

Kuykendall was shocked. "You drank two bottles of vodka?"

Byrd shook his head. "No, I killed them. I shot them in my backyard. Put them, and me, out of our misery."

"Was it Violet leaving or almost getting killed that was the bigger trigger?" she asked.

Byrd met her eyes. "Violet is a junkie. A pill junkie but a junkie nonetheless."

"That sounds harsh."

Byrd sighed. "But it's true. I can't live with someone who I know is actively committing felonies. She was seeing several doctors to get her pain pills and that's a felony in Georgia."

"You see what she did as a betrayal?"

"I see what I did as a weakness. I should have called things off and moved on. I knew she was probably over the line. I ignored it because of my feelings."

She sat forward. "Danny, it's okay to have feelings for someone else. Especially someone who's flawed."

Byrd scowled. "Is it?"

"Of course. You can't go through life keeping everything inside. You need a partner to confide in. Someone to enjoy the good times with and to work through the bad times."

"I thought that's what I pay you for."

She answered sharply. "Don't play that. You need a companion. And if your comeback is 'I'll get a dog,' I'll get out of this chair and slap you."

Byrd pressed back into the chair trying to distance

himself from her. "I get it. But I took an oath. I took a solemn oath before God to enforce the laws of the State of Georgia and the United States. That should be pretty black and white. I let shades of gray creep into all of this. I just feel like I let two women get the drop on me."

"In one case you had feelings for her. She had her own demons, I guess. You let your guard down because you were attracted to her. Has that changed?"

Byrd stared at the ceiling. "I'm not sure the feelings were that deep, yet. But I thought our relationship had promise. As far as the hitwoman goes, we hadn't really developed a relationship."

"Very funny," Kuykendall remarked. "You understand that you see the world as black and white, when it's really shades of gray. Nothing is all black or all white."

Byrd frowned. "Well, it should be. I see good and I see evil. I get that a person who is pure evil is rare, thank God. And I know that the best person can have a darker side. But I also see the lines the law draws. I see my work as defending the good from the bad."

Kuykendall pursed her lips. "Danny, your life is your own. If work is the most important thing in it, that's for you to decide."

Byrd leaned back. "I think that ship has sailed. I turned thirty-five on October seventh. I'm afraid the defenses I've built up make relationships hard. Maybe too hard."

"Men live to be seventy-five or eighty, nowadays. And a man or woman can find a relationship from childhood to death."

Byrd closed his eyes. "I can't imagine I'll make it to eighty. I'm actually surprised I'm still alive."

Anne remarked. "Me too."

"Thanks," Byrd said with a grin. "I always leave here wondering why I came."

"If you ignore what I say, then you could be right. And I sold you my lunch hour out of the goodness of my heart."

Byrd avoided her stare. "Thanks, Anne. You help me keep my life between the ditches."

"Between the lines the law draws?" Anne asked.

Byrd got the point. He looked up and gave her his most disarming smile.

"Will you see family for Christmas?" she wondered.

"My parents, for sure."

Anne stood up. "Get some rest and enjoy the holidays. Celebrate the way you see fit."

Byrd stood and pulled on his overcoat. "Oh, I believe in Christ. He's had angels tied up pretty much full-time keeping me safe. It's a time to think about the sacrifice He made for the rest of us. It makes any sacrifice I've made seem insignificant."

"Don't underestimate your contribution to the world, Daniel Byrd. If you believe, then you know we were all put here for a reason."

Byrd stood in the door. He smiled at Anne. "You know what my prayer is every night?"

Anne smiled. "What?"

"That whatever I was put on this earth to do; I hope I didn't do it today."

Anne shook her head. "I think you told me that before."

Byrd chuckled. "Still true."

"Turn off the charm and get out of here." Anne closed her office door.

SATURDAY, DECEMBER 24, 2005
11:44 A.M.
WESTMINSTER, LONDON, ENGLAND

Steve Loftis mused working on Christmas Eve was above and beyond. Loftis had grown up in South London and was not a child of privilege. Loftis had joined MI-6 after university by virtue of his intellect and work. He was part of the first wave of hires into British Intelligence who hadn't been groomed for membership in the elite international organization by the "good old boy" network. The old guard had been beaten down by the intelligence debacles of the 1960s and 1970s.

As he climbed the steps out of the tube station, pushed and shoved by last-minute shoppers and revelers, he wrapped his topcoat tighter against the cold. He planned to make quick work of the meeting and then get home to his family. A senior executive in MI-6 deserved that much.

The park was empty, and the air was moist with the promise of snow or sleet in the next few hours. Loftis spotted General Warren where he said he would be. The General sat alone on a park bench near the Embankment Station in the quiet park which adjoined his hotel. Loftis thought Warren looked old and tired. Warren was sitting with his eyes closed.

Loftis walked over and sat beside him. "Isn't it cold to be meeting out here, General?"

Warren didn't respond. Loftis looked closer. The man's skin was turning blue. "Bloody hell," Loftis exclaimed. He felt for a pulse and got nothing.

Loftis opened his phone and dialed a number he knew

by heart. "I need a team at the north entrance to Whitehall Garden. Across from Embankment Station. No need for medics. Just make sure Scotland Yard is aware."

Loftis looked toward the overcast sky. He was a man of faith who, like soldiers and policemen everywhere, believed in a God he could not see in spite of the evil he *could* see. He laid his hand on Warren's shoulder and prayed silently for the soul of the man he had come to meet on the eve of the celebration of Christ's birth. Loftis was moved by the symbolism.

The MI-6 man mused about all the old man sitting on the bench had seen, all the wars he had fought, and all the secret things he'd done the world would never know about. He smiled to himself when he thought about the operations Warren had organized which would be considered criminal by some. For a moment, Loftis felt the weight of his own world, his own secrets, as he sat in the lonely park.

Those who chose to live this life, soldiers until the very end, he thought.

SUNDAY, DECEMBER 25, 2005
6:55 P.M.
CIUDAD JUÁREZ, CHIHUAHUA, MEXICO

Rojo dropped into the chair behind his desk. He muttered to himself about the news from his men in Georgia. "This mess is worse than I could have imagined. And once more, the CIA man and his son had escaped the net," Rojo remarked and shook his head. "A man with my power shouldn't have to endure these setbacks," Rojo declared.

The old man cleaning his office stood in front of his desk. "What is your power when you only exercise it against the powerless?"

Rojo seemed surprised to see the defiance in the old man's eyes.

Rojo sneered. "What do you know, old man?"

The man dropped into one of the plush leather chairs reserved for visitors. "I know that I am ready to be finished with my job."

"You want a bigger Christmas bonus?" Rojo laughed bitterly. "Then go. I can find a hundred like you."

The man sat still. His face was like a stone wall. "You have spent your life finding people like me and then grinding them under your boot heel."

Rojo stood up. "Get out of my office, you gnat of a man."

The old man pulled a long-barreled revolver from under his sweatshirt. He pointed it at Rojo's chest. "A gnat, huh? And was my brother a gnat to you?"

Rojo smirked. "Who is your brother to me? Did I wrong him? Or do you just want to feel the power of holding a gun on me?" Rojo moved around the desk as he spoke. He wanted to reach the shotgun hanging from the wall.

"My brother did not kill your son. Your son died of his own ignorance and his own arrogance. Your son was a fool."

Rojo stopped in his tracks. His face reddened with anger. "Who was your brother?" he asked.

"Nobody. Just an old man who spent his life repairing appliances for the poor people of our city. An old man you tortured and killed because he drove your son across the border on the day the American police killed him. My brother did nothing except what he was asked. You tortured and killed a powerless old man to remind yourself of *your* power." The old man dropped the barrel of the gun down and shot Rojo in the groin.

Rojo stumbled, fighting through the pain, and dived for the shotgun. The old man shot him again in the torso. This bullet traveled through Rojo's right lung, tearing a path narrowly missing the drug lord's heart. Rojo slumped to the floor laboring to breathe. "You old fool. What do you think you are doing? My guards will not let you leave this place."

The old man had taken the precaution of locking them into the big room that was Rojo's office. He expected the pounding on the locked office door. He knew it would take the guards a full minute or more to breach the heavy oak panel entrance.

The old man took the shotgun off the wall and swung it around. Rojo raised his hands up. "What are you doing, you fool? I can make you rich."

"I'm killing a gnat."

The old man pulled the trigger of the shotgun as the big door swung open. The pellets of double-ought buckshot tore the top of Rojo's head off, neatly ripping the brain from its stem and dropping it on the floor.

The old man dropped the shotgun and turned to face a hail of bullets from the guards. *Too little, too late*, he thought as he braced for the impact.

"*Feliz Navidad*," the old man mumbled as he fell.

CHAPTER 23
UGLY TRUTHS

TUESDAY, JULY 25, 2006
4:18 P.M.
CANTON, GEORGIA

Daniel Byrd stood on the steps of the Cherokee County Courthouse. The three-story edifice to justice was bathed in sunlight and the white marble shone brightly. The day was blazing hot without the slightest wind. Byrd used his Bureau cell phone to call Clete Petterson.

"Ranger Petterson."

"Clete. Danny Byrd. How goes it?"

The connection was intermittent. "Waiting for you," were the only words he got. He pulled the flimsy antenna up on the unit and turned to see if that helped the connection. He tried walking around in front of the building.

"I just got out of court," Byrd said.

"I can hear you now. How did court go?" Petterson asked.

"Good," Byrd declared. "Reyes entered a plea today. He will be in prison for a few years. Will the State of Texas want him when Georgia is finished?"

"Good question," Clete replied. "I doubt it. How long did he end up with?"

"Twenty do ten. Then he'll be on probation for the remainder. Pretty good for someone with no priors. The rest of the crew from Woodstock were sentenced a couple of weeks ago. They're all illegals with several prior drug offenses. They ended up with twenty to serve and then deportation."

"What about your friends Felisha and the GBI man?"

Byrd chuckled. "Felisha has been spilling her guts to everybody from the GBI to the FBI. DEA wants to talk to her next. She'll end up entering a plea here but I understand the legendary Texas Rangers would like to try her for some murders out there."

"Right," Clete replied. "That's one the State of Texas will want to get hold of. She'll be facing several murder charges. Once she was fingerprinted out there in Georgia, we used her prints to tie her to murders all over West Texas. All of them happened to have done something to piss Rojo off. Two were officers and we don't go light on cop killers." Clete continued, "We have a death penalty in Texas."

"And you use it! As far as Gary Thomasson goes, he'll be serving five years in prison and then ten more on probation. I still don't understand how he passed the background for the GBI."

"Any word on Omar?" Clete asked.

"Nothing. He evaporated. I've been working with the US Marshals and Homeland Security and nothing has turned up. Just like a year ago. Did you find out the real deal with Rojo's death?"

"All we know is that it was some kind of vendetta. A worker in Rojo's house killed him. The guy who took Rojo's place, and we're still trying to figure out who's the new leader, had all Rojo's guards killed for letting the shooter get away with it. The Federales are finding bodies all over the area they think are part of the in-fighting," Clete remarked.

"Couldn't have happened to a nicer bunch," Byrd observed.

"How are you doing? We haven't talked much since we were out there." Clete was tentative as he broached the sensitive subject.

"I'm good. I've enrolled in a master's program at the college up the road. And I've gone back to judo lessons. I took classes in college, but I thought it would be a good way to stay fit. That keeps me out of trouble."

Clete seemed in a rush. "And on that note, I'll get off the phone. I've got a pregnant wife at home who's ready to pop. Can you send me disposition paperwork for our files?"

"Soon as I get my hands on it. Good to talking to you, my friend."

Byrd disconnected the call and walked to his car. He was on the second level of the parking deck and hoped the height would improve his phone service. He knew the number by heart as he dialed the phone.

The call took several seconds to connect. "Hello?"

"Violet? How are you doing?" Byrd asked.

She sounded weak and far away. "Better. I'm in rehab in Jacksonville. I tried to make a go of things in Savannah, but I couldn't shake the pain meds. I've been sober for two months. I'm hoping to get a pass to get out for the weekend."

Byrd was genuinely happy for her. "That's great. Will you be able to go back to your law practice once you're out?"

"They tell us to take it one day at a time. That's all I can do, Danny."

Byrd was at a loss for what to talk to her about. Their lives had taken divergent paths and coming back together would be difficult. "I just wanted to check on you. Your mother called me back in September to let me know you were working on your problem. I hope I'm not intruding on anything."

"I do need to go, but it was nice to hear from you." Byrd didn't hear any enthusiasm in her voice.

Byrd broke the connection.

He fired up his car and backed out of the parking space. As he circled around the parking lot, he stole a glance at the window that had once been Violet Childs's office.

FRIDAY, NOVEMBER 17, 2006
12:55 P.M.
CANTON, GEORGIA

Byrd was driving toward Dahlonega. He had been deep in thought, worrying over his approach to a suspect in an armed robbery case. The first interview, if the man talked at all, was most likely his only interview. When his cell phone rang, he pulled his government car to the side of the road. "Byrd?"

"Danny, this is Clete. What kind of prisons do y'all have in Georgia, anyway?"

"Same kind as in Texas. Lots of concrete, barbed wire, and chain link fences. Why?" Byrd asked.

Clete chuckled. "We picked up our friend Reyes on a wiretap. He's brokering drug deals from prison."

"You're kidding."

"Nope. He now works for Rojo's successor. Guy named Ismael Luis Salazar. They call him El Mayo. He just cut a deal for fifty kilos of meth to be delivered to New York from a conversion lab in Greensboro, North Carolina."

Byrd sat back in his seat and shook his head. "Nothing surprises me. How'd he get a phone?"

"Same way as in Texas. Bribed a guard. One of the task force teams is working with your Department of Corrections. They searched his cell yesterday and took a cell phone, but he was back at it today, using another cell phone. It beats a horse flying!" Clete sounded more amused than exasperated.

"How does he broker the deals?" Byrd asked.

Clete was shuffling papers. When he answered it sounded to Byrd like he was reading a report. "He takes a call from Mexico, usually one of El Mayo's top people. They tell him how much to send and what price to quote. We think he then walks down the hall and has another prisoner who worked for Rojo call a stash house and order up. We are having trouble putting the pieces together since they use a cut-out. No wiretap will get the conversation between the two prisoners."

"It never gets simpler," Byrd observed, then changed the subject. "How's the new baby?"

"She's named Alma. We sent you a birth notice, I thought."

"Sorry, you did. Alma is a beautiful name. And how's mom?"

Clete sounded flustered. "She wants to go back on the road right away. I told her Alma needs her mother at home for as long as we can afford it. She's missing the action."

"I just hope she takes after her mom. Even a wonderful name like Alma won't make up for having your face."

Clete laughed good-naturedly. "You're an asshole, Danny Byrd. But we love you! Come out to see the baby when you can."

"Will do. Give Montana a hug for me." Byrd clicked his phone shut and pulled back onto the road.

Clete pulled his government truck into the driveway. He jumped out and rushed to the house. He couldn't wait to grab Alma and hold her in his arms.

When he got in the door, Montana and her mother were cleaning up a rug Alma had thrown up on. The two women paused when Clete came in. "Glad to see you home early, cowboy. Your daughter has had a bad tummy all day. Mom and I need a break."

Clete crossed the room to his daughter, lying on her back in the pack-and-play in the living room. He leaned into the crib and pulled Alma to his chest. His rapture was interrupted when he got a whiff of his child.

He laid her on their couch and opened her diaper. Before he could stop himself, Clete was gagging. "My God! I can't believe that mess came out of my sweet girl."

"You got it on your shirt too!" Montana told him.

Clete almost dropped Alma. He shook his head vigorously and tried to get past the smell.

Montana poked her mother. "That's what a big, bad Texas Ranger looks like."

MONDAY, NOVEMBER 20, 2006
8:22 A.M.
CANTON, GEORGIA

Byrd had a big day ahead of him as he bundled up. He had an office meeting in Gainesville and his car was cold. Byrd pushed his door open when his phone buzzed in his pocket. He stopped short of going outside. The day was blustery and there was no point in going out until he dealt with the call.

The number was unfamiliar. "Daniel Byrd."

"Mr. Byrd?" the voice was weak and timid. "Is that you?"

"Yes, ma'am. What can I do for you?"

The lady seemed to struggle for words. "I don't know if you remember me. I'm Violet's mother. Betty Sanders."

"Oh yes, Mrs. Sanders. How are you?"

The line was quiet, and Byrd thought the call might have disconnected. "Are you there, Mrs. Sanders?"

"She's gone," the words were almost a whisper.

"Violet? She left rehab?" Byrd was listening intently.

"Well, yes. She got a weekend pass. She came back to Savannah this weekend. She seemed to be doing so much better. But . . ."

"What happened?"

"She's gone. She's dead. She called one of her old friends who brought her some pills to the house. She had crushed the pills up and injected them in her arm. Since we thought she was doing better, we didn't check on her until it was too late. We found her last night in her bathroom. She was gone. Just gone. So young." Byrd heard the tormented woman start to cry loudly.

"I'm so sorry," he tried to say. But he could tell the connection was broken.

Byrd walked back inside and sat on his couch. He was stunned. He stared at the wall for a moment and then got down on his knees. He prayed silently for Violet's soul and for her family. Then he begged forgiveness for not doing enough for her. He started to cry quietly.

Byrd finished his prayer and then stood up. He walked to the front of his house and looked out on the creek. He decided to walk to the burbling water and stand for a few minutes.

With his overcoat tightly wrapped around him, Byrd made the trek to the edge of his property. Clete had been right; the water sound was soothing. He mused about how lonely Violet must have been in that bathroom as her life slipped away. For a moment he felt angry at her and then he just felt sad. A deep sadness he thought he was immune to. As he listened to the rippling water, he dialed Tina Blackwell.

"Danny, what's going on?" Blackwell asked.

"I'm going to be late for the office meeting this morning. I hope that's okay."

"Is everything all right?"

"I'll explain when I get there. I should be there by nine thirty."

Tina must have heard something in his voice. "We'll hold the meeting 'till you get here. Are you sure everything's okay?"

"A drive will do me good. I'll see you soon."

He broke the call and walked up the hill to his car.

EPILOGUE

"You're Omar Warren?" Byrd asked.

Omar started to answer when the older man in the back of the room interrupted. "Names aren't important at this juncture."

Byrd stared at the older man. "Who are you and what's your part of this?"

The man stood. "My name is Steven Loftis. I am a retired civil servant who, on occasion, consults with the Royal Family. I am here to explore the circumstances around his," he pointed at Omar, "history in the States."

Byrd looked from Omar to Detective Chief Superintendent Baker to Detective Chief Inspector Ashwood. Each was stoney-faced.

Byrd looked back at the photos in the file. Suddenly, it hit him. "The man in the pictures is Mitch Warren. Mitchell L. Warren, to be exact."

"The man you knew as Warren was a resident of London when he died suddenly just before Christmas in 2005."

Byrd dug deeper into the file. He found an autopsy report. The verbiage was different than the ones he was accustomed to, but he comprehended the details. "He was poisoned? By who?"

"The man you knew as Rojo, we believe. He shipped a case of expensive scotch whisky to the General's room. He actually made it appear his son had sent it. We were able to track the package's origins to Mexico. One bottle was loaded with a very powerful drug called carfentanyl. It is used to sedate elephants."

Byrd watched Omar's face. "Poetic that Rojo and Warren died a day apart," Byrd remarked. Then, ever the southern gentleman, he addressed Omar: "Sorry for your loss."

"If the General were related to this man in any way," Detective Chief Superintendent Baker offered.

Byrd stared at the file for a moment. When he looked up, he made eye contact with Omar. He knitted his eyebrows as he asked, "The King wants to knight Omar here, and you want me to give you the thumbs up. To promise that we won't try to deport him for the old charges? Is that about it?"

"My name is Bill Kleinman, originally from Midland, Texas. Eighteen years ago, I moved to a place outside of London called Herefordshire. Ever heard of it?"

Byrd nodded. "Special Air Service is based there."

"Are you former military?" Loftis asked.

"No, but I read a lot."

Omar continued. "I opened what turned out to be a very successful business in England. It was called, simply, the Quartermaster. I sell tactical equipment to the military and to certain civilian organizations who are seeking specialized products."

Byrd said nothing.

Omar soldiered on. "My sisters and my mother are actually still living in the US. They established a manufacturing company in Georgia on some land they acquired."

Byrd nodded. "Let me guess. Is it near Fitzgerald? On some land that used to belong to Mitchell Warren?"

"They actually have a contract with the GBI. They manufacture your mesh vests with the gold letters on the back. The ones your agents wear for raids and things of that nature," Omar pointed out with obvious pride.

Byrd refused to comment.

Loftis stood with some effort. He stepped up to the table. "This situation is, as you see, muddy at best. We have used the services of Mr. Kleinman and the man you referred to as Mitchell Warren. Their services have been above and beyond the pale, if you will. We owe them a great, albeit secret, debt."

"I get the sales pitch. What's the tab?" Byrd asked, frustrated with the innuendos and euphemisms.

Loftis looked confused. "I'm sorry?"

Omar leaned forward. "He's asking what it is we want, am I right?"

Byrd nodded curtly.

Detective Superintendent Chief Baker pursed his lips. "I believe it falls to me to answer that particular question. We have enjoyed this special relationship with Mr. Kleinman for his tenure in our country. Now he wishes to return to the family fold in Georgia. His sisters are ill, and he would like to help with their care."

Byrd interrupted. "Can't the CIA handle this? According to what we've been led to believe, the CIA was in bed with the Warrens for longer than I've been alive."

Baker looked to Loftis. "The situation is complex. While our Secret Intelligence Service works closely with your CIA, there are political ramifications. The CIA is not willing to face the fallout."

"His charges, if he were actually Omar Warren, could be resurrected by your agency. Actually, they could be resurrected by you, Agent Byrd," Steven Loftis observed.

Byrd chuckled. "I certainly could. He tried to have me killed, as I recall events."

"Things were complicated, back then. I certainly hold no animosity toward you," Omar sounded sincere.

"Can we get some sounding from you? Would it be remotely possible for those charges to be forgotten?" Steven Loftis asked.

"I took an oath to do certain things. Part of that oath is that I can't shirk my duty. Mr. Kleinman, as you call him, is a wanted man in the US." Byrd had no intentions of bending.

Baker stood and walked closer to Byrd. "Agent Byrd, we understand your feelings, but we are hoping you will reconsider your position on this matter. We, in this country, take into consideration the positive impact this family has had in many circles, including in the US, since the unfortunate events in Georgia."

Byrd stood and faced Baker. "You'll forgive me if my take on crime is different from yours in this country. I seem to recall our countries have disagreed about the judiciary, among other matters, for a number of years now. In fact, my state was among those who were instrumental in fighting for those distinctions."

Baker nodded. "Touché, Agent Byrd. I hope you understand that our intent is to help the Warren family, not to diminish the deeds done in 2005. Nor to place you in a situation that requires you to dishonor your oath of office."

Byrd took a deep breath. "I'm being a poor guest. And an asshole. Forgive me for getting angry. You gentlemen have caught me off guard, is all."

Byrd stretched his neck. Then he turned to Loftis. "I assume you have some knowledge of the case? You are aware of the details? You probably know better than I do the number of people who died in this case."

Loftis shrugged. "We have a certain understanding of the facts, of course."

Byrd turned to Omar. "And you know what these people are asking of me?"

Omar glanced at Baker, keeping his mouth firmly shut.

Byrd shook his head, disgusted. "You're not even the first one to ask me to do something like this. Then, it was a judge looking to move up in the world."

Byrd made up his mind. He stepped closer to Baker. Byrd was as tall as Baker and stared into his eyes. "I want to talk to Omar alone. Or Bill Kleinman. Whichever one is here in this meeting."

Detective Chief Superintendent Baker shook his head. "I don't think that's a good idea, Agent Byrd."

Omar interrupted. "Let us talk. Should we clear the room?"

Byrd shook his head. "No recordings. Strictly off the record. Let's go for a walk."

Baker turned to Loftis, obviously seeking guidance. Loftis nodded curtly.

Byrd grabbed his topcoat and Omar followed behind him. Ashwood led the two Americans down to the main entrance, escorted them through security, and left them on their own. Once they were away from the building, Byrd nodded toward the Parliament Building. "Since I'm here, I might as well make the most of it."

The two men walked side-by-side, bundled in their overcoats against the cold wind coming off the Thames. Byrd pulled his head into his overcoat collar, missing Georgia where the temperature was already in the midseventies.

"Have you cleaned up your act?" Byrd asked.

"I'm out of all that secret life. After my father's death, my work was strictly above board. I never did anything else for the CIA, or any other spook agency, since I left Georgia that night. Almost Christmas, as I recall, in 2005."

"How can I be sure of that? Those men in that room would lie for you. It's obvious you've done work for them. Which means, by extension, work for the CIA. And it's obvious I'll never get the full story."

Omar stared up at Big Ben as they came to Bridge Street. Byrd stopped to look. "This is an amazing city," Omar opined.

Byrd tried not to sound gruff when he remarked, "If you like big cities."

They turned right, making their way toward Buckingham Palace. "My dad pulled me into the dark world. I'm not proud of what I did, but it was the only world I knew. I was young and reckless. I had some great adventures, but I also did some very stupid things." Omar stopped and stood looking at Byrd. "I got some friends killed."

Byrd interrupted. "I'm sorry about Adam Benjamin."

Omar nodded, "You did your job. I see that now. I don't blame you. I won't lie; there was a time when I wanted you dead. Wanted you to pay for what happened to Adam. But this business took off. I made it into something, and I never stepped over that line again. My value was in my business's ability to make specialized gear at a reasonable price. We didn't invent anything as much as we perfected them. Rain gear that could be easily packed into a problem area, and that was really waterproof. Rafts that would carry several men and would fit into a small backpack. Soldiers get issued substandard equipment, Agent Byrd. Soldiers who are members of the SAS and the Special Boat Service are willing to pay out of pocket for quality gear. And I made the best quality around. Soon governments were issuing purchase orders from here to America. Then Israel. Then business was booming."

"Made a lot of money?" Byrd asked.

Omar shrugged. "Everything is relative. The money isn't worth much if you aren't free to be with family. My sisters aren't healthy and can't travel."

Byrd stopped and faced Omar. "I've spent my entire adult life believing in right and wrong. Good guys versus bad guys. I can't give you a pass. And I wouldn't if I could. You and your father did a lot of damage."

Omar hung his head and continued to walk. Byrd hustled to catch up. They were away from traffic now, in St. James's Park. A drizzle of cold rain began falling. It occurred to Byrd he could have used one of those special rain suits right now.

"Did you really expect a pass?" Byrd asked Omar's back.

Omar stopped and turned. He hung his head. "No, not really."

Byrd took a deep breath. "What I will do for you is get in touch with the district attorney. She won't have any idea about this case. She was probably in college when it all happened. I'll see if she'll take a deal. I would be surprised if she wouldn't do it." Byrd waved his hand dismissively. "A nineteen-year-old drug case."

"Will I have to do jail time?" Omar asked.

Byrd put his hands on his hips, fists clenched. "I can't tell you. If I had to guess, they'll ask for some time in the county jail. Not prison, probably. And a fine."

"A big fine?" Omar asked.

"Damned straight. You brought in several million dollars worth of product. Reyes Hernadez got hard time. He's still in a Georgia prison to this day. And don't bullshit a bullshitter. I know you ran with a big chunk of money that night."

When Omar didn't answer, Byrd started walking. He remarked over his shoulder, "That's the best I can do. And I can't guarantee that."

"When would I have to surrender?" Omar asked as he struggled to catch up.

"I can work all the details out with Cherokee County." Byrd stopped walking. "By the way, what is your name? If Warren isn't it, and I know Kleinman isn't it, what is?"

Omar shook his head. "I really don't know. My dad probably had a real birth certificate somewhere, but I never saw it."

Byrd wrapped his overcoat tighter. His tie had been tugged out by the wind and was flapping in his face. He tried to hold Omar's eyes, but Omar looked away. Byrd was about to turn away when Omar reached out and touched his arm.

"What happened to Stacey Carter?" Omar seemed embarrassed to ask, Byrd thought.

"Who?" Byrd asked.

"One of the truck drivers from Texas."

The name clicked. "She's still in jail," Byrd remarked.

Omar seemed crushed. He turned away from Byrd.

"Omar. She's in jail because that's where her office is. She's the Sheriff of El Paso County, Texas. She was working undercover nineteen years ago."

Omar shook his head and laughed. "I figured if any-body was a cop, it was that little banty rooster of a driver, Dawn."

Byrd nodded. "Women are hard to figure, I'll give you that. Now, I'm going sightseeing for the rest of the day. Tomorrow I'll do my best to have an answer for you from the DA. I can't fly back home until the day after tomorrow. I'm going to look the city over before I go home for Thanksgiving."

Omar stuck out his hand to shake. Byrd hesitated, then he shook hands with the younger man.

"Do you have a family?" Byrd asked.

"A wife and two boys. It will be hard to explain to them, but I'll be happy to get this behind me. What about you, Agent Byrd? Wife? Children?"

Byrd suddenly felt sad to be alone in this big city. He shook his head without comment.

"Take care of your family," Byrd said and then started walking toward Buckingham Palace. The rain stopped, but the temperature had dropped noticeably. He bundled tightly against the cold, walking through the park toward the royal palace in the distance. His steps echoed in the tree-lined walk.

ACKNOWLEDGMENTS

While writing is a solitary endeavor, pulling a book together requires a family. As always, I appreciate the people who enjoy my stories. I must thank my first readers, Mark and Shelia Hodge, Jesse Hampton, and Mike Crosby. And my loyal sounding board, Emma Price, who is my staunchest supporter and my toughest critic.

And I couldn't feel right without thanking my loyal family. My wife, Grace, my son and daughter-in-law, Zack and Erika Price, and my wonderful grandchildren. It's a coincidence that their names are Adeline, Raelynn, and Stetson.

And last, but not least, to the wonderful, brave, and dedicated men and women of the Georgia Bureau of Investigation. My time with the agency now seems brief. I had no idea the wild ride in store for me when I raised my right hand and took the oath that shaped my life.

ABOUT THE AUTHOR

Phillip W. Price began his law enforcement career with the City of Canton, Georgia, Police Department in late 1974 (at the age of nineteen). On January 1, 1976, Price was hired as a Radio Operator for the Georgia State Patrol assigned to the Headquarters Communications Center. On January 8, 1978, Price transferred to the Georgia Bureau of Investigation (GBI) as a Special Agent. Price retired as a Special Agent in Charge (SAC) in 2006.

After a stint as a traveling consultant, conducting training on methamphetamine manufacture, in May of 2010, Price was hired as the task force commander for the Cherokee Multi-Agency Narcotics Squad (CMANS). Price re-retired on December 17, 2021.

In 2021, Price completed his first novel, *Mountain Justice*. The setting for the story is the North Georgia Mountains and the story follows a young GBI agent, Daniel Byrd, who uncovers corruption and murder in the otherwise idyllic setting.

Price followed the first novel with *A Little Bit Kin*, the tale of a methamphetamine cook who gets in over his head. The drug disruption scheme spirals out of control and GBI Agent Byrd is left to pick up the pieces. Much of the novel revolves around the world of methamphetamine abuse and the lifestyle that goes with it.

Price's third novel, *Self Rescue*, follows Byrd around Georgia as he pursues a CIA contract officer who dabbles in methamphetamine smuggling from the Mexican border to the Peach State. Soon, Byrd ends up on the Texas/Mexican border in a fight for his life.

Price's fourth novel, *Asphalt Blues*, continues the investigation into the drug enterprise the GBI and Texas authorities uncovered between El Paso and Atlanta.

Each one of Price's novels are based on real events and experiences from his professional career.

Price has an associate in arts degree from Reinhardt University, a bachelor of science degree from North Georgia University, and a master's in public administration from Columbus State University.

Price has appeared on One America News Network and Salem Cable News Network.